THE SCHOOL AT

Elinor M. Brent-Dyer was born Gladys Eleanor May Dyer on 6th April 1894, in South Shields, an industrial town in Tyneside. Unlike many of her heroines, she was one of only two children, and – the product of a broken home – she did not have a happy childhood.

On her eighteenth birthday Elinor became a teacher, and for many years she taught in a variety of schools, both state and private, becoming headmistress of her own school in Hereford in 1938. It was called The Margaret Roper School (named after Sir Thomas More's accomplished daughter), and shared many ideals and customs with the fictional Chalet School.

Elinor's first book, *Gerry Goes to School*, was published in 1922, and her first Chalet School book in 1925. During the next forty-seven years she produced more than a hundred novels as well as several plays and two collections of poems, and a massive historical novel about Sir Thomas More.

After the death of her mother, with whom she had lived for many years, Elinor moved to a house in Redhill in Surrey. There she wrote five further Chalet School books, the last of which was published six months after she died.

Other Collins Modern Classics:

Collins Modern Classics

The School at the Chalet

by

Elinor M. Brent-Dyer

illustrated by
Linda Clark

An imprint of HarperCollinsPublishers

First published in Great Britain by W. & R. Chambers Ltd 1925
First published as a Collins Modern Classic 1999

3 5 7 9 10 8 6 4 2

Collins Modern Classics is an imprint of
HarperCollins*Publishers* Ltd, 77-85 Fulham Palace Road,
Hammersmith, London W6 8JB.

The HarperCollins website address is www.**fire**and**water**.com

ISBN 0 00 694592-9

Printed and bound in Great Britain by
Omnia Books Limited, Glasgow

CONTENTS

Chapter One

MADGE DECIDES

"IF ONLY I knew what to do with you girls!" said Dick in worried tones.

"Oh, you needn't worry about us!" replied Madge.

"Talk sense! I'm the only man there is in the family – except Great-Uncle William: and he's not much use!"

"Jolly well he isn't! Poor dear! He's all gout and crutches." And Madge threw back her head with a merry laugh.

"Well then! I ask you!"

She got up from her seat on the settee and walked across the room to her brother. "Dear old Dick! You really mustn't worry about Joey and me. We shall be all right!"

He lifted his fair boyish head to look at her. Not pretty in the strict sense of the word, yet Madge Bettany was good to look at. She was slight to the verge of thinness, with a well-poised head covered by a mop of curly dark brown hair. Her eyes were dark brown too, the colour of old brown sherry, and were shaded by long, upcurling, black lashes. Dark eyes and hair presupposed an olive complexion, but there Madge had deserted the tradition of the Bettany women, and her skin showed the wonderful Saxon fairness of her mother's family. Her mouth was wide, but with well-cut lips, and her slender figure was as erect as a young poplar. There was enough likeness between her and Dick, despite the disparity of colouring, to proclaim them unmistakably brother and sister. Now she slipped a hand through his arm as she announced, "I've got a plan all ready for us."

"Let's hear it," he commanded.

"Well, the best thing is to go over all the possibilities."

"Oh, for heaven's sake, don't make a long story of it!" he implored.

"All right. But I want you to see my point, so—"

"That means it's something you think I shan't approve of," he said shrewdly. "Well, get on and let's hear the worst."

"You see," began his sister, balancing herself on her toes, "whatever happens, Joey and I must keep together. We are all agreed on that point. But there's no money; or, at any rate, very little. You can't keep us on your pay; that's quite out of the question! So last night, I thought and thought after I had gone to bed; and, honestly, I think my plan's the only one possible."

"Oh, for heaven's sake, cut all that!" groaned her brother. "What do you want to do?"

"Start a school," was the sufficiently startling reply.

"Start a school!" He stared at her. "My good girl, that sort of thing requires capital – which we haven't got."

"Yes, I know that as well as you do!" retorted his sister. "At least, it does in England. But I wasn't thinking of England."

"My dear girl, it's an awful undertaking to run a school. And you look such a kid! Who on earth would have you as Head? And anyway, you haven't told me yet where you want your blessed school!" he protested. "You don't suggest coming out with me to India and starting there, do you?"

"No, of course not. Though, if there hadn't been Jo to consider, I might have done it. But we couldn't keep her there; and I won't leave her in England. So what I've thought of is this. D'you remember that little lake in the Austrian Tyrol where we spent the summer five years ago – the Tiernsee?"

"Rather! Topping little place, right up in the mountains, 'bout an hour's train run from Innsbruck, wasn't it? You went up in a mountain railway from some rummy little town or other – I forget its name!"

"Spärtz," supplied his sister. "Yes, that's the place. It was gorgeous air up there; and you could live for next to nothing."

"Is that where you mean to have your school?"

She nodded. "Yes. There was a big chalet there which would be topping. It was not too far from the lake; fairly near the steamer, and yet it was away from the paths. I shouldn't want a large number, not at first any rate – about twelve at most, and counting Joey. I should want girls from twelve to fourteen or fifteen. I would teach English subjects;

Mademoiselle Lepâttre would come with us, and she would take the French and German, and the sewing too. Music we could get in Innsbruck."

She stopped and looked at Dick somewhat doubtfully at this juncture. A frown was robbing his face of half its boyishness. He knew very well that Madge had set her heart on this project, and that he had neither the strength of will nor the authority to turn her from her purpose. They were twins, and all their lives long she had been the one to plan for them both. If she had determined to start this school, nothing he could say or do could prevent her. Their only relatives besides Great-Uncle William, before mentioned, were two aunts, both married, and both with large families and small means.

"It's no use appealing to the aunts," she said. "Just consider how we are situated. We are orphans, with a sister twelve years younger than ourselves to be responsible for. Our guardian got his affairs into a frantic muddle and then conveniently, for him, died, leaving us to face the music. You're in the Forests, and your furlough is up in three weeks' time; Joey is delicate and shouldn't live in a wet climate; and between us we seem to have some fairly decent furniture, this house, and six thousand pounds in East India Stock at four per cent – or something over two hundred pounds a year."

"Forty over," interjected Dick.

"We can't live on that in England," she went on, unheeding the interruption. "Even if I did get a post in a school, it would mean school fees for Jo. But we could manage in Austria. It's healthy, the Tiernsee, and it's a new idea. I know of one child I could have for the asking – Grizel Cochrane; and we'd have to advertise for the others. I don't see why we shouldn't make it pay in time."

"What about apparatus?" suggested Dick. "You'd want desks, and books, and so on, I suppose?"

"Get them in Innsbruck. My suggestion is that we sell most of the things here, keeping only what we absolutely need, and buy out there. I went over the chalet while we were there, Dick. A fortnight ago I wrote to Frau Pfeifen. Her answer came this morning. I wanted to know if the chalet was vacant, and, if it was not, if there was any other place she could recommend. It is vacant, and she thinks the owner-manager of the Kron Prinz Karl – that big hotel not far from the boat-landing – would let me have it all right."

"I wouldn't have agreed to the idea if you had consulted me," he replied. "As it is, I suppose I must say 'yes'. You'll do as you like, whether I agree or not. I know that! But you've got to promise me one thing."

"I'll see," returned his sister, cautiously. "What is it?"

"That you'll cable me at once if anything goes wrong, and that you'll write at least once a week – oftener if you can."

"All right, I agree to that. Now will you go and fetch Joey, and we'll tell her. I know she's a bit anxious about what's going to happen, but I couldn't say anything till I'd discussed it with you first of all. She's upstairs reading."

"Jo reads entirely too much," he grumbled as he went to the door. "That's one thing I hope you'll alter a little."

"She'll have plenty to take her out of doors," replied his sister serenely. "She really needs other companions. Call her, old thing."

His yell of "Joey!" resounded through the house a second later, and was answered by a shriek of "Coming!" There was the sound of flying footsteps, a thud in the hall, and then Joey, or, to give her her proper name, Josephine, fell rather than ran into the room.

Anything less like Madge and Dick it would have been hard to imagine. Her cropped black hair was so straight as almost to be described as lank, her big black eyes made the intense whiteness of her face even more startling than it need have been, and her cheeks and temples were hollow with continual ill health. Like her brother and sister, she had been born in India; but, unlike them, had come home at the early age of seven months. The frail baby who had never known her mother or father had thriven in the soft Cornish air of their home till she was four years old. Then a neglected cold had brought on an attack of pleuropneumonia, from which she had barely struggled back to life. Since then, her health had been a constant worry to those who had charge of her. What made things still more difficult was the fact that Miss Joey possessed at least five times as much spirit as strength, and fretted continually at the restrictions they were obliged to enforce. The exertion of her flight downstairs brought on a bad fit of coughing, and until it was over, and she was lying back on the sofa, whiter than ever with exhaustion, there was no thought of telling her the news.

"I say, old lady," Dick began, "you mustn't sprint about like that!"

Jo lifted her eyes to his. "I'm sick of 'don't'!" she remarked. "Why did you call me, Dick? Anything settled about us yet?"

"I suppose so," he growled. "But just listen to me for a minute. I'm sorry you're sick of 'don't', but I think you might have a little more consideration for Madge. You know how she worries when you cough."

"Sorry, old thing!" Jo sent up a little smile at her sister. "I was so anxious to hear, I forgot about not dashing round. What are we going to do? I can see it's all fixed."

"Yes, it's fixed," replied Madge. "It's my own idea, and I hope you'll like it."

"Well, what is it?"

"Madge is going to run a school."

"Madge run a school!" Jo sat bolt upright "No! She's much too young!"

"I'm twenty-four—" began Madge heatedly, when Dick interrupted her.

"You listen to me, my kid. Remember the Tiernsee?"

"Rather!"

"Well, you're going there. Madge will open the school in that big chalet not far from the lake. Mademoiselle Lepâttre will come with you to look after you both, and help with the school."

"What a simply ripping idea! When are we going? Before you do, Dick? Who are the pupils?"

"Don't be silly! Of course you can't go yet! There's this house and furniture to see about, and Madge will have to buy her paraphernalia in Innsbruck—"

"Dick," Madge interrupted, "I don't think there'll be much trouble about selling the house. You know, the Corah Mine people want a place for their managers to live in, and it's within quite decent distance of the mine. Don't you think they might buy it?"

"Good idea! Yes, I should think they might. It's the sort of place they want, of course. I'll take a stroll up to old Everson and get him to see it through. Since we're all going, the sooner we get the business over and quit the better."

"I'll go and see the Cochranes," decided Madge. "I know they'll be thankful to get rid of poor little Grizel. What fees shall I ask, Dick? D'you think £360 a year would be too much?"

"Sounds rather a lot," said Dick dubiously.

"It's only what most decent schools charge. I've got some prospectuses to see."

"Well, I'll get along and see old Everson while you interview the Cochranes. What are you going to do, Joey? It's too wet for you to go out," said Dick.

"I'm going back to finish *Quentin Durward*," returned Jo firmly. "You'll take all our books, won't you, Madge?"

"Most of them, anyway. But you needn't start to pack them yet. This is only March, and we shan't be going till next month at the earliest."

Jo returned to her little bedroom, where a blazing fire

relieved the gloom of the rainy day, and her well-beloved books awaited her.

"Best thing in the world for her," observed Dick when she had gone. "Well, I'm off to settle old Everson."

"Insist on his doing things at once, Dick. I want to get off and be settled before the summer visitors arrive at the Tiernsee. He'll want us to play round till September if I know anything about lawyers, and it makes no difference really, because I've made up my mind to go. Mademoiselle will be thankful to get away from England too."

"You're sure it's all right about her coming?"

"Yes. I spoke to her a week ago, and she said if you consented, she would come."

"Righto! Well, so long! Hope you get the Grizel kid!" And with this, Dick turned and left the room, while Madge ran upstairs to get her raincoat and hat, before she, too, ventured out into the hurricane of wind and rain with which March had arrived that year, to seek her first pupil for the Chalet School.

Chapter Two

GRIZEL

SEATED AT THE old schoolroom piano, Grizel Cochrane was diligently practising scales and exercises. She had no real love of music, but her father insisted that she must learn; and since she must learn, then, also, she must practise. Her stepmother, whom Grizel hated with all the intensity of her childish soul, had decreed that, although this was her last day at home, the dreary hour of scales and exercises must he done as usual.

"Thank goodness, I shall be away from all this after tomorrow," she thought. "I love Miss Bettany, and Jo is a dear. I'm glad I'm going away from England – glad I'm leaving them! They don't want me, and I can't endure them!" Tears pricked at the back of her eyes at this thought, but she resolutely drove them back. At fourteen and a half Grizel Cochrane had realized she was decidedly an unwanted member of the Cochrane family. Her mother had died when she was five After her death, Mr Cochrane had sent the child to his mother's, and led a bachelor life for the next five years. On Grizel's tenth birthday he had married again, most unaccountably, without informing his second wife of the fact that he had a daughter. That she discovered when they reached home after the honeymoon, to find Grizel awaiting them on the steps. At first, Mrs Cochrane insisted that the child must go to boarding school. Her husband calmly replied that one reason for his second marriage was that he wanted Grizel under his own roof. He also pointed out that if she were sent away at once people would talk. She desired that less than anything, so she gave way. Grizel went daily to a big high school in the neighbourhood, and, nominally at any rate, received the same care and attention as any of her friends. But life at her grandmother's had spoilt her in many ways, and before long she and her stepmother were at daggers drawn with each other. Mr Cochrane, never a particularly loving parent, refused to interfere. By slow degrees the wilful, high-spirited child gradually became a frightened, nervous creature, who did as she was bidden with a painful readiness.

Later, she became the excuse for many "scenes", and on the day when Madge Bettany set off in the wind and rain to secure her for the Chalet School, Mr Cochrane had at last given way, and agreed to send her away. Then the great question had been "where?" To them, considering the point, had come Madge, and with her a complete solution of the problem. It was satisfactory from all points of view. Grizel's father realized that if she were sent away with such an old friend as Madge Bettany, it would give rise to no gossip in the little town, which was beginning to conjecture at the causes for her loss of spirit. Mrs Cochrane rejoiced in the fact that it would be sheer absurdity for her to make the long journey from Innsbruck to Cornwall for any holidays but the summer holidays. Grizel herself only wanted to get right away from her present surroundings, and Madge went home thrilling to the fact that she had gained her first pupil.

For the next fortnight or so everyone had been kept busy. Grizel found herself condemned to sitting and sewing name tapes on to new stockings and gloves and handkerchiefs, as well as having to endure various "tryings-on". At any other time she would have resented all this intensely. Now it was, for her, just part of the joy of going away. Madge had been unable to say, at first, when they would go; but Dick, having applied for and received a month's longer furlough, bustled their old solicitor to such an extent that the middle of April found them with house and furniture sold, boxes packed, and everything ready. What was more, the Chalet School had two other pupils in prospect. Mademoiselle was bringing a little cousin, Simone Lecoutier, from Paris, and a business friend of Mr Cochrane's, an American, had been fired with enthusiasm over the school, and had written asking Miss Bettany if she could find room for his twelve-year-old Evadne next term.

To Grizel it seemed almost impossible that it could be she who, on the morrow, would he taken up to London by her father, unusually indulgent, and there given over to Miss Bettany's charge. Madge and Jo had left their old home early in the previous week, in order to pay farewell visits to such relatives as remained to them.

"It's too good to be true!" thought Grizel ecstatically; "and that's ten o'clock, thank goodness!"

She finished off the scale of A flat melodic minor in grand style, and then shut down the lid of the piano with a bang. She had heard her stepmother go out a few minutes previously, so she ran down to the kitchen, where the cook, who adored her, and spoilt her when it was possible, welcomed her with a wide smile, and made haste to proffer a rock bun.

"Just out of the oven, Miss Grizel, love," she said.

Grizel accepted it and, sitting on the table, munched it with good appetite.

"This time tomorrow I shan't be here," she said, when it was disposed of.

"No, lovey. It'll be the train this time tomorrow," replied the good woman in her soft, sing-song voice.

"And then Paris the next day — and then Innsbruck next week!" Grizel spoke exultingly. "Oh, Cookie! I'm so thrilled, I'm so thrilled I can't keep still!"

"Eh, it's a lot you'll be seeing, Miss Grizel. And you'll write to Cookie and tell her all about the grand sights in them furrin cities, won't you?"

"Of course I will, Cookie dear! I'll write to you as often as I can." And Grizel jumped down from her perch and, flinging her arms round Cook's neck, gave her a hearty hug. "I'll write to you every week if I can."

"There's a love! And, Miss Grizel, dearie, I was over to

Bodmin last night, and I got this for you to remember your Cookie by."

"Oh, Cookie! How dear and kind of you! Whatever can it be?"

Grizel took the narrow parcel, feeling its shape with childish curiosity before she opened it. A little scream of ecstasy broke from her as she realized what it was – a beautiful Waterman fountain pen.

"Oh, Cookie! And I've always wanted one so much!"

The tears stood in her grey eyes as she carefully examined it. Cook, looking down at the small flushed face, felt rewarded for her long tramp of the night before, and for the sacrifice of a new spring hat, which had been necessary to buy the pen.

"I've nothing to give you," said Grizel, sudden sadness in her tones.

"You'll be giving me your news, lovey – maybe a picture postcard or two! That's all I'll be wanting from you. Now you'd better go, Miss Grizel. The mistress only went down to the butcher's, and she won't like it if she finds you here."

Grizel nodded. With a final hug and a kiss she turned and ran upstairs to her own little room, cuddling her new possession. Some paper lay on the little dressing table, and she tried the pen on it. Cook had had it filled ready, and it was a beauty – neither too fine nor too broad. She wrote her name with a flourish several times, and then, hearing Mrs Cochrane's step on the stairs, tucked it away into her attaché case, and screwed up the bits of paper, thrusting them into her pocket just in time. When her stepmother entered the room she was standing gazing out of the window, and whistling softly. Mrs Cochrane frowned at her.

"Grizel! I have told you before that I will not allow whistling! Kindly obey me! As long as you are under this roof you will do as I tell you!"

Grizel obeyed. The disciplining of the past three years had taught her the value of unquestioning obedience, if it had taught her nothing else.

"You had better put on your outdoor things and come with me," went on her stepmother. "You ought to say goodbye to the Rector and Miss Fareham; and I have to go to the Rectory. Hurry up now, and brush your hair, and be downstairs in ten minutes' time."

She left the room, and Grizel did as she was bidden; but all the time that she was putting on the new blue travelling coat, and changing into her outdoor shoes, she was murmuring softly to herself, "Only today left! Only just today! Tomorrow will soon be here now."

Walking demurely at her stepmother's side, she went down the garden path, which was already bordered with wallflowers and tulips, gaily a-nod in the spring breeze, and out into the street, where they met two of the girls from her old school.

"You will want to say goodbye to your friends," said Mrs Cochrane graciously – she was always gracious in public. "I will wait for you at the Rectory; but don't be long, as there are still one or two things I want to do."

She passed on, and Grizel was left with them.

"It's tomorrow you go, Grizel, isn't it?" said the elder of the two, a pretty fair child of fourteen, Rosalie Dene by name. "Aren't you sorry to leave home?"

Hitherto Grizel's pride had kept her from making any revelations about home matters. Now, somehow, it didn't seem to matter. She would not come home for more than a year, for she was to stay with the Bettanys all the summer.

"Sorry?" she said fervently. "I'm not sorry; I'm glad – glad, I tell you!"

"Grizel!" gasped Rosalie. "Glad to leave home and go right away!"

"'Tisn't like your home," replied Grizel sombrely. "You've a mother!"

"Well, but you have Mrs Cochrane, and I'm sure she's awfully sweet to you."

"Yes, when there's anyone there to see it," replied Grizel recklessly.

The two schoolgirls stood in horrified silence. They didn't know what to say.

Grizel broke the spell. She held out her hand.

"I must be going," she said briefly. "Goodbye. Write to me sometimes."

"Goodbye," said Rosalie flatly. "Of course I'll write if you will."

"I'll send you some postcards," responded Grizel. "Goodbye, Mary!"

Mary, the other child, mumbled something in farewell, and then Grizel ran off, leaving them still staring after her. "Well!" ejaculated Rosalie at last. "Did you ever?"

"Never!" replied Mary with finality. "I didn't think Grizel Cochrane was like that!"

"I wonder what Mother will say," said Rosalie thoughtfully.

What Mrs Dene actually said when she heard her daughter's story was, "Poor little dear! I hope she will be happy in Austria, then."

Meanwhile, Grizel hurried to the Rectory, where her stepmother was waiting for her, and took leave of the Rector and his sister, both of whom were fond of her. They had farewell gifts for her too, in the shape of a new Kipling and a big box of chocolates, and she said goodbye to them with real regret. They had always been kind to her.

After the Rectory visit, Mrs Cochrane took her into the town to do some shopping, and it seemed to the little girl that never before had they met so many acquaintances in one morning. Everyone was very kind, and wished her good luck and a pleasant journey. One or two told her that they envied her her visit to foreign countries, and most people begged for postcards. Grizel promised them to all and sundry, and all the time her heart was beating madly with delight to think that this was the last time for many a long month that she would be here. Then they went home to lunch, and after it was over, her stepmother dismissed her to the moors, where she ran about like a wild thing till the little silver watch on her wrist warned her that it was nearly tea-time, and she had better be turning homewards. Her father came in for tea, and brought with him a folding Brownie Kodak in a neat leather case with a strap to sling across her shoulders. The general atmosphere of kindness seemed to have infected even Mrs Cochrane, and so that last evening passed off well. The next day Mr Cochrane took her up to town, and gave her into Madge Bettany's charge at Victoria.

Chapter Three

THE JOYS OF PARIS

"RIEN À DECLARER?"

"*Rien à declarer!*" replied Madge firmly, with one eye on her two charges. The custom-house official grunted as he chalked the mark on the three suitcases. which was all the luggage they had with them, Mademoiselle Lepâttre and Dick having gone out to the Tiernsee early in the previous week with the trunks and cases of books, ornaments and pictures, which were all they were taking with them from England. Experienced Joey promptly helped to fasten the cases again, while Grizel, flushed and excited, gazed round her, wonder in her big grey eyes. She had never been out of England in her life before, so even the draughty, prosaic *douane* of Boulogne, where everyone had to go in a queue with their cases, was invested with a certain pleasure glamour for her. The hoarse voices of the *douaniers*, the clamour of their fellow passengers, the unusual trains with their funny, high engines, and little steps up into the carriages, were all fresh and new to her. Madge cast an amused glance at her absorbed face as they settled down in their second-class carriage. The only other occupant was a little fat man in a loud check suit. He was mopping his face with a white handkerchief adorned with scarlet spots.

"Eh, it's 'ot," he said, his accent at once betraying him for a Yorkshire man. "'Ot for this time o' t'year it is."

Madge was always interested in people, so instead of snubbing the good-hearted little man's advances with frosty good breeding, she answered him pleasantly. He had had little education, as was evident, but he felt a kindly, if curious, interest in the trio in his carriage, and when, a little later, they produced sandwiches and milk, he vanished, to return with some magnificent gooseberries, which he begged them to share with him. Again, Grizel looked for the icily polite snub her stepmother would have given him. Madge only thanked him for his kindness with the direct simplicity which was so much a part of her charm, and offered him sandwiches in return.

Over their meal they became quite friendly, and, before they reached Paris, he had found out that she proposed running a school in the Tyrol. He commended the scheme, and offered to try to find her pupils among his customers – he was a wool manufacturer from Bradford, as it turned out. They were quite sorry to say goodbye to him when they reached Paris; but he was going on to Lyons that night, and they were to spend the next two or three days in the jolliest city in the world. It was five o'clock – or seventeen, if you cared to take French time – by the time they had arrived, and both Jo and Grizel were tired, so Madge made no attempt to do anything that night. They went to their hotel, a quiet one, not far from the Madeleine, and after having arranged for the remainder of the week, they were shown to their rooms, where *thé à l'Anglais* was sent up. They all woke early next morning, and after *petit déjeuner* of coffee and rolls, prepared to go out. Naturally, since they were so near, the Madeleine was their first objective. Jo had seen it before, but she was perfectly willing to visit the great church which Napoleon had begun as a "Temple of Glory", and which he was destined never to finish. Grizel looked at it with wonder in her face.

"Somehow, I didn't think Napoleon was a religious man," she observed thoughtfully. "Whatever made him want to build a church?"

"He wasn't; and he didn't," explained Madge. "I forget what his idea was, but it certinly wasn't the idea of the average man. But then he wasn't an average man, of course! Anyway, it's rather a wonderful thing, isn't it? Not to be compared with Notre Dame, of course!"

"Is he buried here?" asked Grizel.

"No, in the Invalides," replied Jo, who was an enthusiastic admirer of the great Emperor.

"Well, I think we've seen everything here, so we may as well go to the Champs Elysées," said Madge. "We'll take a bus there. Then we'll go up it a little way, and get another bus to the Pont Alexandre. From there, it's easy to get to the Invalides. We'll have *déjeuner*, and after that, we go to the Louvre by the Métro."

"And the opera tonight," supplemented Joey. "Oh, topping!"

Madge nodded. Mr Cochrane had given her an additional cheque, with the request that she would take Grizel about as much as possible. He was not a devoted father, but some strange feeling of regret that he meant so little to his only child had prompted him to do this.

"Children always enjoy that sort of thing better when someone of their own age is with them," he had said. "Please include Miss Joey in the party."

"Are we really going to the opera?" asked Grizel incredulously.

"Yes, it's *La Bohême* tonight. I don't know how much of it you'll understand, but the music is lovely," replied Madge, as they boarded a bus. "Look out of the window, Grizel. We're coming to the Place de la Concorde, where the guillotine stood during the Reign of Terror."

Joey, the insatiable reader, murmured softly, "Sydney Carton!" But Grizel's knowledge of the French Revolution was confined to that gained from the Scarlet Pimpernel stories, and when, as they reached the famous space, the younger girl softly quoted the closing sentences from *A Tale of Two Cities*, she paid no heed. The Champs Elysées pleased her far more with their bustle and life. Madge chuckled softly to herself as she walked between them. The outlook of the two children was so totally different. Joey always saw Paris through a rose mist of history and legend; Grizel, now that her first wonder was over, so obviously took all that side of it for granted; and devoted herself to its life and people.

After Les Invalides, they had *déjeuner* at one of the many restaurants, and then took the Métro to the Louvre. The opera was an entire success. True, neither of the girls understood much of the story, but the exquisite music appealed to both, and even matter-of-fact Grizel felt a lump come into her throat when Mimi died. The next day was devoted to a trip up the river to St Cloud and Sèvres, which pleased Miss Cochrane far more than the Louvre.

"I like to see things done," she explained to Joey. "Of course, pictures and statues are all right but they're not half so interesting as seeing people do things now. And I think St Cloud is awfully jolly! I wish we'd been able to go up the Eiffel Tower, though."

"You've done quite enough for today," declared Madge, with an anxious eye on Joey's white face. "Tomorrow we'll go out to Versailles, and then on Monday we must be getting on."

On the next day they went to Versailles, and spent long, happy hours wandering about that magnificent extravagance of Louis XIV. The gardens filled them with admiration, and Grizel thrilled at seeing the Hall of Mirrors, where the Peace Treaty had ended the Great War. From there, they went on to the Trianons, with their dainty artificiality, where poor Marie

Antoinette and her court ladies had played at being milkmaids and shepherdesses clad in flowered silks, while, less than twenty miles away, the Paris mob was beginning to cry aloud for bread. The whole place was peopled with exquisite ghosts for both Madge and Jo, and even Grizel became infected by them, and half expected to see some hooped and powdered lady, with raised fan and brilliant eyes, beckon to her from behind one of the statues. Madge was wise enough to take them back early, after they had seen the famous fountains playing, and the next day was spent in visiting Notre Dame and looking at the shops.

Grizel was anxious to buy nearly everything she saw, but Madge kept a tight rein on her. She would only allow her to change a little of her money into francs, and then she insisted that choice must be carefully made. Finally, at the Louvre, a lace collar was chosen for Cook; several postcards were bought and sent off; then, at Jo's suggestion, they went to the Luxembourg Gardens, which lay bathed in April sunshine. Grizel was deeply interested in the French children who romped about there, carefully watched by mothers and nurses. The *carousel*, with its lions and elephants, and little hurdy-gurdy, took her fancy completely, and she insisted on having several 'goes', rather to the amusement of Jo, who strayed off to the fountain, where several bare-legged and crop-haired small boys were sailing their boats to a general chorus of "*Quel est beau!*" "*Ah, mon Dieu!*" "*C'est bien que possible!*" "*Voleur!* "*C'est le mien!*" And, more than once, "*Fermes le bec, toi!*"

Here Madge and Grizel found her when they came a little later, haranguing two small, bewildered-looking boys in a polyglot mixture of French and English.

Grizel laughed, "Oh, Joey, I think it's lovely! I caught the ring five times, and the man said it was superb!"

"Well, now let's have *déjeuner*," suggested Madge. "I'm hungry, if you aren't."

Déjeuner over, they strolled along to the Champs Elysées, and joined in the merry throng round "Guignol", which is a French version of Punch and Judy. Tea they had at a *pâtisserie*, where Grizel rejoiced once more in the delightful custom which ordains that each customer shall take a plate and fork to the counter and help himself to delicious sandwiches and cakes before settling down.

"So much more sensible than English shops," she said. "They always bring the things you don't want—"

"Like horrid spongy cakes with butter icing!" chimed in Jo. "I loathe them! Now éclairs, I could go on eating for ever!"

"And beautifully sick you would be," said Madge firmly. "No, you don't, Joey, my child! Remember, our train leaves at nine. Finished? – *Le comptoir, s'il vous plaît.*" This last to the pretty waitress who stood near. After that, they returned to their hotel to pack up and have dinner, and half-past eight saw them at the Gare de l'Est, climbing into the Paris–Wien express train.

"Here start our Austrian adventures," observed Jo, as she curled herself up comfortably in a corner. "You can't count Paris!"

"Can't you? I do!" replied Grizel. "It's all been absolutely thrilling, so far!"

"Go to sleep and don't talk," ordered Miss Bettany. "We shall be in Switzerland, I hope, when you wake tomorrow."

"Switzerland?" Grizel sat bolt upright in her excitement.

"Yes; we reach Basle about six in the morning. Now, be quiet!"

And she refused to say another word or to let them talk, so they subsided, and before long all three were fast asleep, while the great train hurtled onwards through the darkness.

Chapter Four

AUSTRIA AT LAST!

IT WAS HALF-PAST seven on the Wednesday evening when the Vienna express slackened speed before entering Innsbruck station. By this time Grizel was weary of the train, while Jo's tongue had long ceased wagging, and she lay in her corner of the carriage gazing dreamily out at the darkening landscape.

"We're only an hour late," observed Madge, as she collected their belongings together. "We've missed the last train of the mountain railway, so we'll have to go to a hotel somewhere for the night."

"I shan't be sorry," replied Grizel decidedly. "Will Mr Bettany meet us, or shall we have to fish for ourselves?"

"Dick will meet us all right," said Jo, rousing herself up to answer this question. "Where shall we put up, Madge — at the Europe?"

"I suppose so," replied her sister. "Or there's the Kreide, only it's further away."

"I hope it's somewhere near," returned Jo wearily. "I should like to have a bath and go to bed! Hello, we're slackening!"

"There's Dick!" exclaimed Madge, as she hung out of the window. But Dick had seen her, and was already running along by the side of the carriage, shouting a cheery greeting to them.

"Shove the cases through the window!" he called, as the train stopped. "Bustle the kids out! I've got a porter here! Rooms booked at the Europe!"

Dick was an experienced traveller, and both he and Madge spoke German fluently, so they were soon past the barrier and out into the big square, where carriages intended for two horses, but drawn by one only, were waiting for hire, while the coachmen, picturesque enough figures in their short open jackets, full shirts, and little green Tyrolese hats with the inevitable feather at the back, leant up against the wheels, shouting chaff to each other, or smoking their long china-bowled pipes. Beyond, they could see the great snowcapped mountains towering up on all sides, while round them thronged tow-headed, grey-eyed children, begging for kronen with a persistence which suddenly died away as Dick addressed them with a ready flow of language.

"Awful little beggars!" he said as they dispersed. "They're nearly as bad as the natives at Port Said. Tired, Grizel? Here's our hotel; nice and handy for the station, you see!"

"Is everything all right at the Chalet?" asked Madge, as they entered the big hotel. "Has Mademoiselle's cousin arrived? I've got another pupil – an American called Evadne Lannis. She's coming in September."

"Good for you," replied her brother. "Yes, everything's all right and the kid – Simone, her name is – arrived Friday of last week. Mademoiselle stayed down here till today, and sent up the things by rail. I got the place scrubbed out, and dear old Frau Pfeifen came along, and her eldest girl, and we've got it quite shipshape. There's a big room they had built on for a *Speisesaal*, and we've turned that into a classroom. I knocked up some shelves, and we've got the books up. Two little rooms we've given to you and Mademoiselle, and a huge loft affair we've put the kids' beds in. It holds eight easily, so you'd better buck up and get four more. There's a landing-stage just opposite, and the water's quite shallow. Old Braun at the Kron Prinz Karl says you can bathe from there in the summer. Now I'll get your keys, and then you can go and beautify yourselves while I order some food for you. Come down to the *Speisesaal* when you are ready."

"What's a *Speisesaal*?" asked Grizel, as they went up in the lift.

"It's German for dining room," explained Madge. "Here we are! Now buck up, you two, and make yourselves tidy, and then come and tap at my door."

They hastened joyously, and in a marvellously short time they were ready.

Then they went down to the *Speisesaal*, where they found

Dick and a delightful meal awaiting them, together with a most obsequious waiter.

"Nothing really exciting," said Dick. "Only *Kalbsbraten* – all right, Grizel! That's German for roast veal! and *Kartoffeln*, otherwise spuds, and *Apfeltorte*, which isn't apple tart, although it sounds like it."

"What is it, then?" Grizel wanted to know.

"Sort of cake with cooked apples on it," said Jo swiftly. "Oh, it is nice to have the funny things again! I think foreign food is much more interesting than English! Must we really go to bed after supper? I don't want to in the least."

"It'll be nine o'clock before you're settled," retorted her brother. "You can trot round Innsbruck tomorrow if you're so keen! It won't run away in the night, you know."

"When do we go up to the Tiernsee?" asked Grizel.

"Not till the half-past seven train tomorrow evening," replied Madge. "There are one or two things I want to get, and you really must see a little of Innsbruck while you are here. We will go to the Ferdinandeum Museum and the Hof-Kirche, and you must see the old house with the golden roof."

"Is it really gold?" asked Grizel in awestruck tones.

"Oh dear no! And it is really just the roof of the balcony to a window. But it's very famous, and you ought to see it."

"Then there's the Maria Theresien Strasse with its swagger shops," chimed in Dick, "and the great Triumphal Arch. And you must go down and have a look at the Inn. You'll have plenty to do tomorrow, I can assure you. I'll go up during the morning, Madge, and take the cases, then you and the kids can come on later."

Everyone agreed to this programme, and Jo and Grizel went off to bed quite happily, while their elders took a stroll up to the little station, where the electric railway, which is known as the Stubai Bahn, begins.

"You ought to take the kids up here some day," observed Dick.

"Some day," agreed Madge; "but do remember that I'm here to start a school in the first place!"

"Geography," he said shortly, with a twinkle in his eye. "You might make a weekend expedition of it in the summer and take them to the edges of the Stubai glacier. You could get rooms in Fulpmes, and the Stubai valley is lovely."

"I know," said Madge, sighing. "It all is! But oh, Dick! Supposing it isn't a success! Supposing I fail!"

"Tosh!" he said easily. "You won't fail! You've too much grit for that. Other people might; but you'll go on! Buck up, old thing!"

"But I'm so young," she said, "only twenty-four, Dick!"

He gave her arm a reassuring squeeze.

"You'll pull through all right! Keep your hair on, old girl! We'd better be getting back now. You're tired, and ought to be in bed."

"Yes, I am," acknowledged Madge. "Oh, Dick, I shall be so thankful to get to our own house! I must say it sounds attractive. What is little Simone like?"

"Didn't see much of her," he replied. "She struck me as

jolly quiet. Very dark, of course; not a bit pretty like that Grizel kid."

"Yes, Grizel will be lovely when she's grown up," said his sister. "I should think she's clever, too. Oh, Dick, she and Jo were too funny for anything in Paris! Joey was dreaming it all into history, and Grizel is so absolutely matter of fact. She simply couldn't understand Joey and her dream pictures."

"Jolly good job," said Dick austerely. "Jo dreams far too much."

"Well, she hasn't had much chance to do anything else," replied Madge. "Perhaps Grizel and Simone, and Evadne when she comes, will make her different."

"Oh, she'll be better in the mountains," was his answer. "Half the trouble has been her health. She's better already, I think, even though she's tired."

"It can rain at the Tiernsee," Madge reminded him.

"I know that. But she'll have companions of her own age. And don't you worry, my chicken! Everything's going grandly!"

With this assurance the subject was dropped, and presently they reached the hotel, and Madge retired to bed.

The next day was spent in shopping and sightseeing. Dick left them early in the day, and went up to the Tiernsee with the cases and the rugs, while the three girls explored the city to their hearts' content. Grizel, quick to learn, was already picking up phrases in German, and she took the greatest delight in practising them. Jo, whose German had been fluent in the past, found it coming back to her, even as her French had begun to do in Paris. She instructed her friend as they went about, and eventually poured so much information into her, that it was small wonder that Grizel became muddled. The result was a mistake that the Bettanys remembered against her for long enough.

Madge had decided to take both children to have their hair shampooed before going up to the lake. She remembered, from their last sojourn in the Tyrol, a very good hairdresser's shop in the Museum Strasse, and thither she took them. The hairdresser had a little English, but not much. When the shampooing was over, he asked them whether the final rinsing should be of hot or cold water. The German for "hot water" is "*heisses Wasser*". Jo came through the ordeal all right, demanding a lukewarm rinsing for the last. Not so Grizel. She forgot what the German for "cold" was, but remembered, as she imagined, the word for "hot". The temptation to exhibit her knowledge of his language was too great to be resisted, and she reduced the man to horrified silence, and the Bettany girls to helpless laughter, by boldly demanding "*heiliges Wasser*".

It was the expression of outrage on Herr Alphen's face as much as anything that rendered it impossible for Madge to do anything but choke wildly; while he himself, a most devout Catholic, decided that this was only one more example of the madness of the English. It struck him as profane in the extreme that anyone should demand to have her hair rinsed with holy water. Still, doubtless these poor creatures knew no better. With a resigned expression and outspread hands, he carefully explained that it was impossible to give her what she asked. He assured her, however, that he would put some of his very best toilet preparations into what was used if she would only say whether she would have it hot or cold, or, like the other *Fräulein*, lukewarm.

Of all this harangue, which was poured forth at top speed, Grizel understood not one word. Finally Madge, choking back her laughter with great difficulty, came to the rescue, and the shampoo was finished.

"But I don't see what there was to giggle at," observed Grizel to Joey when they had finally left the shop. "And why did that man get so fussy when I asked for hot rinsing water? Did he think I should catch cold after it? I wanted a cold rinse, as a matter of fact, but I couldn't remember the word for it, so I asked for hot."

"That's just what you didn't do," Joey informed her solemnly. "You've shocked poor Herr Alphen most horribly, and I'm not surprised! I only wonder he finished you at all!"

"But why? What did I do?" demanded the bewildered Grizel.

"Oh, you only asked for a final rinsing of holy water! And he a Catholic – at least I suppose so!"

"But I only said what you told me," protested Grizel.

"They're rather alike in sound," admitted Joey. "The beginnings are the same anyhow. I wonder if he's got over it yet?"

At first, Grizel was inclined to accuse her friend of pulling her leg, but when she finally realized that the mistake was her own, she cheerfully joined in the laugh against herself.

"Well, anyhow, that's one thing I shan't forget," she said, as they made their way to the station. "I couldn't if I tried after that!"

"I don't believe you could," agreed Jo – Madge was buying their tickets to Spärtz. "If you'd insisted, I wonder if he would have tried to get some for you! They're awfully obliging here, you know. Hello, Madge! Got them all right? Doesn't it feel grand to count in hundreds and thousands?"

"No, rather a nuisance," replied her sister. "Now come along. Our train is over here. Have you got those books safe, Joey?"

The journey from Innsbruck to Spärtz is of no particular interest, but the little mountain railway, which carries you up to a height of three thousand feet and more above the sea level, is something to remember. Higher and higher they climbed, now and then stopping at a tiny wayside station, till at last they reached the great alm, and there before them, dark, beautiful, and clear as a mirror, spread the Tiernsee, with its three tiny hamlets and two little villages round its shores, and towering round on all sides the mighty limestone crags and peaks of the mountains.

The railway terminus is known as Seespitz, and here the steamer was waiting for the passengers. Dick was there too, ready to help with the parcels.

"It's a jolly walk round the lake," he said, "but tonight I

think we'll take the steamer. It's about a quarter of a mile nearer from the Briesau landing-stage than it is from here, and I know you're all tired."

The little steamer waited ten minutes, then her whistle blew, and off she went, first to Buchau at the opposite side of the lake, and then to Briesau, where they were welcomed by good Frau Pfeifen, who almost wept for joy at beholding Madge and Joey once more. From the landing-stage to the Chalet was a good ten minutes' walk, and then they saw the welcoming lights, and heard Mademoiselle's warm French greeting. They were at the Chalet School at last.

Chapter Five

THE CHALET SCHOOL OPENS

BY DEGREES THEY settled down in the Chalet. The end of
April found them ready to begin work. The huge room,
which had been built to accommodate eighty people at
meals, had been partitioned off into two good-sized
classrooms. A third next to them had been made of a small
room which had been used as a lounge. Another one, on the
opposite side of the door, had been turned into a sitting
room, sacred to Madge and Mademoiselle. There were no
carpets on the floors, but they were brought to a fine polish
with beeswax and hard rubbing. The furniture, with the
exception of the schoolroom appointments, was all old. There
was but little as yet; Miss Bettany intended buying here and
there, and having it as good as might be. In the long kitchen
at the back of the house Marie Pfeifen reigned, with a
younger sister and a cousin to help her, while Brother Hans

cleaned shoes and knives, and attended to the huge porcelain stoves which warmed the place throughout.

Dick Bettany's furlough was up on 29th April, and he had to say goodbye to them before getting the Paris express, since he intended joining the boat at Marseilles. Actual school work would start on the following Monday, and Madge was very thrilled over that for, in addition to Joey, Grizel, and Simone, she had four day pupils whose parents lived round about. So they would begin with a very fair number.

Joey and Grizel were just as thrilled as she was. Simone, though quite nice, was very shy and quiet.

So, when Monday came, they were all agog to meet the strangers.

School began at nine thirty, when a little body of schoolgirls were to be seen coming along the lake road, carrying books and chattering.

"There they are!" cried Joey from her vantage point at the window. Then a minute later, in amazed tones, she added, "I thought Madge – my sister, I mean – said there were only four!"

"So she did," replied Grizel, joining her.

"Well, there's six there anyhow, and one's quite a tiny one!"

"Let's go down and meet them," suggested Grizel.

"Good scheme! Come along, Simone!"

"Hello!" she said, holding out her hand in welcome, "I'm Jo Bettany, and I know you are coming to the Chalet School. Do tell me your names, won't you? And why there's six of you, when we only expected four."

One, who was obviously the eldest, came forward and took Jo's hand.

"How do you do?" she said in careful English. "You are Fräulein Bettany's sister, are you not? I am Gisela Marani, and these are Gertrud Steinbrücke, Bernhilda and Frieda Mensch, Bette Rincini, and my younger sister Maria."

"These are Grizel Cochrane and Simone Lecoutier," said Joey.

The two Maranis and Bette Rincini were slight, graceful girls; Gisela and Maria very dark; Bette, brown, with wavy brown hair, brown eyes, and a warm brown skin. Gertrud was brown-haired, grey-eyed, and very pretty, and the two Mensches were of the fair German type. They were all between the ages of twelve and sixteen, with the exception of Maria, who was obviously not more than nine. Seeing Jo's eyes fasten on her small sister, Gisela apologetically explained her presence amongst them, and also Gertrud's.

"Mamma thought that perhaps Fräulein – ah, but you say 'Mees', do you not? – Bettany would be so kind as to permit Maria to come also. She is younger than we are, but it would be dull for her at home, and she is clever. And Frau Steinbrücke has long wanted to send Gertrud to an English school, so she is with us, and her mother will come herself to explain."

"Well, come in and take your things off," said Joey, wondering to herself how Madge would take it. "This way in. This is our cloakroom. Have you brought slippers to change? Righto! We shan't do much in the way of lessons today, you know! Just get to know what we know, and about books, and so on. You're the oldest, aren't you, Gisela?"

"Yes, I have sixteen years," replied Gisela, "and Bernhilda is next."

Bernhilda smiled at Joey, but she was obviously too shy to say anything just at present. She and Frieda rather reminded Joey of two dolls with their fair hair, blue eyes, and rosy faces. She knew, because Madge had told her, that Bernhilda was fifteen and Frieda twelve. Bette looked about fourteen and a half, and Gertrud was evidently much the same age. When they had all changed, she led them into the first of the big schoolrooms, whither Grizel and Simone had already gone.

"Now we're all here," she said. "Shall we sit down? I expect my sister and Mademoiselle will be here presently."

They sorted themselves out, Gisela, Gertrud, and Bernhilda taking three desks at the back, while Bette, Grizel, and herself sat in the next row, and Frieda, Simone, and little Maria occupied the front row. There was a minute's silence. Then came the sound of light, swift footsteps, and a moment later Madge entered the room. head well up, although her heart was beating rather quickly. She welcomed them all with a pretty, shy dignity, listened to Gisela's explanation of Gertrud and Maria, and assured her she was very pleased to have them, and then turned her attention to the business of the day.

Prayers were followed by the working of some exam questions by all the girls, so that she might have some idea as to how to arrange them. As all lessons, save French and German, were to be taken in English, she found the foreign girls worked rather more slowly than would otherwise have been the case, and little Maria did nothing at all. The arithmetic was not done in the ways to which she was accustomed, and there were many quaint turns of speech in the short English compositions; but, on the other hand, both Joey and Grizel rather came to grief over the French, while Simone's German was dreadful, and Grizel's worse. Finally, after much consideration, she decided to work all of them, save Simone, Maria, and Frieda, together in English subjects. Maria, Joey, Grizel, and Bette would form one French class, while the others would make another; and for German, Grizel and Simone would have to be specially coached. It was also obvious that she must get another assistant as soon as possible. "We are growing quickly," she mused. "I only hope it continues."

At twelve o'clock she finished work for the morning, and bidding the Tyroleans to bring some sewing for the afternoon, dismissed them for two hours, during which she saw that the children had their lunch, insisted on Jo's practising for an hour and, finally, entertained Frau Steinbrücke, a stout, cheery lady, who informed her that all the Tiernsee was talking about her, and who prophesied that, in the summer at least, she would have quite a large number of pupils.

At half-past two punctually all the girls were settled in their places again, each with some sewing, and Mademoiselle took charge. Here, both Jo and Grizel came off badly, since both hated their needles, and even little Maria was more expert than they were.

Grizel mused, "I wonder who will be appointed head girl? The first head girl of the Chalet School!"

"Ah, yes; I have read of the head girl in your English school stories," replied Gisela pleasantly. "And also prefects."

"Yes. I know Miss Bettany means to have this exactly like an English school, so I expect we shall have them too." Then she began to giggle. "Rather weird to have prefects when there are only nine of us!"

"But soon there will be more," observed Bette Rincini, who up till then had worked in silence on Gisela's other side. "Mamma said at *Mittagessen*—"

"'Lunch'," corrected Gisela.

"Ah, yes, lunch – that already many of our friends are tailing about us, she makes no doubt that many more girls will come."

"How jolly!" commented Grizel. "I like a big school. Do you have big schools in Innsbruck?"

"But yes. The public schools are very large. I did not go to them; Gisela and Maria and I had a Mamsell. But our Mamsell has gone away to be married, so Mamma is very pleased for me to come here."

"Bernhilda and Frieda went to the public school," observed Gisela, "but they, too, are pleased to leave it. My father says that the English schools are deficient in education, but they give girls a more healthy life, and Herr

Mensch agrees with him. There are others, too, who think the same, so, as Bette has said, we shall, without doubt, soon become a large school."

"But our schools aren't deficient in education!" said Grizel, firing up. "You get a jolly good education at the high schools!"

"But you have such a short period in school," returned Bette. "You work for no more than five or six hours. Now we begin at eight o'clock in the morning and work till twelve. Then we begin again at thirteen and go on for another four hours."

"How ghastly!" said Grizel sincerely. "Almost as bad as Germany!"

"But in Germany, so my cousin Amalie has told me, they work even harder than that. And they have no games as you have."

"Well, we certainly shan't work like that," replied Grizel decidedly. "I'm sure Miss Bettany would never hear of it!"

"No; she is English," agreed Gisela.

At four o'clock the command came to fold up the work, and then the six day-girls got ready for their walk home. The Maranis and Gertrud lived at Torteswald, a small village about twenty minutes' walk from Seespitz, and the Mensches were at Seespitz *Gasthaus* for the summer, while Bette had to go all the way to Buchau. As it was a fine day, she meant to walk instead of taking the steamer, and Grizel and Jo volunteered to accompany them to the Seespitz landing – Simone had disappeared as soon as they were dismissed, and they could not find her, though Joey ran, calling, through the house.

It was a delightful walk, and they found each other very friendly, although shy Frieda only smiled and scarcely spoke at all. Gisela, Bette, and Gertrud were anxious to find out all they could about English schools, and they asked many questions.

They chattered on about school topics till they reached the Seespitz *Gasthaus*, where Bernhilda and Frieda said goodbye to them.

"Will you, perhaps, come and eat an English tea with us on Saturday?" asked Bernhilda, just before they parted. "Mamma would be so pleased if you would come; and Simone also."

"Thank you, we'd love it," replied Joey.

"Our first invite," she said gleefully to Grizel as they trotted back to the Chalet. "Well, what do you think of them all?"

"I like them," returned Grizel with fervour. "Gisela's a dear, isn't she? Do you think Miss Bettany will make her head girl?"

"Oh, I expect so; she's the eldest. I say, there's Simone! Hello, Simone! Why didn't you come with us?"

"I went for a little promenade," replied Simone.

"Well, why didn't you promenade with us?" demanded Grizel. "There's no need for you to go off by yourself like that!"

"You had enough," returned Simone.

"Oh, tosh!" declared Joey in friendly fashion. "You

mustn't go raking off by yourself. There's only us three boarders at present, and we must stick together!"

Simone looked wistfully at them, but made no remark, and as they had reached the Chalet, the conversation was dropped.

Chapter Six

JOEY GIVES A PROMISE

By Saturday it was quite obvious that the Chalet School would have to enlarge both its premises and its staff. It had started actual work with nine pupils. In five days' time these had swelled to seventeen, two of them being English girls whose parents wanted to go to Norway, and were not anxious to take their children on such a tiresome journey. So, as Joey said, there were two more boarders straight off.

Amy and Margia Stevens were nice little people of eight and eleven, who had spent most of their short lives in travelling, since their father was foreign correspondent to one of the great London dailies. Margia, the elder child, was a motherly person, who adored her small sister; Amy was a dainty, fairy-like little creature, who thought Margia was all that was wonderful.

"It really is time they mixed with other girls," said Mrs

Stevens, as she sat talking to Madge and Mademoiselle; "but until this year, Amy has been so delicate, I did not like to leave her anywhere, and it was out of the question for Margia to go alone. We must to to Bergen, but I did not want to send them to a convent school. When we heard of you, it seemed quite providential."

Bette Rincini's cousins came from Innsbruck to live at Buchau with their uncle and aunt for the summer months, and it was taken quite as a matter of course that they should come with her. Then two sisters came from Scholastika at the other end of the lake, and two small children came from the Kron Prinz Karl, where they were staying with their parents.

"It is awfully thrilling!" said Joey to Madge on the Saturday morning as she sat curled up on her sister's bed. "I didn't think schools grew as quickly!"

"They don't generally," replied Madge. "It just happens that we've made a lucky pitch. Joey, is Simone Lecoutier happy? She's such a quiet little thing, and those eyes of hers look naturally tragic. Are you and Grizel kind to her? I hope you don't go off together and leave her alone?"

"Do you really think we'd be so mean?" demanded Joey, righteously indignant. "Why, we haul her along wherever we go when we can find her! But she's so weird! Soon as ever lessons are over, she slides off by herself, and where she gets to is more than I can say."

Madge let the subject drop, and suggested instead that Joey had better go to her own quarters.

Joey left the room and went downstairs to the big dining

room, where Marie was just putting a big dish of honey on the table. Simone was there already, looking, as she usually did, almost painfully tidy in her blue and white checked frock and long black pigtails. The Chalet School uniform was to be a short brown tunic with shantung top, but so far, Joey and Grizel were its only members to have them, although the others were getting them made, and Simone's, at any rate, would be ready by Monday.

Her sister's question had aroused fresh interest in the little French girl in Joey, and she regarded the younger child gravely as she saluted her with the pretty Tyrolean greeting, "*Grüss Gott!*"

"*Bonjour,*" said Simone soberly. She was rather white, and her eyes looked as though she had been crying.

"Why don't you give me 'God's greeting'?" asked Joey laughingly. "I think it's such a nice thing to say to anyone." She came closer. "Simone, why have you been howling? Aren't you happy?"

"I am ver' 'appee, zank you," replied Simone with dignity.

"Then you don't look it," retorted Joe in her most down-right manner. "If you're happy, why don't you chirk up a bit?"

Simone lifted tragic dark eyes to her face, but anything she might have said was lost, for Grizel came running in at that moment, followed in more stately fashion by Mademoiselle, and Simone promptly became muter than any oyster.

As a matter of fact, all that was wrong with her was that she was dreadfully homesick. She had never been away from her mother before in her life, and wanted her badly. She slipped off again as soon as breakfast was over, while the other two were chatting. Jo missed her presently as she went off, quite cheerfully, to what was, for the moment, known as the Junior formroom.

"Slipped off again!" she thought. "Simone! Si-mo-one!" She raised her voice in a long melodious call, but no Simone answered it. "Si-i-i-mo-one! Where are you? Simone!"

No response came, so she dashed upstairs – in complete defiance to rules – to see if the small girl had taken refuge in the dormitory. But when she pulled aside the pale yellow cubicle curtains, she found the cubicle quite empty. A hasty rush through all the living rooms helped her no further, for Simone was not there. Marie, when questioned, declared she had not seen the young lady since breakfast, and she was sure she was with neither Mademoiselle nor Fräulein Bettany, for they had gone off to Spärtz half an hour before. Jo wandered out into the warm sunshine, and turned to gaze at the Bärenkopf, a mountain which greatly took her fancy, although they had not climbed it yet, since it was considered dangerous, at any rate for amateurs.

"I'll have a shot at that some day," she thought, as she looked at the bold, rugged outlines. Then she gave an exclamation, for among the trees which clustered at the foot of the slope of the Bärenbad, another mountain, she had caught a flash of the blue and white frock which Simone wore.

"So that's where she goes!" she thought as she raced across the flower-besprinkled grass which lay between her and the woods. She soon reached them, but by that time Simone had disappeared, and although Joey shouted again and again, there was no answer. Finally, just as she decided to give up the hunt and return home, she stumbled over the root of a large tree, and went headlong onto a nest of old leaves, and there was Simone, sobbing as if her heart would break.

"Simone! What's up? Don't cry like that, old thing! Aren't you well?"

At the first sound of her voice Simone had half sprung up, then she collapsed again into the little huddle she had been when Jo found her.

"Is anything up?" asked the latter again, as she made a valiant effort to pull the other child into her arms. "Tell me, Simone, old thing!"

"I want my mother!" sobbed Simone in French, so that it was all Joey could do to make it out. "I want my mother and my home!"

"You poor kid!" Simone was exactly ten weeks younger than Joey, but for the present the English girl felt very maternal towards her. "You poor kid! There, don't cry, old dear! You'll be all right soon!"

Simone stretched out a hot, sticky hand and grabbed Joey's.

"I am so lonelee!" she sobbed. "You and Grizel are such friends!"

"I say, we didn't mean to make you feel out of it," replied Joey, whose conscience was very busily at work. "Honour bright, we didn't!"

"You are of the same nationality," went on Simone, who, once she had started to make confidences, evidently meant to go on. "You live in the same town, and know each other well, and me, I am only one. And now there will be two more, and I shall still be only one."

"Simone," Joey said, "I'm awfully sorry Grizel and I have been such beasts. I quite see we have been beasts, even though we didn't mean it! Now I want you to mop up – here's a hankie! – and come back with me, and we'll start again. I'm sure Grizel will see it, and we'll all be pally together."

But this was not what Simone wanted. Truth to tell, she had conceived a violent affection for Jo, and Grizel, with her vivid prettiness and more obvious qualities, repelled her. So she sobbed on, while Joey sat, nearly distracted, and not knowing what to do.

"Simone, I do wish you'd stop!" she said finally. "Do stop crying, old thing! I'll do anything I can for you; honest, I will!"

Simone made a big effort. "Will you be… my friend?" she choked out.

"Of course I will! I am! We both are!"

"No; I mean… my *amie intime*! Oh, Jo, if you only would, I think I should be happier! Grizel makes friends with everyone. Gisela Marani loves her, and so does Bette Rincini! I don't want her; I want only you!"

Jo promptly hugged the younger girl, and said, "Righto! we'll be pals. And now, do mop up, there's a gem!"

"You will be my *amie intime*?" persisted Simone, even as

she scrubbed her eyes hard with Joey's handkerchief. "You will relate to me all your secrets, and walk with me?"

"Yes, as long as it doesn't interfere with other people," responded Joey. "I can't tell you other people's affairs, Simone! And look here, you mustn't come rushing off by yourself. It might come on a thunderstorm or anything, and we shouldn't know where you were. At least, I should now, but others wouldn't, and it might worry them."

"I will p-romise to do it no more," replied Simone soberly.

Simone accepted the hand Joey stretched out to her, and got on to her feet.

"You're all leaves; you'd better let me brush you down!" said Jo. "You'll have to change before we go over to the Mensches this afternoon; you can't go in that frock now! It looks as though you'd slept in it!"

They went slowly down the slope, and crossed the grass to the Chalet, where they were met at the door by Grizel, who had just finished her practice.

"Hello!" she said. "I've just finished. What shall we do?"

"I'm going to practise," replied Jo. "I haven't touched the keys yet!"

"Not practised? But you went when I did!"

"Well, I changed my mind. I've been out with Simone, so I've got to do it now instead; and she's got to change her frock. Come on, Simone!" And Joey vanished into the house, leaving Grizel looking after her in startled fashion.

Simone followed her, and Grizel was left alone to wonder,

first, what on earth the French child had been crying about; second, why Joey had left her practice till this hour. She could come to no satisfactory conclusion, so she gave it up, and wandered off to the landing-stage to see if any visitors were coming, as the steamer was just crossing from Buchau. She was rewarded for her interest by seeing a party, unmistakably English, leave the boat and, giving their luggage in charge of the porter, make for the Tyroler Hof, one of the largest hotels in Briesau. What interested her most was the fact that, besides a lady and gentleman who looked very bored, there was also a girl of about her own age.

"I wonder if they are staying long?" she thought to herself, as she turned and went back to the Chalet to see if the other two were ready to come out. "P'raps it'll be another pupil for the Chalet School. Oh, I do hope so!"

Chapter Seven

THE TIERNJOCH

"SOME NEW PEOPLE came this morning," said Grizel.

They were all five – Joey, Simone, Bernhilda, Frieda, and herself – gathering flowers in the stretch of meadow that lies between Seespitz and Torteswald. The flowers in the Tyrol are wonderful, and now, in mid-May, the place was a veritable fairyland. Even Grizel and Joey, fresh from Cornwall, where the wealth of bloom is almost as rich as it is in Devon, were thrilled with the riches at their feet, and gathered armfuls of gentian, anemone, hepatice, heartsease, narcissi, and daisies, which they would later arrange in the bowls and jars at the Chalet.

There had been a good deal of chatter about school affairs, or rather, Joey and Grizel had done the chattering, and the others had put in an occasional word. Now Grizel changed the conversation.

"Some new people came this morning."

"How interesting!" said Bernhilda politely. "Were they English?"

"They looked like it," replied Grizel. "There were three of them – father, mother, and a girl about fourteen, I should think."

"Perhaps another pupil for the Chalet School," suggested the elder girl, glancing at her watch as she spoke. "I think, if you do not mind, that we had better return now, as we shall have tea at—"

"Four o'clock!" put in Joey. "You told us the time before, Bernhilda, and it is so muddling when you talk of sixteen o'clock."

Bernhilda laughed. She was a rather sedate, well mannered girl, and Miss Bettany had already decided to appoint her as second prefect. Gisela was to be head girl, and Bette and Gertrud would be subs. Madge would have preferred an English girl as Head, but Grizel was too irresponsible, and Joey too childish for her to dream of it.

Bernhilda now led the way to the *Gasthaus*, her arm slipped through Grizel's, while the other three followed, Joey keeping up a lively flow of conversation, to which shy Frieda only responded by smiles. Simone had remained glued to her side the whole afternoon, and it was beginning to dawn on Joey that she might have undertaken a friendship which was to prove rather tiresome on occasion.

In this order they reached the hotel, where kindly Frau Mensch was awaiting them with tea, accompanied by great platefuls of delicious-looking little cakes which, Joey knew, must have come from Innsbruck, since such things were unprocurable in the lake villages. She welcomed them cheerily, and soon they were all sitting round the table, while their hostess inquired, "*Thee mit Zitrone oder mit Rhum?*"

With a sudden shock Joey realized that she was being asked whether she would have tea with lemon in it or rum. She hated the one, and had no idea of taking the other, so she was not very sure what to do. Luckily, Bernhilda came to the rescue.

"Oh, Mamma," she said. "I think Joey and Grizel prefer *Thee mit Milch*, do you not?" turning to them.

"Yes, if you please," replied Joey promptly.

Frau Mensch smiled kindly. "Of course, if that is what you desire, my children. – *Kellnerin*," she called to the waitress, "*bitte, Milch!*"

The milk was brought and the tea was made, the Mensches taking it in the same way, though Frieda evidently disliked it. Towards the end of the meal Herr Mensch appeared. He was a big, jolly man, with fair hair and grey eyes, and, since he was in one of the big banks in Innsbruck, his English was much more fluent than his wife's. His children obviously adored him, and he sat down, pulling Frieda on to his knee with a loud and hearty kiss.

"What hast thou done today, *Mädchen*?"

"I have studied my lessons for Monday," replied Frieda seriously, "and I have helped our guests to gather flowers."

"Such glorious flowers!" put in Joey eagerly. "I do think the Tiernsee is lovely!"

"Thou lovest it already, Fräulein?" He looked pleased. "It is my home – where I was born. I fished yonder," – he pointed at the blue lake waters – "many a day ere I was thine age. I climbed the Tiernjoch when I was but eleven, and brought my mother home some Edelweiss. *Ei!* But my father was angry! I had gone in disobedience, you understand, and his stick was ready for me; but my mother begged me off, and there was no punishment that time." He broke into a great roar of laughter, and the girls joined with him.

"Why should you be punished for climbing the Tiernjoch?" asked Grizel curiously. "Which is it, Herr Mensch?"

"The Tiernjoch is dangerous for all but the most experienced climbers," he replied, "and the Edelweiss grows only in one part, which is the most dangerous of all. Thou dost not know it, *mein Kind*? Come then, and I will show it to thee. We will walk to Buchau – canst thou walk so far? And Fräulein Joey, and the little one? – then we will go to Buchau, and from there I will name you the mountains, and all three shall see them."

They set off through the thick grass, listening eagerly while Herr Mensch told them about the time when he was a boy here.

"We did not then think of the hundreds of tourists from all countries who would come and visit our little lake," he said. "And now we have even a school!"

"Papa, Grizel saw some English people come today," said Bernhilda. "They are at the Tyroler Hof, and there is a girl of our age. Perhaps she may come to the Chalet School."

"That would be very pleasant – another compatriot," he replied seriously. "Now see, my children, there is the Tiernjoch, that large one who lifts his head into the clouds. In front of him stands the Bernjoch, and that one, to the side, is the Mittelberge – all very difficult to climb. That one that seems to watch over Briesau – see how he bends protectingly! – is the Mondscheinspitze, quite easy to climb, and there is a hut on the alm where one can obtain milk and butter and cheese. We will climb there some day if Fräulein Bettany will permit it. It is a walk up the valley, and then it is very pleasant on the mountain, with flowers growing, and butterflies so tame, they will not flutter when one approaches."

"How topping!" said Joey. "I should love that!"

"I want to climb the Tiernjoch," said Grizel suddenly. "I like difficult things!"

The kindly giant – he really was almost a giant! – looked down at her with a smile. "*Na-na, mein Kind!* A good *Mädchen* will wait till there is time for a whole day and a guide. That cannot be until the summer. Then, perhaps, it may be possible. But the little expedition up the Mondscheinspitze can be made on a Saturday, and we will take the herdsmen some tobacco, and drink of their milk, which is very rich with cream, and so come back. To climb the Tiernjoch one must start very early in the morning, before the sun has risen, and climb for six to eight hours before one reaches the summit. But the Mondscheinspitze, that is a nice little climb."

Grizel said nothing further, but her lips set in obstinate lines, and Joey, looking at her, felt assured that it would take more than Herr Mensch's speech to make her change her mind.

"I wish we hadn't said anything about it," she thought to herself. "I know Grizel will think of nothing else now, and I shall have to spend half my time trying to persuade her not to!"

How heartily she was to wish this thing before the summer was over Joey did not then know – which was, perhaps, just as well. Now she turned her attention to Herr Mensch, who was pointing out the mountains behind them, and naming them: "Sonnenscheinspitze, Alpengluckjoch, Maria-Theresienspitze, Wolfkopf, Schneekoppen. But these are not such mountains," he went on, "as the Dolomites. Some day you will doubtless see those too."

"Papa took us there two years ago," observed Bernhilda. "We stayed in the *Gasthaus* at Primiero, and our cousins came too. It was very pleasant there, and they have many lovely flowers. You would like those, Grizel."

"Did you climb any of them?" asked Joey.

"Oh, no! The Dolomites are very difficult to climb," explained her young hostess. "But Papa and Onkel Paul used to go for days. Once or twice they took my brother with them—"

"Brother! I didn't know you had a brother!" interrupted Grizel, somewhat rudely, it must be admitted.

"Oh, yes; my brother is eighteen, nearly nineteen. He is at

the University of Bonn," replied Bernhilda. "He will be a doctor some day, and perhaps I shall be his *Hausfrau* till he marries."

"Perhaps he won't," suggested Joey. "I know Dick, my brother, says he won't. He says the Deccan is no place for women, and he loves his work too well to give it up."

"Oh, I hope Gottfried will marry some day!" said his sister earnestly.

"We all hope that," said her father. "And now we must be returning, for there is quite a long walk, and the little one looks weary."

He reached out a big hand and pinched Simone's cheek as he spoke.

She blushed, and edged nearer to Joey, who felt suddenly cross with her. If Simone was going to be so idiotically shy, and stick to her like glue all day, Joey felt things were going to be tiresome. And why, oh, why didn't she talk instead of standing there deathly silent?

"It's been awfully jolly of you to show us all these things, Herr Mensch," she said, with a surreptitious poke at Simone. "It makes it seem twice as nice to know the names of all the places; doesn't it, Simone?"

"Yes," replied Simone faintly.

"We are going up the Bärenbad Alpe some Saturday soon and have cream," went on Joey. "Marie, Marie Pfeifen, who does the work for us, says that it is awfully nice cream; and it's an easy climb, so we shall all be able to go, even the new little boarders. Did you know we were to have two new boarders on Monday, Bernhilda?"

"No, I had not heard of it," responded Bernhilda.

"Well, we are – Margia and Amy Stevens. Margia is eleven, and Amy is about the same age as Maria Marani. That makes five of us boarders, and p'raps we shall get some more."

Suddenly Grizel caught her arm. "Look!" she cried. "There are those people I told you about this morning that I saw going to the Tyroler Hof! See – coming this way!"

They all looked with interest at the trio who were walking in their direction – a tall, bronzed man, with erect, soldierly bearing; a small, slight woman, sallow of skin and fashionable of dress; and a schoolgirl of fifteen or thereabouts, whose most noticeable features were a pair of enormous dark eyes, and a long, fair pigtail swinging to her waist. She was walking slightly behind the others, and there was a sullen, unhappy look in her face. Just as the two parties met, the woman turned to her, saying sharply, "Juliet! Hold yourself up! Good gracious me, child, you look positively deformed! Put your shoulders back at once!"

The sharp, scolding tones brought back her stepmother to Grizel, and involuntarily she shivered. Joey, noticing, slipped an arm through hers with a little squeeze. The girl Juliet looked at them curiously as she passed them. She had made no effort to straighten herself, and Bernhilda commented on this when they were out of hearing.

"But how disobedient!" she remarked.

"I can tell you their name," said her father. "He is a Herr Captain of the Indian army – Captain Carrick. He came into the bank this morning to change some money."

"I don't think he looks kind," said Joey. "What a pretty name the girl has – Juliet! Don't you think so, Grizel?"

"I thought she looked dreadfully unhappy," replied Grizel. "And how funny to have fair hair with those dark eyes!"

"Do you think so?" asked Bernhilda. "There are a great number of people living in Wien who are like that. But as for unhappy, she did not do as she was told."

Herr Mensch approved of this. "The young should always obey," he said. "Is it not so, my little Frieda?"

Frieda, who would as soon have thought of flying as of disobeying her parents, said in her shy, soft voice, "Yes, Papa!"

Grizel made a little impatient movement, but Joey's hand on her arm checked any remarks she might have made, and they went on to the *Gasthaus*, talking about the mountains. The girls went in, and the three boarders got their flowers and said goodbye to Frau Mensch. She kissed them all, and told them to come back whenever they liked. Then, accompanied by Bernhilda and Frieda, they went out, to find Herr Mensch waiting for them at the boathouse.

"Come!" he said. "It is a long walk, and *die Kleine* looks tired! I will row you across to your own landing-stage. Bernhilda and Frieda, you may come too. Run, Frieda, and tell Mamma!"

Frieda ran quickly back, and presently returned, and they pushed off.

It was glorious on the lake. The day had been very warm for mid-May, but now, with the evening, had come a little cool breeze that ruffled the surface of the water into tiny ripples, and set the curly ends round Grizel's face dancing gaily.

They rowed out into the centre, and then Herr Mensch rested on his oars, and nodded towards the mountain he had named for them – Alpengluckjoch.

"Look!" he said. "Alpengluck tonight!"

They turned and looked. As they did so, they saw the grey limestone crags flush into rosy life with the reflected light from the setting sun. All along the westward side of the Tiernsee the peaks caught the glory. It reflected on the silver thread of a mountain cataract high up in the Sonnen-scheinspitze, and even cast a faint glow over the lake. For five minutes the wonder lasted, then it began to fade, and Herr Mensch took up his oars again and rowed them in leisurely fashion to the Chalet landing-stage.

"It is beautiful!" said Joey in low tones. Her imaginative temperament had been fired by the loveliness of what she had just seen. "I have seen it once or twice from the windows, but never from the water before."

"Yes, it is a glory," replied Herr Mensch; "but it always brings bad weather with it. We shall have rain tomorrow."

He brought the boat up to the landing-stage as he spoke, and helped them out. Madge had seen them coming, and came running down the path to meet them. When the Mensches had gone and were beyond calling range, she turned to the three.

"Girls," she said, "I have news for you! We have another

day-girl. She is an English girl, whose parents are Anglo-Indians. They have just come to the Tiernsee. When they heard of us, they came at once, and she starts on Monday. She is fifteen and a half, and has only been to school in the Hills. Her people are army people, and her name is—"

"Juliet Carrick!" burst out Grizel impatiently. "Oh, Miss Bettany, is it – is it? Do say it is!"

Madge looked at her in amazement. "Yes, it is," she answered. "But how do you know?"

They explained to her about the meeting near Buchau, and Grizel enlarged on the way Mrs Carrick had spoken to the girl.

"I believe she's her stepmother!" she concluded.

"No," said Madge, "she isn't. Don't get wild ideas into your head, Grizel. If they only came to the Tiernsee today, I expect they are tired, and that is why Mrs Carrick scolded."

Grizel said nothing further, and Madge thought no more of it. But when Herr Mensch heard, he looked thoughtful.

"I hope things will go well with Fräulein Bettany," he said to his wife. "I did not like that man. I do not trust him."

And he resolved to advise Madge to write to her brother at the earliest opportunity, and see if any information could be gathered about these people who had come so suddenly.

However, when he spoke about it some days later, he found that she had done that very thing already.

"I know it seems mad to take anyone so abruptly," she said, "but they were so anxious, and… well, somehow he persuaded me. And they have paid a term's fees, of course, and if I find from my brother that she is not a desirable pupil, I can get rid of her quite easily by saying that we are full up. Anyhow, it is probably for this term only, as they expect to go to England in September; but they had heard of the Tiernsee, and thought they would like to see it, so they broke their journey home."

And after that the good-natured Austrian felt he had nothing left to say for the present.

Chapter Eight

A First Prefects' Meeting

"Gisela!"

"Yes? Do you want me, Gertrud?"

"I should be glad if you would summon a prefects' meeting."

Gisela lifted a surprised and inquiring face to her friend.

"A meeting, Gertrud? Oh, but why? Nothing has gone wrong?"

"No," agreed Gertrud, "but I am afraid something will go wrong very soon."

In her earnestness, she forgot the school rule which said that, during school hours, and save in French and German lessons, nothing but English was to be used, and dropped into her native tongue.

"Oh, Gertrud! You have forgotten," said Gisela reproachfully.

"I am sorry, Gisela! I was thinking about the meeting," apologized Gertrud. "Shall I enter my name in the Order Book?"

"No," said the head girl firmly. "It is not good for the Juniors that they see a prefect's name there. You had better report yourself to Miss Maynard. And now, tell me, why do you wish this meeting?"

"There is mischief going on in the school," returned Gertrud, perching herself on her friend's desk. "It is partly that new girl, Juliet Carrick, but I think Grizel Cochrane is making it also."

"How tiresome!" Gisela knitted her black brows at this information.

During the seven weeks that she had been head girl, there had been no real difficulty to meet. This was partly because of the novelty of things to all the girls; but also her own personal character had a great deal to do with it. Miss Bettany had chosen wisely in choosing her as Head of the girls. Bernhilda made a very good second, and Bette and Gertrud were rapidly learning their duties as subs, but the most reliable person was Gisela.

"Ready?" said Gertrud. "Then shall we call the others? They are by the landing-stage."

"Yes. Would you ask them to come to our room, Gertrud?" said Gisela. "I will await you there."

Three weeks previously, Madge Bettany, after a long discussion with Mademoiselle and Miss Maynard, who had been added to the staff as mathematics mistress, had given over to the prefects a small room on the first floor for their own.

"Even if they have just four chairs in it, it will give them a feeling of being a little different from the rest of the school," she said.

Miss Maynard, herself a high school girl, had agreed, and the four delighted girls had, accordingly, that possession of which they had read so much in their English school stories – a prefects' room.

Miss Bettany had explained to them that, beyond chairs and a small table, she could give them no furniture yet; but they had promptly joined forces. While Gisela brought some pictures and a couple of bowls of flowers, Gertrud produced a set of bookshelves which she had induced her brother to make; Bernhilda contributed a pretty blue and white tablecloth and a fancy inkstand, and Bette presented a little clock and a bracket on which to place it. In one book Gertrud had read of the prefects' notice board. Careful questioning had soon drawn from Joey all there was to know about this, and now a similar board hung over the book-shelves, with notices of various kinds on it, all written in Gisela's pointed Italian handwriting. The two big bowls were full of Alpen roses, and on this sunny afternoon it was as charming a girls' room as could be wished. The head girl pulled up the four chairs round the table, and seated herself at the head, paper and pencil before her. Presently there came the sound of footsteps on the stairs, and then the other three entered. Very smart and businesslike they looked in their school uniform, which every girl now wore as a matter of course. Gisela looked at them with approval. The most English of English prefects could not have looked more orthodox, she thought.

"Gertrud tells me you wish a prefects' meeting," began Bernhilda, as she took her seat on Gisela's right hand. "What is it that you wish to discuss with us?"

"It is Gertrud's idea," replied the head girl. "She thinks that things are going rather—"

"Wonky," supplemented Bette, as Gisela paused to search for the right word.

The head girl now made a little bow to her sub, and continued:

"Apparently Gertrud fears that Grizel Cochrane and Juliet Carrick are about to cause trouble. Myself, I have noticed nothing."

"But I have," said Bette composedly. "I quite agree with Gertrud, and I think Juliet Carrick is at the bottom of it."

"Why should you think that?" demanded Gisela.

"Because, until she came, Grizel Cochrane never rebelled against our authority. But now she is tiresome," replied Bette. "She is even rude."

"How so? She has not been rude to me as yet. How has she been rude to you?"

"I told her to go and put her shoes away," said Bette, "and she said it was sickening having fussy foreigners always at you."

"That was very rude," said Gisela slowly. "What did you do?"

"I said I was sorry she looked at it in that way," returned Bette, "but as I was a sub-prefect, and one of my duties was to see that the cloakroom was kept tidy, I was going to see that it was kept tidy."

"What did she say then?" queried Bernhilda with interest.

"Said I thought myself everybody," replied Bette. "I told her not to be impertinent, and saw that she put the shoes away, and that was all."

"I think it was sufficient," said Gisela quietly. "And you, Gertrud?"

"Talking after the silence bell had been rung," said Gertrud. "I told her to be quiet, and she looked at Juliet and laughed."

"What did Juliet do? Laugh too?"

"Yes, and shrugged her shoulders. It is not good for the Juniors to see that in a girl as old as Grizel or Juliet."

"I don't think you need worry about the Juniors," said Bette. "Amy and Margia would never behave like that, and Maria is too fond of you, Gisela, to worry you that way. Nor would Suzanne and Yvette. Giovanna will be good, because she doesn't want a fuss with me, and I couldn't imagine either Frieda or Simone doing anything but keeping the rules. Joey, of course, will do as she's told, too. It really is only Grizel, and she wouldn't if Juliet didn't encourage her!"

"Well, I must make a punishment," said Gisela. "I am sorry, but Grizel must not be so rude to the prefects." She thought deeply for a minute. "I shall send for her and make her apologize to you, Bette, and you, Gertrud. Then I shall say she is to learn some German poetry in her play hours. Yes, that is what I shall do! Will you fetch her, Bette?"

Bette got up and left the room, to return ten minutes later by herself.

"She refuses to come," she said briefly.

"Refuses to come?" There was consternation in Gisela's voice. "But did you tell her that the prefects wanted her?"

"Yes," said Bette. "She just laughed, and said if we wanted her we could go to her; she wasn't coming to us!"

There was a silence. No one has foreseen that Grizel would go to quite such lengths as this, and they were uncertain how to deal with it. It was, had they but known it, the testing point of the prefect system in the Chalet School. Had they given way, or taken no notice of the English girl's defiance, it would have been goodbye to all hope of self-government. Luckily for the school, Gisela Marani was made of too fine stuff to throw up the game weakly. To her mind there was only one course to follow, and she followed it.

"I must report the matter to Miss Bettany," she said quietly. "Bette, will you come with me? She will want to hear what you have to say."

"Shall we wait till you come back?" asked Gertrud.

"Yes, I think it would be better, if you do not mind. We will make haste."

The two girls left the room, and went downstairs to the sitting room.

Madge Bettany, enjoying a much-deserved rest, looked up

with surprise when, in answer to her "Come in!" they entered, closing the door.

"Well," she said with a smile, "what is it that you want? Anything wrong, Gisela?"

"I have come to make a report to you," replied Gisela steadily.

Madge's face sobered. "To report a breach of rules? Must you, Gisela?"

All indecision had vanished from Gisela's mind now.

"Yes, I must," she answered firmly.

"Well, what is it then, dear? Sit down, both of you, and tell me."

They sat down, and then Gisela unfolded her story, looking every now and then to Bette for corroboration. Miss Bettany grew more and more serious as they progressed, and when, finally, they had finished, she sat for a minute or two without speaking. As a matter of fact, she had herself noticed a change in Grizel's manner of late. She realized, of course, that after four years of such rigorous training as the child had had, reaction must follow with the greater freedom; but she had not expected anything quite so bad as this. She had no desire to punish Grizel, but this sort of thing could not be allowed. As for Juliet, she sincerely hoped that September would see her far enough away from the Tiernsee.

"I will send for her," she said at length. "Where are you? In the prefects' room? Very well, then! I will come back with you, and she shall come and apologize for her rudeness to you. I am sorry this has occurred, Gisela."

"I, too, am sorry," replied Gisela. "I wish it had not been necessary to trouble you with it, Madame."

"You were quite right to report it," returned her headmistress. "We cannot have this sort of thing occurring. Will you find a Junior, Bette, and send her for Grizel? Then I will follow you upstairs."

Thus dismissed, they left the room. In the passage they met Amy Stevens.

"Please tell Grizel Cochrane that Miss Bettany wants her in the prefects' room at once," said Bette, while Gisela passed on in silence.

"Yes, Bette," said little Amy. "In the prefects' room? All right."

She ran off, and Bette followed Gisela upstairs. They were greeted by a duet of "Well?" as they entered the room.

"Miss Bettany has sent for Grizel, and she is coming here herself," replied Gisela.

A minute later the headmistress appeared, looking sterner than they had ever seen her before. She had just taken her seat, when there was a tap at the door, and Grizel entered with an air of somewhat forced defiance.

Left to herself, she would never have behaved as she had done. But there was a certain weakness in Grizel's character, and she was easily led. Juliet Carrick was just the type of girl to exercise a good deal of influence over Grizel. In the first place, the child's generous pity had been aroused by what she had seen and heard of Juliet's family life. There was no doubt that Captain and Mrs Carrick found their daughter a good deal of a nuisance, and the girl had a most unhappy time. Then again, Juliet had grown up in the class of Anglo-Indian society that considers the English the only nation worth mentioning, and her training in a Hill school, where nine-tenths of the girls were Eurasians who looked down on their native cousins with a bitter contempt, had helped to foster this feeling. She had sneered at "foreigner prefects", asserting that they could not possibly act adequately. Grizel was feeling sore at what she considered Joey's extraordinary fancy for Simone Lecoutier – and all the time poor Joey would have given much to be rid of this friendship! And she therefore followed Juliet's lead, with disastrous results to herself, and to others later on.

Madge wasted few words on her when she appeared.

"You have been rude to the prefects, Grizel?" she asked.

A mumble was the only reply. Madge took it as meaning "yes".

"You will apologize at once," she said coldly. "I will allow no rudeness from you younger children to my prefects. You had better understand that at once. Ask their pardon, and then do whatever they give you for punishment." There was a silence. "Come, Grizel!"

There was that in the headmistress's voice which compelled Grizel to obedience.

Without raising her eyes, she muttered, "I'm sorry!"

Miss Bettany was wise enough to realize that it would be well to accept this. She waited till Gisela had accepted the apology, and had set the culprit a short German poem to learn. Then she said, "You may go, Grizel!" And when the child had dashed away, she left the room.

As for Grizel, she had rushed off to the pine woods, where she vowed, amidst her tears of shame and anger, that she would pay them all out for treating her in this way.

Chapter Nine

SIMONE'S EXPLOIT

IF ANY OF the girls had been inclined to defy the prefects, Miss Bettany's prompt action over Grizel Cochrane's behaviour had put an end to any such ideas. The school was rapidly settling down, and the twenty girls who made it up already felt a great pride in it. All the day-girls stayed for lunch now, arriving at the Chalet by half-past eight in the morning and staying till six o'clock in the evening. Lessons began at nine and went on till twelve, when there was a break for the midday meal. At two o'clock they started work again, and went on till four. Tea was at ten past four, and then, from five to six, the Seniors did preparation and the Juniors practised. Twice a week Herr Anserl came up from Spärtz and gave music lessons to the more advanced pupils, while the others learnt with Mademoiselle. Miss Maynard taught mathematics and geography through the school, and Miss Bettany herself undertook the Engish subjects. French, German and sewing were Mademoiselle's department, and she was form mistress of the Junior form. At present they had only the three forms – Senior, Middle and Junior.

Two days after the prefects' meeting, a long letter came from England from Mrs Dene. Mr Dene had been the senior curate of the parish church at home, but he had accepted a chaplaincy in the West Indies, and they were not anxious to take Rosalie there. Then Mrs Dene had thought of the Chalet School at the Tiernsee, and she wrote to ask if Rosalie might join them in September. If so, would Miss Bettany also have room for Rosalie's cousin, Mary Burnett?

Miss Bettany wrote back saying that she would be pleased to have them both.

The same day, an Italian lady whose acquaintance she had made came to make inquiries with regard to her little daughter. Signora di Ricci was a charming person, and she was obviously very anxious that Vanna should come. Madge knew Vanna, and liked her; so, with Evadne Lannis, there were four more pupils for the Chalet School.

Sitting on her desk in the Middle schoolroom, Joey Bettany proclaimed the news of the coming of two more English girls in the autumn.

"How old are they?" asked Margia Stevens.

"Rosalie's about fourteen and Mary's twelve," replied Joey.

"Oh! One for the Seniors and one for us," observed Frieda Mensch, who was beginning to get over her shyness. "That will be jolly!"

"Top-hole!" agreed Joey. "We are spreading, aren't we? You'll love Mary, Frieda. She's such a dear, steady old thing! I'm glad she's coming!'

Simone, who was, as usual, glued to her side, changed colour at this, but for once Joey took no notice. Truth to tell, she was getting thoroughly tired of Simone's jealousy and all-in-all friendship, and there had already been more than one scene, when Simone had accused Jo of hurting her on purpose, and not liking her any more. The last time, unsentimental Jo had very nearly declared that she didn't; that she was fed up with all these fusses! But Simone had melted into tears at the least harshness, and cried so piteously, that Joey hadn't the heart to do it. Now, unheeding of the little French girl at her side, she went on enthusiastically: "Mary was a form below me at the high school, but they lived near us, and we used to play together. We were in the same netball team too."

"And the other girl – Rosalie; is she, too, pleasant?" asked Frieda.

"Oh, yes, quite jolly!" replied Joey. "She's awfully pretty too, and jolly clever as well! Oh, bother! There's the five-to-nine bell, and I haven't got my books out! Mind, Simone!"

She brushed past Simone as she jumped down, and dashed to her locker to collect her possessions. The French child looked at her with big, mournful eyes, but Joey took no notice.

At lessons that morning Simone seemed unusually stupid. All her arithmetic was wrongly worked; her dictation was full of mistakes; and she knew not one word about history, although as Joey well knew, she had thoroughly prepared it on the previous evening. As question after question passed the little girl, and she either did not answer at all, or else talked utter rubbish, Miss Bettany's brow grew blacker and blacker. She had just left the Seniors after a tussle with Grizel, who seemed to have taken leave of her senses lately, and she wondered whether that young lady's spirit of lawlessness were infecting Simone. Finally, she closed her book with an angry snap.

"Simone! Why have you not prepared your work? I am surprised at you! You must do this lesson over again at half-past four, and please never give me such disgraceful work again!"

Simone said nothing. She felt utterly miserable and unhappy, and only longed to fly away somewhere where she could cry her heart out. The others were looking at her with startled faces. It was so unlike Simone to have to be spoken to like this. Meanwhile the bell rang, and, under their Head's watchful eyes, they were forced to file out of the room in proper order. Nor were they able to speak until they had escaped with their glasses of lemonade into the open air.

Then Simone was discovered to have disappeared.

"What on earth can be the matter with her?" demanded Joey of a select group, composed of herself, Margia Stevens, Frieda Mensch, and Suzanne Mercia. "D'you think she's ill or anything?"

"She was all right at first," replied Margia. "She was talking like anything at breakfast, and she ate heaps!"

"But look here! She knew that history last night, I know she did! And she never gets returned work! Why, she's top of the form every time!" protested Joey.

"Let's try and find her," proposed Margia. "If she isn't well, Miss Bettany ought to know. She might be going to have measles or anything."

At that moment the bell for the end of break went, so they had to return to their form room and French composition. Simone did not put in an appearance; but then, as Joey said afterwards, they all thought that she must be poorly and have gone to tell the Head, who had sent her to bed. Mademoiselle herself did not miss the child. Simone was always so very quiet and inconspicuous, and naturally she did not require nearly as much attention as the others. The last lesson was geometry with Miss Maynard, and as the little French girl's arithmetic was appallingly backward, it had been decided that, for the present, she should concentrate on that. When, however, she did not put in an appearance at *Mittagessen*, Miss Bettany promptly inquired where she was.

"In bed, I think," replied Joey with equal promptness.

The Head's black brows were drawn together in a frown of perplexity.

"Bed? But why? Who sent her? Isn't she well? Mademoiselle—"

"I know nothing," replied Mademoiselle. "I have not seen her since this morning."

"Nor I," replied Miss Maynard. "She came to my arithmetic lesson, of course, but she doesn't take geometry, and I haven't seen her since before recreation."

Miss Bettany got up, looking disturbed. "Joey, why do you think she has gone to bed? Did she tell you she felt poorly?"

"Oh, no," replied Joey. "Only, she got all her work wrong, and it isn't like her, so we thought she must be ill."

"Run upstairs and see if she is there."

Joey vanished, to come back a few minutes later looking flushed and startled.

"She isn't there, Madge," she said, using the forbidden Christian name in her earnestness. "There's no one there. But in her cubicle I found this!" And she held up a long, thick plait of black hair.

A gasp sounded through the room. Madge, Mademoiselle, and Miss Maynard stood as if they were transfixed to the spot, while Joey Bettany stood holding that awful relic of Simone before their eyes.

As if someone had released a spring which was holding her, Mademoiselle leapt forward and snatched the plait from the trembling Joey.

"And where, then, is Simone?" she shrieked in her native tongue. "What has become of her?"

"Nothing very terrible can have happened, Mademoiselle," said Madge, coming forward hastily. "She must have done it for a joke or for mischief, and now is probably ashamed to show herself!"

Mademoiselle turned on Joey. "Josephine, you are the friend of Simone! Why has she done this thing?"

Joey shook her head helplessly. "I don't know,

Mademoiselle, honest injun, I don't! I'd have stopped her if I'd known."

Things certainly seemed at a deadlock. Amy had stopped crying, mainly because no one was taking any notice of her, and the rest just sat in stricken silence.

"Well," said Miss Bettany at length, "we had better try to find her. Miss Maynard, will you take the table while Mademoiselle and I go to search? Yes, Joey, what is it?"

"Oh, please, may I come too?" asked Joey breathlessly. "I've just remembered where she might be – in the pines. I can find it in a second."

"Very well," said her sister. "Mademoiselle and I will go through the house, and you can try this hidey-hole you say she has in the pine woods. Put your hat on, though – the sun is very hot today."

Joey only waited long enough to snatch her hat from its peg in the cloakroom before dashing off to the pine-covered slopes at full speed. As she ran, her brain busied itself with the question of why Simone should have cut her hair, of which, as a matter of plain fact, she had been rather vain. She reached the hollow between the big roots, where she had found Simone before, but it was empty. There was no sign at all of the little French girl, and Joey's heart stood still for a moment. She had been so sure she would find Simone there. As she stood, wondering whatever she should do now, a little sob caught her ear. At once she swung round, and scrambled over the sticks and dead pine needles in its direction. There, in a little heap, lay Simone, crying as even Joey had never seen her cry before. The ends of her hair where she had sawn off her plait stood up like little drake's tails, an effect which would have made her friend giggle helplessly at any other time. Now, however, she only tumbled down beside her, flinging an arm round her, and hauling her up on to her knee.

"Simone! Oh, Simone! What is the matter with you?"

"Go away!" sobbed Simone, in her own language. "Go away, Joey!"

"No fear!" replied Joey. "I'm not going till you're ready to come with me. And anyhow, I want to know why you've chopped your wig like that. You once told me you wouldn't have your hair cut for anything. Why on earth did you do it?"

"I… I thought you would like it!" Simone choked out. "You have often laughed at me because my hair was long, and I thought if I cut it short you would love me, and not leave me when those new English girls come next term!"

"Well!" Joey sat back and gasped. "Of all the mad ideas!" she said, when she had got her breath back. "I don't care whether you wear your hair cropped like a convict or trailing round your feet like Lady Godiva! Really, Simone, you are a perfect idiot! And why did you rush off here like that? I nearly had a fit when I went to find you in your cubicle and found only your pigtail!"

"I look so terrible!" sobbed Simone. "And then I thought of what Cousin Elise would say, and how Miss Bettany would be angry and you and all the other girls would laugh, and so I ran away."

"Well, now you're coming back," said Joey firmly. "I don't know what Madge will say to you, or Mademoiselle! But you can't stay here for ever, and I want my lunch – I came out in the middle of it! As for laughing at you, I shan't; and I don't suppose the others will either. Now do stop howling and come on!"

At first Simone refused to budge, but finally Joey succeeded in getting her to come back with her, and they reached the Chalet, both of them feeling hot and tired. After one glance at the French child's face, Miss Bettany packed her off to bed without one word of scolding; and when she had finally dragged the whole ridiculous story out of her sister, she sent that young lady up to her cubicle with strict instructions to go to sleep. Then she betook herself to Mademoiselle and unfolded the tale to her.

"In a way, it's just as well," she said, "for all that mass of hair was far too much for her in hot weather; but of course she had no business to cut it herself like that. You had better take her over to the Kron Prinz tomorrow and let the hairdresser there trim it. Now I must go to my class."

The next day Simone was taken to have her hair properly cut and, much to her relief, the other girls said very little about the whole affair, although her cousin scolded her roundly. Altogether, Simone deeply regretted the fact that she had ever touched her hair – the more so, since Joey Bettany, instead of being impressed by what she had done, characterized the whole thing as "idiotic nonsense!"

Chapter Ten

THE CINEMA ACTRESSES

IT WAS A mercy, as Madge Bettany said, that for the next week or two everything went quite ordinarily. Grizel and Juliet gave the prefects no further trouble; Simone ceased, for the moment, to behave in a sentimental way; Amy Stevens gave up crying on the smallest provocation; and there was peace in the Chalet School. The only event of any note was an accident Bernhilda had with the red ink.

All the stationery was in one cupboard, the key of which Miss Maynard kept. Bernhilda had been appointed stationery prefect, and she went every Friday and gave out the new stationery as it was required. It was not a very heavy task as yet, since everyone had started with new books at the beginning of the term. Scribblers and little notebooks were what were mainly required, with a very occasional exercise book, and Grizel Cochrane, in her capacity as ink monitor, came on Mondays for the week's supply.

On the Monday following Simone's exploit, Grizel came as usual with her ink can. She found Bernhilda, who took her duties very seriously, engaged in tidying the top shelf of the cupboard. The prefect, sitting on the top of the stepladder, looked down at her Junior.

"Oh, Grizel, will you please take the ink?" she said. "I want to finish this before the bell rings! It is in the big jar at the bottom."

"All right, Bernhilda! Don't you worry; I'll get it all right," replied Grizel cheerfully. Juliet had been absent on the Thursday and Friday of the previous week, and had not yet turned up, so Grizel was a much nicer girl in consequence.

Having directed the Junior's attention to the big ink jar Bernhilda returned to her task, while Grizel uncorked the jar and, carefully tilting it on one side, began to fill her can. Both were absorbed in their work. Grizel had very nearly finished, when Bernhilda gave a sudden shriek, and dived forward, nearly collapsing on to Grizel, who echoed her shriek. At the same time there was a crash as the large pint bottle of red ink fell heavily against the stepladder, and smashed, sending a fountain of red ink in every direction. Bernhilda's tunic suffered, but the one who came off worst was Grizel, who was almost directly underneath. In her dive forward, the prefect managed to catch the bottom portion of the bottle, and the rest fell clear of the Junior; but the ink deluged her – hair, frock, hands, even her legs were dripping with it.

The combined shrieks of the two drew the staff hastily to the spot. Mademoiselle, under the impression that there had been a fearful accident, rushed forward with a cry of "Where, then, is the injury?"

Miss Maynard and the headmistress, who had both realized almost at once what had occurred, were hard put to it to keep from laughing, although the latter promptly produced a handkerchief, and set to work to try to wipe off some of the ink. By this time Bernhilda had reached the ground, and was giving a somewhat incoherent account of what had occurred.

According to her story, she had turned some books round sharply, and had caught the ink bottle with a corner. She had tried to catch it, but had not been in time to prevent its breaking. The rest they could see for themselves. Grizel, who had not been actually hurt, was furious.

"I'm all ink, and my tunic is ruined!" she said in choked accents.

"No, I don't think so," replied Miss Bettany gravely. "You must get out of it at once, of course, and Marie must wash it immediately. Then I think it will be all right. Luckily it's your cotton tunic. And you must go and get a bath. I'll come and wash your hair, and then you'll be all right by recreation. Don't look so distressed, Bernhilda. It was an accident, and you couldn't help it. But I advise you, for the future, to put all liquids on the floor of the cupboard."

When recreation came, a very clean and exceedingly indignant Grizel joined the others, secretly expecting to be well teased about her unexpected bath. Luckily for her, however, she found everyone buzzing with excitement over some news Juliet Carrick had brought that morning.

It appeared that a certain well-known firm of film producers had decided to use the Tiernsee as part of the setting for a film called *Life in the Austrian Tyrol*. It was one of a series of educational films that they were doing; and since it was not, of course, always possible to get the natives of the country to pose for them, they had sent the "principals" over from America. These six important people, together with the director, the camera man, and a business manager, were making the Tyroler Hof their headquarters for the time being. They were going to use all the villages and hamlets round the lake as settings, and also some of the alms, where the cowherds lived during the summer in wooden huts, while the cows browsed contentedly on the sweet, short grass of the upland pastures. They intended to go beyond the lake and, following the course of the little Tiern, take some of the hamlets and villages on its banks. Just why they should have hit on the Tiernsee was hard to say. Juliet was not occupied with that question. It was the whole idea which appealed to her, and she was full of it

"They are going to the Zillerthal after this," she chattered eagerly, "and Kufstein as well, before they go south to the Dolomites. They've done Innsbruck and Stubaithal and round about there, and Mr Eades — that's the camera man — said they had some glorious close-ups of Hall and Spärtz. He was awfully interested in us, and I think they mean to ask

Miss Bettany to let them take us. Isn't it thrilling?"

Miss Bettany, however, when approached on the subject by the said Mr Eades and a Mr Sindon, the business manager, refused to hear of it. She was icily courteous and absolutely decided. Nothing would induce her to reconsider the matter, and the two gentlemen left the Chalet, realizing that, as one of them later expressed it to Juliet, "It was abso. N.G. Nix on the 'movies' stunt!"

Most of the girls cared very little either one way or the other, but Juliet herself, Grizel, and one or two of the more thoughtless ones were bitterly disappointed. They had already, in imagination, seen themselves on the screen. People all over Europe and the British Isles, at any rate, would know them, and now it was all spoilt by Miss Bettany's refusal.

"It's a shame!" cried Juliet, to a select gathering on the afternoon of the day on which she learnt of her head-mistress's decision. "Why couldn't we be filmed? Big schools like Eton and Winchester are! But Miss Bettany always does that sort of thing! She's thoroughly narrow-minded!"

"No, she isn't!" returned Grizel, who had moments when she realized that her present behaviour was anything but what Madge had the right to expect of her. "It's different photographing boys at sports, and doing us here by the lake. Oh, I can't tell you how, but it is!" And from this position she refused to budge.

Juliet gave it up, for she was clever enough to realize that once Grizel had made up her mind to a thing, wild horses wouldn't move her. However, Anita Rincini, Sophie Hamel and Suzanne Mercier were more easily swayed, and were soon persuaded into thinking that they had a grievance against Miss Bettany. The manager of the "movies" also felt he had a grievance. He had foreseen a glorious advertisement in the school. It was, so far as he knew, an entirely new idea, and the girls looked so fresh and dainty in their uniform, and the whole thing would have made an excellent foil to his Continental scenes.

"If only I could get just one or two of you kids!" he said to Juliet. "It would be an easy matter to rig up a schoolroom scenario. And we could take you sculling, and swimming, and so on."

These words gave Juliet an idea. "Could you really do it?" she asked. "If I got some of the girls together in our uniform, could you really manage?"

"Of course I could!" he said impatiently. "Come to that, I suppose I could rig up something in the States when we get back."

"But it wouldn't be the same scenery," said Juliet earnestly.

"We could fake it near enough for the public," he replied.

"But it would be better with the same backgrounds, wouldn't it?" she asked.

"Of course it would! But that school-ma'am of yours won't even listen to the idea, so where's the good of talking about it?" he returned irritably.

"Supposing I were to get two or three of the others to come, couldn't you take us?" queried Juliet.

Mr Sindon's face lit up at the idea. "I could manage it, of

course," he said slowly. "When could you arrange for it? Because we are off next Friday, so it would have to be before then."

"Would Saturday do?"

"Yes, that would do very well. Saturday, then, at ten o'clock in the morning. Bring your swimming suits, and we'll get you in the water."

Juliet tackled her four satellites, and by dint of flattery, coaxing and, in the case of Sophie Hamel, frank bullying, got them to agree to join her. As she had expected, Grizel was the hardest of them to capture. She gave in when Juliet had alternately scolded and pleaded with her for nearly half an hour, and agreed to be at Geisalm, a little hamlet a mile and a half up the lake-shore, on Saturday morning. It would be an easy matter for her to be there; for, on Saturdays, they were left very much to themselves, Madge Bettany having a theory that it was better to trust girls than to watch them continually. They were not allowed to bathe or go boating unless a mistress was there; but otherwise no one interfered with them, and so far there had been no necessity for interference. Therefore, ten o'clock on Saturday morning found Grizel, in company with Juliet, scrambling along the narrow rocky path that leads from Briesau to Geisalm.

"Aren't you thrilled?" demanded Juliet, as they stopped to rest on the great "fan" of alluvial rock which marks the halfway between the two places. "I am! I've never acted for 'movies' before."

Grizel did not suppose Juliet had, and her conscience was

beginning to wake up very thoroughly, which may have accounted for the vehemence with which she said, "Oh, rather! Awfully!"

Juliet shot a quick glance at her from her strange, dark eyes, but she said nothing, "Well, we'd better be getting on!"

They went on their way – slowly and carefully, for at this part the path was not very wide, and went almost sheer down to the water, whose vivid blueness told how deep it was. At any other time Grizel would have enjoyed that scramble over the rocks, and the rapid run past the place where the mountain water dripped from a crag that overhung the path. She had enjoyed this very walk a score of times. But now she felt half angry and wholly unhappy, and I think that if it had not been for her fear of Juliet's mocking tongue, she would have turned back even then. So absorbed was she in her uneasiness, that she never noticed a broad-bottomed rowing boat with four people in it heading for Scholastika. Juliet, who, at the moment it passed, was gathering a bunch of purple scabious and white moon-daisies, did not notice it either.

The occupants of the boat glanced up, attracted by the splash of brown against the green of the alm which they had reached. Juliet they passed over, but as Joey Bettany's eyes lingered on the other gym-frocked figure, she gave a gasp.

"Herr Mensch!" she cried. "That's Grizel! Whatever is she doing here?"

Herr Mensch turned a placid face towards the place, but the two girls had vanished behind the clump of trees which protects the footpath from the lake at this point.

"So?" he said politely. "Then that is why we could not find her when we came to fetch you? But is it wrong for her to be here?"

"I'm sure my sister doesn't know about it," declared Joey. "She thought Grizel must have gone to buy apples from the old woman at Seespitz, 'cos she said so!"

Herr Mensch's fair, German-looking face became troubled.

"That is very wrong of *das Mädchen*," he said gravely. "Would you like us to land at Geisalm and take her into the boat?"

Joey thought rapidly for a moment. They had never been told that they were not to go to Geisalm by themselves, but she knew that Madge was always a little nervous about that path, especially the narrow bit of it.

"Yes, please! I think it would be better, if you don't mind!"

Without a word, the good-natured Austrian turned the boat towards the little green triangle with its big white *Gasthaus* which forms Geisalm. A group of people were standing there talking together. Joey recognized the cinema folk, but still she didn't guess what was up until Bernhilda cried, "Why, there are Sophie and Anita. How strange for so many of the Chalet girls to meet here today!"

Then Joey understood.

"Oh!" she said, and her face, pale no longer, but tanned by the hot sunshine, flamed with sudden anger. "Oh! How can she, when Madge said not!"

"How can she do what?" asked Bernhilda, who was slow at grasping things. "And of whom are you speaking, Joey?"

"It's Grizel! Juliet's done it, of course! She's mad on them!" replied Joey incoherently. "Oh, Herr Mensch! Please stop them! Madge will be so angry, and it isn't fair when she said she wouldn't!"

Herr Mensch was quicker than his daughter. With a final pull he brought the boat neatly to the landing-stage and sprang out.

"Stay here!" he said curtly to the three girls with him, and then he strode off to the group by the *Gasthaus*.

Mr Sindon was considerably surprised when he found himself confronted by an angry giant of a man, who requested to know, in very good English, if he intended taking photos that day. Something in the angry giant's voice warned him that he had better give an answer at once, and to the point, so he replied that he was. It was at this moment that Grizel and Juliet came upon them. Herr Mensch took not the slightest notice of the elder girl, but he turned to Grizel and, in tones which literally scared her, told her to go to the boat at once. With her he sent Anita and Sophie. Then he spoke to the paralysed Mr Sindon.

"I am sorry, *mein Herr*, if in taking these young ladies away I am causing you any inconvenience, but they are here without the knowledge or permission of their parents and guardians. I wish you good day!" And with this he turned and strode back to the boat, where Anita Rincini, who happened to be the daughter of his own great friend, had dissolved into tears. Sophie looked scared, and Grizel was beginning to recover sufficiently to feel furiously angry at having been treated in this summary fashion. But Herr Mensch took no notice of her at all.

"How did you get here?" he asked the other two in their own language.

Sophie pointed to the light rowing boat moored to the landing-stage. "We rowed across from Scholastika," she explained.

"I see," he said. "Well, now you will row back with me." Then he turned his attention to the English girl. "You will come with us," he said. "Get into the boat."

Grizel gave him one look, and obeyed. Sophie and Anita had already started. In a grim silence they pulled up the lake to Scholastika. Bernhilda and Frieda were too much afraid of their father's anger to speak.

At Scholastika, Herr Mensch grimly marched them before him, first to the Rincinis' villa, and then to the hotel where the Hamels were staying. While there, he rang up the Chalet, and told Madge that, as they had met Grizel, he was taking her with the others to Maria Kirche to see the famous church there, and they would all return in the afternoon. Then he went back to the girls, and sending Bernhilda and Joey on in front, took a hand each of Frieda and Grizel.

It was not a pleasant expedition. And when they returned in the afternoon, Herr Mensch had a long conversation with Miss Bettany, which ended in a more serious scolding for Grizel than she had ever known since she had left England.

What hurt her more than anything was the knowledge that she was not to be trusted by herself, at any rate for the present. As for Juliet, Captain Carrick had made arrangements only that morning for her to be a boarder for the remainder of the term, as he and his wife were going to Munich to visit some friends, and did not want to take her with them. Miss Bettany resolved to keep a watchful eye on the new boarder.

Chapter Eleven

THE HEAD'S BIRTHDAY PARTY

"Joey! Are you busy, or may I come and talk to you?"

Joey Bettany raised her head with a start at the sound of the voice. Looking down from her perch on the fence which shut off the alm of Briesau from the Geisalm path, she saw Gisela Marani standing beside her, book in hand, a very serious expression on her charming face.

"Hello, Gisela! What's the trouble?" she said cheerfully.

"It is this book," explained Gisela, tapping it. "Will you come with me to the seat by the boat-landing? I wish to discuss it with you."

"Rather!" Joey slid down from her seat with great goodwill and, slipping her arm through Gisela's, strolled along by her side.

"Look!" she said suddenly. "There's some new people from the Kron Prinz Karl. They came last night. Father and mother, and two girls and two boys, and a grown-up girl. Don't they look jolly?"

Gisela glanced idly in the direction in which Joey was pointing. Then her face suddenly changed, and her lips curved up in a smile of surprise and pleasure.

"Wanda!" she cried.

The elder girl, a slim, fair person of about fifteen, turned round at the sound of her voice. Then she uttered a little cry and ran towards them.

"Gisela!" she exclaimed.

The younger girl and a small boy of about seven looked up too, and in a minute they also were racing up to the little group.

Gisela embraced them all, while Joey stood on one side, feeling rather in the way. But the Austrian had no idea of leaving her out.

"Wanda – Marie – Wolfram – this is my English friend, Joey Bettany. I am now at her sister's school in the large chalet over there. Joey, these are Wanda and Marie von Eschenau, and their brother Wolfram. I was at school in Vienna with Wanda and Marie when we lived there."

Joey had never been a shy person; she had travelled about too much for that. So now she came forward and shook hands easily.

"Hello!" she said. "Are these your holidays?"

The elder girl, whom Gisela had saluted as Wanda, smiled.

"But no; not holidays," she said, and her careful speech reminded Joey of the first few weeks of the Chalet School.

"We have left our *lycée* and we are resting here until Mamma finds us one where we can be always. Ah! you call it 'boarding school', I remember."

"Oh, Wanda!" cried Gisela. "You must come to the Chalet School!"

"That would be very pleasant," said Wanda politely. "Listen! I hear Mamma calling. *Auf Wiedersehen!* Goodbye, Fräulein Joey."

And she hurried off, followed by the other two.

"What pretties, Gisela!" said Joey enthusiastically. "What did you say their name was?"

"Von Eschenau," replied Gisela. "It would be very jolly if Wanda and Marie came to the Chalet School, for they are nice girls."

Gisela was, at the moment, much more engrossed in the book which she had been reading than in the arrival of her old friends, and as soon as they were comfortably established on one of the white seats by the landing-stage she began her discussion at once.

"Papa brought me this book two days ago," she said, exhibiting to Joey's interested eyes a girls' school story with a brightly-coloured paper jacket.

"*Denise of the Fourth*," read the English girl. "Who's it by? Muriel Bernardine Browne? Never heard of her! What's it like?"

'I find it interesting – in parts," replied Gisela, "though some of it seems to me impossible. But there are descriptions of two things which interest me very much, and I was wondering if we also could not have them.

"The two things are a magazine, first. In the school of this story, the girls had a most interesting magazine. It gives examples from it. See!" And she rapidly found the place, and gave it to Joey, who skimmed through the chapter with a widening grin on her face.

"It is amusing?" queried the head girl. "You find it funny?"

"It's a shriek," pronounced the critic. "But it's rather an idea. We ought to have a magazine. The only trial is, it will be so frightfully difficult to decide what language it will be in."

"But of course it will be in English," said Gisela. "We are an English school."

"It would be rather fun," mused Joey. "Who'd be editor? You, I suppose?"

Gisela shook her head. "Oh, no," she said earnestly. "I do not know enough about it. Perhaps Miss Maynard would do it."

"She might; but it ought really to be a girl. Well, go on! What's the other scheme you liked so awfully?"

"The Head's birthday," replied Gisela, turning over more pages. "See, Joey! In this they had a dance, and they gave the Head beautiful presents, and had a splendid time!"

Joey grinned. "I've never heard of a school where the girls gave the Head a slender gold chain on which was swung an exquisite pendant studded with diamonds! The most we ever rose to at the High was a really decent reading lamp. But the holiday stunt is all right, and so is the dance. Madge's birthday does come this term, as it happens.

I vote we ask her for the holiday, anyhow."

"But she must also have a gift," protested Gisela. "And flowers as well. What day is it, Joey? Soon?"

"It's July the fourth," replied Joey, "next Thursday. It would be a ripping scheme to go for an expedition some-where, wouldn't it? Tell you what! We might go up the Mondscheinspitze and have a picnic there, and then come down and have the dance in the evening! Oh, gorgeous!"

"And the gift?" persisted the head girl. "We all admire and love Miss Bettany so much, we would wish to give her something."

"Oh, well, that's for you to decide!" returned Joey.

"But of course we will! You will want to give your own souvenir; we won't ask you to join unless you wish it. But I know the others will. What would Miss Bettany like?"

"Oh, any old thing! She'd like whatever you give her!"

"The flowers will be easy," pursued Gisela thoughtfully. "We have a garden, Bette has a garden, Anita and Giovanna have a garden, and so has Gertrud. We shall have roses, lilies, and marguerites."

"Let's go and ask the others," proposed Joey. "It's nearly time for prep anyhow. You'll have to ask my sister for the holiday, you know, and you'll have to give whatever you do give her."

Gisela coloured faintly. She was rather inclined to be shy.

"In *Denise of the Fourth*, Mervyn, that's the head girl, asks them to cheer the headmistress," she said. "I should have to do that too?"

"Of course! What do you think? Here's Gertrud and Grizel coming. Let's tell them now, shall we?"

"Don't you think it would be better if we waited till everyone was together?" suggested Gisela diffidently. "And should I not ask the prefects first?"

"Ye… yes, I suppose you should," conceded Joey reluctantly. "All right! You go and call a prefects' meeting, and I'll go and see what Simone is up to. I haven't seen her since *Mittagessen*."

Joey skipped off, leaving Gisela to follow at a more stately rate, as befitted a head girl.

Simone greeted her friend with mournful eyes.

"I looked for you everywhere, Joey," she said reproachfully.

"Well, I was reading on the fence," responded Joey briskly. "Then Gisela came to talk to me about a new book she was reading. Oh, Simone, do you remember those people who came to the Kron Prinz Karl last night by the last boat? We've just met them; they're friends of Gisela's – come from Vienna, and they're here for a while. You remember the two pretty girls like fairy princesses? Their names are Wanda and Marie, and Gisela wants them to come to the Chalet School. What's the matter?" staring in undisguised amazement at Simone, who looked as if she were about to burst into tears. "Aren't you well?"

"Oh, Joey," said Simone pathetically, dropping into her own language in her agitation, "oh, Joey, don't have any more friends! Please, Joey, don't! You've got Grizel, and Gisela and

Bette, and I've only got you! And now you want those two new girls that you don't know at all! Oh, Joey, don't be so selfish!"

Joey stood stock-still in her amazement.

"Selfish!" she repeated. 'Selfish! It's you who are selfish! I've told you over and over again that I'm going to have all the friends I want, and it doesn't make one scrap of difference to my being pally with you! I don't mind your having other friends – I don't see why you don't! Margia would chum with you if you gave her half a chance, and she's a jolly nice kid! It's no use looking like that, Simone! It doesn't make one scrap of difference! If I like Wanda and Marie, I'm going to like them. If they do come to the Chalet and we want to be pally, I shall be!" Then she relented somewhat at the look of misery in Simone's great dark eyes, and slipped an arm round her shoulders, giving her a gentle little shake. "Do buck up, Simone, and be... be a man! You'd be twice as jolly if you only would! Look here! There's five minutes before the bell goes – I forgot my watch is fast – and there's just time to tell you what Gisela was talking to me about. Come along and let's go and sit by the boat-slip and I'll tell you about it. It's awfully thrilling!"

But although Simone allowed herself to be drawn towards the little wooden landing-stage beside the Chalet, the dumb wretchedness of her expression did not relax, and all the time that Joey was enlarging on Gisela's "topping" idea, she sat without making the slightest effort at cheering up. Finally, even happy-go-lucky Jo Bettany gave it up in despair. What could you do with a girl who refused to be interested in birthday parties and sat looking like a chunk of solid misery?

Joey was thankful when the bell went, and she was able to go off to her own form room, where there were plenty of people interested in all she had to say about the newcomers at the Kron Prinz Karl.

"It would be splendid for the school if they did come," said Anita Rincini. "I have heard Papa talk of Herr von Eschenau. They are very well born."

"What a silly reason!" said Grizel crushingly. "The real question is, Will they be all right in school? Are they good at games, for instance?"

"They will not know cricket," laughed Sophie Hamel, coming to the rescue, for Anita was too much squashed by Grizel's remark to say anything. "You will have to teach them that, Grizel. Two more, perhaps, for your team." For Grizel, who was keen on cricket, and had been a shining light of the Junior Eleven at her last school, had been appointed cricket captain, and was proving a very capable coach. Perhaps one reason for her success was that the other girls were all so keen on being an "English" school, that they took her criticisms and sarcasms in good part, and really tried to learn the game. As for the Juniors, they spend most of their free time in fielding practice. The games mistress at the High had been very insistent on the necessity for smart fielding, and Grizel, quite a good, steady bat, had nevertheless excelled in bowling, which naturally made her more determined to have good fielding than if it had been the other way round.

They had tennis, too, for most of the girls played it quite well, and Gisela Marani and Gertrud Steinbrücke were exceptionally good. However, there could be no doubt about it, cricket was the more popular game.

Now, in answer to Sophie's remark, Grizel spoke quite graciously.

"We shan't be playing cricket next term. I don't quite know what we shall play; do you, Joey?"

"Not an earthly!" returned Joey promptly. "I should think it'll be hockey, though. My sister was awfully good at it when she was at school. But isn't there heaps of snow here in the winter?"

"Oh, yes," said Anita readily. "The lake is frozen, too, and there is much skating."

"Girls! Why are you talking?" said Gertrud's voice at that moment. "You ought to be working! Sit down, please!"

They went to their seats, while Gertrud, who had come to take preparation, arranged her books to her liking on the mistress's table. Then there was silence while they got on with their preparation in the cool, quiet room.

As soon as the bell for tea went, Joey literally pitched her books into her locker, and fled along the passage to find Gisela. She wanted to know what Madge had said about the birthday party. However, she had to possess her soul in patience, for the head girl was in the prefects' room.

Luckily, those great people had decided to make all arrangements as soon as possible, and when their own tea, which they were allowed to have by themselves, was over, they came down to the *Speisesaal*, where the others were, and Gisela, blushing furiously, murmured a request to Miss Maynard, who was taking tea. Miss Maynard nodded, and got up at once.

"Yes, certainly, Gisela! We have just finished, so I will say grace and then leave them to you."

She said grace, and then went out of the room.

"Will you all please sit down," said Gisela, when the door was shut.

They all sat down, Joey squeezing her hands together in her excitement; for, of course, this must mean that Madge had agreed, and they would be able to go up the Mondscheinspitze, which she had been longing to do ever since Herr Mensch had told them about it.

Gisela was quite brief. She explained to them about the English custom of celebrating the Head's birthday, and told them that she and the prefects had thought it would be a good plan to celebrate Miss Bettany's. Miss Bettany had no objection to their having the holiday and, subject to the weather being fine, had agreed to their making an expedition up the Mondscheinspitze. If it was wet, they were to have a party in the Chalet.

"Miss Bettany has been very good to us," went on Gisela, "and I think you would all like to join to give her some souvenir of the first term of the Chalet School; would you not? So any who wish it may bring contributions to Bette Rincini or myself tomorrow, and on the Saturday we will go to Innsbruck and purchase something. And on Thursday, will those of you who can, please bring flowers, and come early, so that we may also give her a bouquet."

Then she ceased speaking, and waited. But the burst of enthusiasm which answered her told her that the idea was most popular and, as Joey said later on, "That was that!"

Chapter Twelve

SHOPPING – AND A MEETING

SATURDAY PROVED TO be a gloriously fine day. Joey and Grizel in their short white tennis frocks, with bare brown legs, looked delightfully cool, and the others in their brown gym tunics regarded them enviously.

"You look so nice and fresh!" said Margia Stevens. "I wish I was going into Innsbruck today!"

"You needn't," laughed Madge from the foot of the table, where she was buttering Amy's roll for her. "It will be stewing hot in Innsbruck today. Remember we're three thousand feet above sea level as it is, and there's a delightful breeze from the lake; but there won't be a breath of air down in the valley. What it will be like by noon I can't think. Luckily, Gisela and Bette have enough common sense to make you keep quiet then, or I wouldn't let you go. Finished? Very well. You'd better run along or you'll miss the train, and make the others miss it too. Have you got plenty of money?"

"Heaps!" declared Joey. "Come on, Grizel, buck up! Goodbye, everybody. Expect us when you see us!"

With this she danced out of the room, followed more slowly by Grizel, and soon they were hurrying along by the lake path towards Seespitz and the mountain railway, where Gisela and Bette awaited them impatiently, while Fräulein Helfer, the Rincinis' Mamsell, or mother's help, as we should call her in England, was already sitting in the train.

"Come! You are very late!" cried the head girl. "I had fear that we must await the next train, and Papa says that it will be so hot in Innsbruck later on."

"Awfully sorry," returned Joey in unruffled tones. "I think our clocks must be wrong, because we thought we had oceans of time. Good morning, Fräulein Helfer. Hope we haven't given you spasms! Isn't it a glorious day?"

Fräulein Helfer, who understood about half of this speech, bowed and smiled nervously.

"Joey, have you yet learnt what it is Madame desires?" inquired Gisela presently, as the train puffed its way importantly down the mountainside.

Joey shook her black head vigorously. "Not an idea. I think it'll be best if you just get what you think. Whatever it is, she'll be sure to like it, because you've given it. Hello! Some people at Wachen! I say, what a crowd!"

"Summer visitors," said Bette. "Germans, most of them. That woman in the tartan dress comes from Berlin, I heard her say."

"What a size she is!" commented Grizel, as the lady in question lumbered into the car.

"What a tremendous way up we are! What would happen if anything broke, Gisela?" said Joey.

"I do not think it could happen," replied Gisela seriously. "I have never heard of it. But if it did, we should plunge over the side and onto the path to Spärtz, which lies down there."

"Wouldn't it be awful if the lake were suddenly to overflow? It would come down here like a mill race, wouldn't it?"

"Joey! What horrid things you imagine!" protested Grizel.

Joey laughed, and stopped her imagining, to gaze at the lady from Berlin. She certainly was enormous – far fatter than Frau Mensch. She looked uncomfortably hot, too, in a dress of scarlet, green, and yellow tartan, with a little straw hat adorned with scarlet and green bows perched on the top of her head. Her yellow hair was scraped back off her wide face, making it seem larger than ever, and she stared in front of her with eyes like grey glass. Suddenly, as if attracted by Joey's interested regard, she glared at the small girl.

"*Engländerin!*" she snorted in guttural tones.

"Rather!" responded the irrepressible one. "And proud of it too!"

"Joey! Be quiet!" said Gisela firmly.

"Why should I? She spoke first!"

"It makes no matter. She is much, much older than you!"

Gisela had not intended her remarks to be overheard, but her voice was of the clear, carrying order, and the lady from Berlin not only heard, but understood.

"*Schweine!*" she said, and then heaved her bulk round, nearly upsetting her opposite neighbour, an inoffensive little Tyrolean who was going to market in Spärtz.

"Isn't she rude?" observed Joey. "All right, Gisela! I'm not going to say anything more. Did you say your father was going to meet us at Innsbruck?"

"Yes. Fräulein Helfer wishes to visit her parents, and Papa is going to be our escort. He will see us at the station, and will take us to the shops. Then we are going to have lunch at the Maria Theresien Restaurant, and afterwards we shall go for a drive along the Brenner Road, and go back by the last train. There is a *Gasthaus* up the Brenner where we can have coffee, and we will take cakes with us. Do you like it?"

"Topping! Isn't it, Grizel?"

"Rather!" said Grizel, "It's top-hole of Herr Marani to do it!"

"I am so glad you are pleased!" said Gisela courteously. "Ah, we have arrived at Spärtz and there is our train to Innbruck on the other side of the platform! Come! We must hurry!"

But it was easier to say that than to do it. Frau Berlin, as Grizel had christened her, took her own time about getting out and as she blocked the doorway, the girls had, perforce, to wait until she was well on to the platform.

"Come on! We shall miss the train if we don't buck up!" shouted Joey.

They nearly did miss it, for the Mamsell was not accustomed to dashing from one train to another, and had it not been for Grizel and Gisela, who hauled her up the steps and into the carriage with little ceremony, she would have been left on the platform. As it was, she was gasping and scared.

"But never mind that; we've caught the train!" said Jo practically.

It was full, as it was the Vienna–Paris train, so they had to content themselves in the corridor; however, it was only for a short time, and then they reached the outskirts of the capital of the Tyrol, where tall, flat houses faced them, with *plumeaux* hanging out to air from the open windows, while the hot valley air rushed to meet them as they whirled past.

"Here we are!" exclaimed Grizel, as the train drew up beside the busy platform. "And there's your father, Gisela. Let's get out! There's no horrid fat Frau Berlin to stop us this time!" As she spoke, she swung herself down on the platform, bumping into someone who was going heavily past. The someone turned and glared at her. Horrors! It was Frau Berlin herself! What would have happened it is hard to tell, for she had obviously heard and understood Grizel's indiscreet remarks. Luckily, at that moment Herr Marani came up, and quickly grasping what had occurred, he raised his hat, apologizing courteously to the furious lady for the English child's clumsiness. Frau Berlin was not to be placated, but she rolled onwards, after directing a venomous glare at the impenitent Grizel.

"You must be more careful, my child," said Herr Marani, after he had assisted the others out of the carriage and through the barrier. "You might have hurt that lady very much indeed."

"I'm sorry," murmured Grizel untruthfully; while Gisela added, "Indeed, Papa, she was very rude as we came down, and called us *Schweine*."

"Hush, *mein Liebling*! I do not like to hear such words from thy lips," said her father, as they crossed the station square, which lay white and hot in the brilliant sunshine. "Let us talk of our errands instead. We need not think of an ill-bred Berliner, but only of what is pleasant to us all."

"There is a shop in the Museum Strasse where one can buy beautiful china," said Bette, as Gisela seemed to be reduced to silence by her father's gentle rebuke. "We thought we could give Madame a little coffee service. We have collected enough money for a small one. Would she like it, Joey? Or we can get her a necklace of carved ivory beads?"

"It's topping of you!" said Joey cordially. "She'd rather have the china, I believe. She doesn't care a great deal for jewellery."

"The coffee service then, by all means," agreed Herr Marani. "I must go in here for two little moments to buy some cigars. Then we will go to the china shop and purchase the coffee service."

"How shall we carry it home?" asked Grizel practically, as they waited for Herr Marani outside the shop.

"Gisela, is there anywhere I can buy a picture of the Tiernsee? I think M— my sister would like that best," said Joey.

"Yes, of course! There is a very good shop in the Maria Theresien Strasse where they have pictures and photographs too. We can go there as we go to the restaurant."

Herr Marani came out of the shop at that moment, and taking Joey's hand, and with Bette on his other arm, said, "And now we are all ready for the important part of our holiday. Let us go to the shop." He turned off as he spoke down one of the side streets that lead from the Landhaus Strasse to the Museum Strasse. "Now this is the shop where the china is sold. Let us go in and choose."

It was all very well to say it, but it was dreadfully difficult to decide among so much. There was one coffee service bespattered with pink roses on a black ground, and another with a purple clematis pattern all over it, and they paused a long time before one in gold and black. However, they finally agreed on one with a blue and yellow design on a white ground, which had a quaintly foreign air to both Joey and Grizel, and Herr Marani told the woman in charge to pack it up and have it ready for them to take to the station when they should return from the Brenner drive. Then they left the shop, and turned out of the Museum Strasse into the Maria Theresien Strasse, which is a fine, wide street with very good modern shops. Whether you look down or up it, you see the mountains with which Innsbruck is ringed round. At the south end stands the Triumphal Arch and gate, and beyond them, the Herzog Friedrich Strasse, with its crowning glory of the *goldenes Dach* or Golden Roof.

Grizel loved the great wide sweep of the more modern

street; Joey preferred the history-steeped narrowness of the Emperor Frederick's day — and there you have the difference between the two girls. Herr Marani had discovered it long since, but it amused him to see it once again in their arguments about the two most famous thoroughfares of his beloved native city. However, time was getting on, so he hushed their arguments, and led them across the road to the shop on the opposite side of the street, where Joey soon succeeded in choosing a charming picture of the Tiernsee for her sister. Then they crossed once more, and entered the Maria Theresien Restaurant.

They did not pause in the crowded room which faces on to the street, but went right through to the Garden Room, where palms, a fountain, and creeper-hung trellises gave an open-air atmosphere which was very delightful. Electric fans whirling round kept the air fresh and cool, and they all sat down with sighs of relief. It really was boiling in the streets!

When she was comfortably settled, Joey looked round, and gave a little squeal.

"Gisela! Look! There's that horrid fat woman!"

Gisela, who was opposite her, promptly turned round, nearly overturning her chair as she did so, and saw, sitting a few yards away, their late enemy of the train. She had not seen them, for she was buried in a current number of the *Fliegende Blätter*, which is the German *Punch*, and she looked hotter than ever.

"Horrid old freak!" murmured Grizel. "Doesn't she look awful?"

"Like a scarlet hippopotamus!" suggested Joey. "If I were as fat as that I should go and drown myself."

Herr Marani, who had been discussing the menu with the waiter, turned at this moment, and caught the last speech of his youngest guest.

"Josephine!" he exclaimed in horror.

Joey had the grace to blush. "I know it's rude of me," she mumbled "but… she is fat, isn't she, Herr Marani?"

"Hush, my child," he replied. "It is wrong to say such things of one so much older. Now let us discuss our drive up the Brenner Road. I propose that we go to the Alte Post, where we can get coffee and rolls and butter. Perhaps we may be able to find a zither player, and then you shall hear some of our mountain songs amidst the grandest scenery on earth. Then, when we have had coffee, and you have gathered your flowers, we will come down, and stop at the shops for our parcels, and then we must catch the train. You like that? Yes?"

"Oh, rather!" said Joey enthusiastically. "It's jolly good of you to give us such a ripping treat, Herr Marani."

He laughed. "I, too, like a little holiday. Here comes the soup."

Joey's eyes widened at the thought of soup on so hot a day, but when it came, she discovered that it was iced, and very delicious. From her seat she could see Frau Berlin gobbling up soup also, with small regard for good manners. However, Herr Marani kept her attention occupied, and she soon forgot the fat lady. Frau Berlin, on the other hand, had just seen them, and she looked furious. In her indignation she allowed her temper to overcome her discretion, and she spat vehemently in their direction, just as the head waiter passed between them.

There was an instant uproar; for he, in the shock of the moment, stepped heavily backwards, almost upsetting Gisela, whose plate of soup went flying. Herr Marani sprang to his feet, and a couple of Italians who were lunching near joined in at once, pouring forth a flood of questions and exclamations and, when the angry manager appeared on the scene, explanations of the whole affair. Several people who were sitting near stood up to see better what was happening. The author of all the disturbance snorted out something about *verdammte Engländerinnen*, and demanded her bill. Ten minutes later she had gone, everyone had sat down, the head waiter's feelings had been soothed by a gift of *Trinkgeld* from Herr Marani, and the manager had vanished, with only a very hazy idea of what had occurred, but convinced by everyone that the fault lay with Frau Berlin.

"I hope that is the last time we shall see her," said Gisela.

"She has been horrid all round!" declared Grizel with conviction. "But it was rather fun, wasn't it?"

"Yes, it was," agreed Bette; "but, like Gisela, I hope we shall see her no more."

However, they, were destined to meet her again, though this they could not possibly know just then.

They finished their meal without further disturbance, and

then Herr Marani took them back to the Station Square, where they got into one of the quaint open carriages which always amused the English girls so, and set off for their drive into the mountains.

Chapter Thirteen

AT THE ALTE POST

"Oooh! Isn't this gorgeous?" Joey Bettany drew a long breath as she gazed round her at the mountains which rose on every side in majestic splendour, while below, the pine forests swept down to the valley, where the Inn went brawling past, hurrying down to join Father Danube. Herr Marani smiled kindly down at the little girl. Her enthusiasm pleased him, for like all Tyroleans, he loved his country devotedly.

"It is finer further up," he said. "As we get higher and higher, we see the peaks at the other side; and if we go high enough, we can see the Stubai Glacier. We must take you there some day."

"If it's fine, we're going up the Mondscheinspitze on Madge's birthday, you know," said Joey eagerly.

"So? That is a pleasant little climb."

"I want to climb the Tiernjoch," put in Grizel. "I mean to some day, too!"

Now Grizel had said nothing about climbing the Tiernjoch lately, so Joey had imagined she had forgotten about her desire to make its ascent, and she was thoroughly dismayed at Grizel's remark.

"I wish Herr Mensch had never said anything about it!" she thought.

Herr Marani raised his eyebrows at Grizel's words. "The Tiernjoch? It is not a girl's climb. Best leave it alone – for the present at any rate," he said decisively.

"I mean to go," said Grizel stubbornly. "And I'm not a baby, Herr Marani."

"But will Madame permit it?" put in Gisela somewhat tactlessly. "It is, as Papa says, a very difficult climb – I have not done it yet! It would tire you, Grizel."

Grizel made no answer, but her mouth took its old obstinate lines, and Joey made haste to change the conversation.

Their kindly host pointed out to them a huge, white, barn-like building up the mountainside.

"That is the Alte Post," he said. "We shall be there in half an hour now, and then we will have our coffee—"

"Papa!" Gisela interrupted him with a cry of dismay. "The cakes! We have forgotten the cakes! Now we shall only have rolls and butter."

"*Gott in Himmel!* But how thoughtless!" Herr Marani looked as perturbed as his daughter.

"Perhaps they will have *Kuchen* at the inn," suggested

Bette, not very hopefully.

"And anyway, it doesn't matter," added Joey. "We can get cakes any day when we're in the town."

The big Austrian's face cleared at that. "That is true, *Bübchen*. You shall have cakes for Fräulein Bettany's birthday to make up for your disappointment today. My mother makes delicious honey and nut cakes, and I will ask her to make some for you."

"Oh, that would be ripping of you if you will," said Joey fervently.

"Topping!" agreed Grizel.

"Grandmamma makes wonderful cakes," said Gisela. "We all love them."

"Madge will be bucked!" murmured Madge's small sister. "She is going to have a jolly birthday!"

"It won't be a bit like English birthdays," observed Grizel. "Except the presents, of course, and the flowers!"

"And the birthday cake," added Joey. "She and Mademoiselle have made a huge one, all rich and plummy, with a threepenny and a button and a ring in."

"But why?" demanded Gisela. "I do not understand."

"Don't you? Why, whoever gets the threepenny will be rich, and the ring means marriage, and the button an old maid," explained Joey. "We always did at home; and candles round the cake too – as many candles as you are years old."

"Is Miss Bettany going to have candles?" queried Grizel with interest.

"I don't know; she didn't say. I expect she will, though. Oh, Herr Marani! Just look at those flowers! Can't we get out and gather some?"

"Best to wait till we return," he advised. "Then your flowers will be fresh to take home. We are almost there now. Just one more turn and we reach it."

"I say! Wouldn't it be awful if Frau Berlin were to be there?"

All the others turned to Grizel, who had made this charming suggestion.

"Goodness! I hope not!" This vigorously from Joey.

"What a dreadful idea, Grizel!" Thus Gisela.

While Herr Marani said decidedly, "Oh, I should not expect it!"

"Still she might be," persisted Grizel. "We've met her once already."

"Then, if she should indeed be there, I shall trust you to say nothing, do nothing that may upset her," said the Austrian gravely.

"Supposing she spits at us again?" suggested Joey. "She might!"

"Then you will remember that you are English, and an Englishwoman is not revengeful. Gisela and Bette, you must be careful of what you say. I do not wish a disturbance which might mean that we could not have our coffee at the *Gasthaus*."

"And here we are!" exclaimed Bette. "We will remember, Onkel."

Herr Marani gave orders about the coffee to a pretty dark-eyed girl who had come out on hearing the noise of the wheels.

"Coffee?" she said, in the low-German patois of the country. "Yes, I can give you coffee, very good, and bread and butter too."

"Have you any cakes?" asked Herr Marani.

She shook her head. "*Na; Kuchen, nein! Aber Marmelade,*" she added good naturedly, seeing the disappointment on the four girlish faces. "*Die Marmelade ist sehr gut.*"

"We will have that, then," decided Herr Marani.

She nodded. "*Im Speisesaal – fünf minuten.*" She held up the five fingers of her left hand to emphasise her remark, and then ran off.

"I always think it's so funny to call jam '*marmelade*'," observed Grizel idly. "What a pretty girl, Herr Marani! But she looks quite Italian. Look! There are some more! What heaps of children!" as four or five tow-headed urchins came shyly round the corner of the house to stare wide eyed at the visitors.

"All probably grandchildren of the innkeeper," said Gisela. "Sometimes three or four families will live together in a place like this. Papa, see! How near the mountains seem!"

"It is only seeming," said her father. "Look, Josephine! That is the way you came to Innsbruck. There is the line over there, across the river. And now, our five minutes are up. Let us go and see if our coffee is ready."

Bette and Grizel ran on in front, bursting into the

Speisesaal, only to draw up in amazed silence. There before them sat Frau Berlin, drinking coffee and eating bread at one of the tables!

She looked up as they entered, and her already purple face deepened in colour as she glared at them.

"My only aunt!" gasped Grizel, finding her voice at last.

Herr Marani was equally thunderstruck; but before anything else could be said, Frau Berlin heaved herself to her feet.

"I will *mit* English pig-dogs not eat!" she announced in thunderous tones.

"Well, we don't want to eat with you!" retorted Grizel before Gisela could stop her.

The woman glared at her in stupefied silence. Herr Marani put out a hand, and dragged the English child back with small ceremony.

"Be silent!" he said sternly. "Go outside, all four of you!"

However indulgent he might be in some ways, Gisela knew that her father insisted on obedience, so she hauled Grizel out into the open air, followed by Bette and Joey, who were half scared, half inclined to giggle.

"Grizel!" exclaimed the head girl when they were outside. "How could you speak so rudely! She has right to be annoyed now!"

"I'm not going to be called 'pig-dog' by any measly old German!" retorted Grizel.

Gisela threw out her hands with a little gesture of helplessness.

"You are an idiot, Grizel!" remarked Joey casually. "You're spoiling our fun by being so stupid! If you'd left it alone, she'd have been in the wrong; now it's us!"

"Well, you can let that fat old pig call you names if you like," flashed Grizel, "but I won't! You aren't a bit patriotic!"

"How dare you say that!" Joey was becoming heated now. "I'm as patriotic as you, but I've a little more common sense! If you'd held your tongue, she would have been in the wrong. But now you've been abominably rude and let us down! Patriotic! Huh! If that's your patriotism, I'm glad I don't possess any of it! A nice name she'll give all English girls now, thanks to you being 'patriotic'!" She stopped for sheer lack of breath, and Gisela promptly interfered.

"It is of no use to quarrel now. It is done, and it is a great pity, but it cannot be helped. Joey, will you come with me to gather some of those flowers? And Bette, perhaps you and Grizel will go the other way and see what you can find."

"Certainly," said Bette promptly. "Come along, Grizel!"

Grizel's quick passion had died by this time, and she was feeling rather ashamed of herself, so she meekly followed Bette; while Gisela, taking no notice of Joey's lowering expression, walked up the road, chatting easily about the flowers which grew in glorious splendour everywhere. By the time they returned to the *Gasthaus* in answer to Herr Marani's call, the storm had blown over, and they were able to enjoy the excellent coffee, *Butterbrod*, and *Pflaume Marmelade*, which the pretty girl of the inn laid before them on a table outside. She also produced some apples, and they made an excellent tea. Herr Marani was, apparently, quite undisturbed by his encounter with Frau Berlin, whom they could see in the *Speisesaal* thunderously drinking her coffee, with her enormous back ostentatiously turned towards them. However, Grizel was not to get off quite so lightly, for when the meal was over, and they were gathering flowers to take back to the Tiernsee, their host called her to him.

"*Mein Kindchen*," he said gently, "another time, please do not be so violent in your patriotism. There is no real harm done this time, but it has not made our little expedition the pleasanter, and I do not think Miss Bettany would like it."

"No,"agreed Grizel meekly. "I'm sorry I was so rude, Herr Marani."

"Then we will forget," be said cheerfully. "Come, I will get you some of those ferns for your bouquet, and then we must return, or we shall be too late to catch our train, and I am sure you do not want to walk up the mountain road from Spärtz."

"Don't forget we must call for the picture and the china, Papa," said Gisela, as they were once more seated in the carriage, rattling down the mountainside. "The others will wish to see what we have chosen."

"Of course," he said. "I can understand that."

"It's getting hotter, isn't it?" remarked Joey. "There was a lovely fresh breeze up by the Alte Post, but down here it's quite hot."

"That is because we are lower down," laughed Bette. "Onkel, did you see Herr Rittmeister von Eschenau yesterday? He had bought Wanda and Marie six books of English school stories, all new. Wanda said she would lend them to us."

"Ah, that reminds me," said her uncle. "Josephine, Frau von Eschenau has told me that she wishes to send Wanda and Marie to the Chalet School. Do you think your sister will be able to have them for boarders?"

Joey's face flushed as she said joyfully, "Oh, how gorgeous! I like Wanda and Marie so much; don't you, Grizel? Yes, I'm sure she can have them. Oh, what splendacious news!"

"We are growing! We'll be a big school soon," said Grizel. "There are four more girls coming next term, and with Wanda and Marie, that will make us twenty-two, and there may be more yet!"

"Are we going to live at the Tiernsee all the winter, Papa?" asked Gisela.

"Yes, I think so," he replied. "I shall spend the week with *Grossmutter* in town, and come for the Sunday. Herr Mensch is going to do the same; and Bette, I think you are to live with us."

Bette clapped her hands. "How delightful! Oh, Onkel Florian, I am so glad! It would have been so lonely in Innsbruck without you all!"

"Hasn't this been a day of happenings?" said Joey presently as they reached the town.

They retrieved their purchases and made for the station, where Herr Marani left them for a moment in order to buy a paper. As they stood in a little group waiting for him, Grizel suddenly uttered an exclamation. "Oh, see! Joey! Look! There is Captain Carrick over there!"

Her clear accents carried high above the other noises, and the man at whom she was pointing, in defiance of good manners, heard her, and turned. It was, indeed, Captain Carrick. Raising his soft hat he came over to them.

"Well, girls! Fancy seeing you here! I found I had to run into Innsbruck to go to the bank. I have left Mrs Carrick waiting for me in Munich. How is Juliet? She is not with you, I see."

"No; we came in to buy a birthday present for Miss Bettany," explained Grizel. "We are going back now."

"And so am I – going back to Munich. But your mention of Miss Bettany reminds me that I have a note for her from my wife – something about her summer frocks, I think. I wonder, Miss Joey, if you would mind taking it for me. I forgot to post it, and she will get it all the sooner."

"Oh, rather!" Joey took the note, and then the Captain bade them goodbye and strolled away.

"Joey, you look puzzled," said Bette. "What is it?"

"Nothing," said Joey briefly. "Here's Herr Marani."

They acomplished the rest of the journey without any further happening, and were met at Seespitz by Madge, Miss Maynard, Simone, Juliet, and the Stevens.

"We thought we'd stroll round to meet you," explained Madge. "What lovely flowers! For me? Oh, thank you, girls!"

"Madge, this is for you!" said Joey, producing the note. "It's from Captain Carrick. I saw him in Innsbruck, and he gave it to me to give to you, because he had forgotten to post it. He came in to go to the bank, and was going back to Munich tonight, he said."

Madge's black brows had been drawn together in a quick frown at the sound of the forbidden Christian name, but something in Joey's tone checked her. She glanced irresolutely at the note.

"Read it!" urged Joey. "Read it now, Madge!"

"Oh, yes, Miss Bettany, please read it!" echoed Juliet, who had gone suddenly white on hearing Joey's news. "Yes, read it!"

With a murmured word of excuse, Madge opened the envelope, and began to read, a little puzzled frown on her face. Suddenly she gave vent to an exclamation.

"Oh, how dreadful! What am I to do?"

Chapter Fourteen

JULIET, THE INCUBUS

At once they all closed round her — all, that is, save Juliet. She stood on the outside of the little circle, with white face and eyes full of dread. None of them noticed her; they were too much interested in Madge and the letter.

"What is it?" demanded Joey. "What's the letter say?"

Madge, reading the closely written words on the sheet of thin, foreign paper, did not answer her, so Joey shook her arm slightly.

"Madge, what is it?"

With an effort the elder girl pulled herself together, and took in the startled little crowd of children round her.

"Never mind, Joey," she said sharply. "Miss Maynard, will you take the girls home, please? Tell Mademoiselle I shall be back presently. Herr Marani, I must have a man's advice."

"Certainly, *Fräulein*. I shall be pleased to do anything for you that I can. Will you not come back with us? It is difficult to talk business here. Gisela, you may go to Buchau with Bette, but make haste to return."

The various parties set off, Miss Maynard taking the Chalet girls by the lake road to Briesau, while Bette and Gisela struck off across the water meadows in the direction of Buchau, on the opposite side of the lake, and Miss Bettany and Herr Marani turned towards Torteswald. No one even noticed that Juliet stayed where she had dropped in the long grass in a little heap, shaking with silent sobs.

Herr Marani left the subject of the letter severely alone until they reached the Villa Hubertus, a pretty wooden house just outside Torteswald. Arrived there, he put Madge in a chair on the verandah, and disappeared indoors, to return presently with a cup of coffee, which he insisted on her drinking before they discussed any business whatsoever.

"You have had a shock," he said. "Drink the coffee, *Fräulein*."

Miss Bettany drank it, and felt better. He took the empty cup from her, placing it to one side, and then sat down beside her.

"And now, *Fräulein*, tell me what has troubled you in this letter."

For answer, Madge held it out to him. "Will you read it?" she said.

He took it from her, and read it slowly through.

Dear Miss Bettany, (Captain Carrick had written.)

Perhaps you will be surprised at what I am going to say. Possibly you will think and say very hard things about me. That is my misfortune. However, let me break to you at once the news that I am presenting you with my daughter Juliet. Circumstances over which I have no control force me to leave Europe at once with my wife. A sulky school-girl will only be an encumbrance to us, added to which I have very little money. At least you have been paid a term's fees, and I dare say you can make the girl useful to you, and repay yourself for her food and clothes in that way.

If, in the future, I find myself able to afford to keep her again, I will send for her. Until you hear from me to this effect, she is in your hands and at your mercy.

I regret that I am forced to these measures, but I see nothing else for it. Of course, if you like, you can send her to the nearest orphan asylum; but I have more faith in your goodness of heart. For your own convenience, I may as well tell you that neither my wife nor I have any relatives, so search for them will be as useless as search for us. Juliet can tell you that much herself. Au revoir!

Lindley F. C. Carrick

Herr Marani swore deeply in German when he had finished reading this heartless letter. Then, realizing that Madge could understand him, he apologized hastily.

"I crave your pardon, *Fräulein*. It is the callous impudence of this man! He is not worthy of the name of either 'man' or 'father'! That poor child, to be abandoned thus!"

At these words, a slight figure rose out of the bushes which came up to the edge of the verandah, and a sobbing voice said, "Miss Bettany! Oh, have they left me again?"

"Juliet!" cried her headmistress. "How did you come here?"

Herr Marani made three strides, and was off the verandah and beside the child in a moment. He gripped her by the arm and drew her in to Miss Bettany, who looked at the red-rimmed eyes in the white face with a softening glance.

"What did you mean by 'again'?" demanded the Austrian.

Juliet flung herself down on her knees by Madge's side.

"Oh, I was so afraid when they made me a boarder!" she sobbed. "They did it once before in the Hills; but that time the Head found them and made them take me back. Then we came here, and ever since he told me I was to be a boarder, I have been afraid they meant to leave me. In one way, I'd rather be with you, because you are kind to me. But oh, it's so dreadful to be thrown on people's charity!" she finished with a little dry sob.

Madge slipped an arm round her. "You poor child!"

It was such a pitiful existence the child had shown her in that little, gasping, sobbed-out speech! She was furious at the letter, but she could not vent her anger on the girl kneeling beside her.

"Don't cry, Juliet. We'll fix things up somehow. It's very hard luck on you."

With these few words she had won Juliet's passionate

allegiance, though she was not to find that out till afterwards. Now she turned to her host.

"Herr Marani, I must think what to do. Perhaps you can help me. Meanwhile, Juliet ought to be at home — it's getting late. Here is Gisela coming. I just want to know if you can tell me whether it would be possible to get on to Captain Carrick's tracks. Could we wire them at Munich station?"

Herr Marani shook his head. "I do not think he will have gone back to Munich. He is much more likely to have gone east to Wien, or else straight through to Paris. We can try, but I do not think it would be worth it. Take Juliet home now, and I will think what is best to do. Yes, that is the best plan."

"Thank you, Herr Marani. We will do as you say. Come, Juliet, it is supper-time now. Stop crying, child, and come along."

"You will permit me to row you across the lake?" said their host. "It is growing late, and the last steamer has gone."

Madge thanked him with her prettiest smile. She was, as a matter of fact, thankful to have him with them, for he was right in saying that it was growing late. She had been out all day, and was feeling tired out with exertion and the shock Captain Carrick's letter had given her. So she fell in readily with the kind Austrian's suggestion, and even meekly accepted the loan of a huge shawl belonging to his wife when he brought it to her with the remark that her gown was thin and that, on the lake at any rate, it would be rather chilly now. Juliet was muffled up in a similar wrap, and then they set off down the quiet road over which the occasional chalets cast dark, gloomy shadows in the bright moonlight. Feeling the child beside her still quivering with an occasional sob, Madge slipped one hand from under her shawl, and clasped the thin fingers in a reassuring grip.

'It is very good of you, Herr Marani," she said, addressing her host. "Indeed, I think everyone is kind in Austria."

"Oh, *bitte sehr*," he said, glancing down at her with a smile. "We should be a rude people indeed if we were not grateful to the lady who is doing so much for our girls. And we are not Prussians, you know!"

"It's funny," said Madge slowly, "but the only discourtesies I have met with have been from Prussians. The Bavarians I know are all delightful, and as for the Tyrolese, I cannot say how much I like them. But the Prussians seem to be filled with a hatred as bitter and venomous as vitriol."

Herr Marani laughed. "We had a good example of that today. The little Grizel makes a worthy opponent."

"An opponent? Why, what do you mean? What on earth has Grizel been doing?" demanded Madge with a feeling of dismay.

"Oh, she was not really to blame," he replied. "It was a Frau Berliner who created most of the disturbance, and *das Mädchen* is patriotic – and hot-headed. Here is the boat, *mein Fräulein*. Will you sit in the stern, please, and steer?"

He helped them in, and pushed off from the land. When they were well away, he told them of Grizel's encounter with the fat lady of Berlin, describing it with a good deal of humour, and glossing over Grizel's behaviour as much as might be.

"Oh, dear! I'm afraid Grizel has been dreadfully rude," sighed the young headmistress. Then, with a sudden change, she began to laugh. "I should like to have seen it, all the same! I can just imagine it! She is a thorough little John Bull. The result, I suppose, of never having left her own country before. Joey, my little sister, is much more of a cosmopolitan. But then, she has travelled fairly widely."

"It was very funny," agreed Herr Marani with a reminiscent chuckle, as he drew up by the Chalet boat-landing. "No, thank you, *Fräulein*," as Madge invited him to come in for coffee. "I must return. My wife is away, and the children will be expecting me. *Auf Wiedersehen!*"

"*Auf Wiedersehen*," called Madge softly, as the boat shot out into the moonlight once more. Then she turned to Juliet. "Come, Juliet! It's appallingly late, and you ought to have been in bed an hour ago."

Juliet clung to her arm a moment, her face gleaming white in the dusk.

"Miss Bettany, you've been awfully good to me! I'm so sorry I was ever horrid to you! If you'll keep me, I'll do my level best to help you and… and not be a nuisance! I promise you I will!"

Madge looked down at her with a little smile. "I shouldn't turn you out even if we were in England, Juliet. Certainly not in a foreign land. Your father guessed rightly when he guessed that!"

Juliet looked at her with an expression in her eyes which made the elder girl exclaim sharply, "Juliet! What are you thinking?"

"I was thinking… oh, Miss Bettany, do you think they are really my father and mother? Do you think perhaps I am a foundling, and that's why?"

"Nonsense," replied her headmistress firmly. "That's all rubbish, my dear child. Of course they are your father and mother! Now come along in, and then you must have some hot milk and go to bed and to sleep. Come!"

She turned towards the house as she spoke, and Juliet, her mind set at rest on this point which had troubled her for long, followed obediently. At the door they were met by Mademoiselle, who was looking anxious.

"I had begun to have fears for you, *ma cherie*," said the little Frenchwoman as they entered. "It is so late, and Juliet will be so weary. Go straight upstairs to bed, *ma petite*, and I will bring thee a cup of warm milk. Go quietly, for all are now asleep."

"Yes, Juliet, go," said Madge. "Goodnight, child! Sleep well, and don't worry!"

"Goodnight, Miss Bettany," replied Juliet. "And… and thank you." She turned and vanished up the stairs, while Madge and Mademoiselle went on to their sitting room.

"There is a cablegram, Marguérite," said Mademoiselle, as the English girl dropped limply into the nearest chair. "Drink this coffee, *ma mignonne*. Thou art weary."

"I'm completely done," replied Madge candidly, as she opened the cablegram.

She read it aloud. "'Have nothing to with Carrick. Writing. – Dick.' Oh, well, it's done now! Read this, Elise, and see what you think of it."

She tossed Captain Carrick's letter across to her friend, and then turned her attention to the coffee, eggs, and rolls Mademoiselle had provided for her.

Meanwhile, the Frenchwoman read the remarkable communication with many ejaculations, but of horror and surprise. When she had finished it, she turned back to the beginning and read it over again.

"But, *ma mie*," she cried in her own language, "it is villainy, this!"

"Villainy pure and simple," agreed Madge. "As for that poor child Juliet, what do you think she had got into her head? That she was a foundling, and that was why they had done it. Apparently it isn't the first time either. They did it once before in India, she says." And she repeated Juliet's pitiful story, while Mademoiselle uttered little cries of sympathy.

"Of course he is quite right," finished the girl soberly. "I shall most certainly keep her! But imagine the poor child's feelings! Of course it's a silly, morbid idea, and there is no foundation for it except this abominably callous treatment of her; still, that's what she was thinking."

"Oh, there can be no truth there," agreed Mademoiselle. "There is a most clear likeness to both parents. But, my Marguérite, have you thought that there will be now another mouth to fill and another body to clothe? Soon it will be winter, already it grows colder at nights, and she has no winter garments at all."

"Well, what do you propose I should do?" demanded Madge. "Follow the delightful suggestion he offers as an alternative to keeping her, and place her in an institution? You know you wouldn't hear of it! No, I shall keep her. Next term I shall let her help with the little ones, so that she need not feel under too great an obligation to us. She can do quite a lot without interfering with her own work, and as she will be the oldest of our boarders, it need surprise nobody. Now I vote that we go to bed. It's eleven o'clock, and I'm dead tired. What a blessing tomorrow is Sunday and we can take things easily!"

At the head of the stairs she turned before going to her own room.

"Don't let the others know about this," she said earnestly. "It would make it so dreadfully uncomfortable for Juliet. I will go and see her tomorrow early, and warn her to say nothing. *Bonne nuit*, Elise."

"*Bonne nuit, ma mie. Le bon Dieu te garde*," responded Mademoiselle.

Then they went to their own rooms, and presently darkness and silence reigned over the Chalet.

Chapter Fifteen

SUNDAY

THE BOARDERS OF the Chalet School always declared that Sunday was quite one of the best days of the week. To begin with, they could stay in bed until nine o'clock if they were so minded. Then, after their breakfast of coffee, rolls, and honey, they all assembled in the meadow which ran up from the lake edge to the pine wood, and Madge read aloud to them for an hour. The Catholics generally attended High Mass, but the service was held only once in three weeks. After the reading, they were allowed to wander about as they liked, so long as they kept within call, and they were summoned to lunch at twelve o'clock. In the afternoon, they generally took books and lay outside, reading, or talking quietly, or sleeping; and in the evening Madge took the English girls, and Mademoiselle the Catholics, and they had quiet talks which never lasted more than an hour. Then they were once more free to do as

146

they pleased until Marie's bell called them to supper and bed.

On this particular Sunday, the first person to awaken was Jo Bettany. She had a funny trick of opening her eyes to their widest extent and then sitting bolt upright, wide awake in an instant. This morning, as she sat up in her little wooden bed, gazing straight out of the window, she suddenly remembered Madge's expression as she had read Captain Carrick's letter the night before, and her hands clenched.

"If he's worried Madge, I... I'll take it out on Juliet!" she thought. "I hate him, horrid man! Poor old Madge! I wonder if I could wake her? What time is it?" She burrowed under the pillow and found her watch. Seven o'clock and much too early to disturb anyone on a Sunday! Joey tucked it back and turned her attention to the book at the bedside, which Dick had presented to her just before he had departed for India. The sight of the green covers of the book recalled her brother's cablegram to her memory, and she began to wonder what news it had contained. Obviously it had been nothing serious, or her sister would have let her know before this.

At this point the sound of a light footstep aroused her, and, turning her head, she saw Madge come in, moving cautiously as she skirted the other beds. Her face lit up as she met Joey's gaze.

"So you are awake!" she said in low tones. "I thought you might be. Fetch your things along to my room, and we'll dress and go out. I want to talk to you."

Joey slipped out of bed, clutched at her garments, and

then tiptoed along to her sister's room. Miss Bettany was standing in front of the mirror brushing out her hair. She turned round as her small sister entered, and smiled involuntarily at the funny little figure in the yellow dressing-gown.

"You do look a fright, Jo!" she said in true sisterly fashion. "Now hurry up and get dressed. I had my tub before I came to fetch you, and I've filled it up again for you."

Joey deposited her clothes on the bed and departed.

Madge then left the bedrom to make a raid on the larder. When she came back, bearing two large chunks of currant cake, Jo was ready, and her bed had been stripped and the *plumeau* hung over the balcony. The Bettanys were not demonstrative as a rule, preferring to show their affection by deeds rather than words, so Madge understood what that act was intended to convey, though all she said was, "Here, catch! That's all I could find. There isn't any milk either, so if you're thirsty, you'll have to drink water."

"Thanks awfully," said Jo, with her mouth full. "Ripping cake Marie makes, doesn't she? Are we going for a trot?"

"Just a short one. It's a glorious morning – going to be boiling later."

"I'm glad. I love hot weather," replied Joey, as she crept downstairs after her sister.

"Be quiet! You'll wake the whole house if you yell like that!" returned Madge, the headmistress completely merged in the elder sister.

Joey gave a subdued giggle, but moderated her tones at

once. Madge, glancing at her, felt a throb of joy. The three months in a dry climate had already made a great difference to her. The cough had vanished, and the warm sun and clean mountain air had wiped out the unnatural pallor which her constant illnesses in England had produced. She was getting plumper, too, and her eyes were bright. Pretty she would never be, not even with the elusive prettiness of her elder sister, but she had lost her goblin-like appearance.

"You look pounds better," decided Miss Bettany. "The Tiernsee suits you."

"Rather!" aged Jo. "Suits you too, old thing! You're a bit more freckly, of course, but I'm not sure it isn't an improvement."

"Freckly! You little horror!" exclaimed her sister. "It's a mercy the girls don't hear you! And that reminds me, Joey, you really must try to remember not to use my Christian name before them. You did it again last night. Yes, I know it was because you were excited; but you mustn't do it, even if you are thrilled about something."

"Awfully sorry," murmured Joey. Then she slipped her hand through Madge's arm. "Madge, what was in the cablegram from India?"

"Business," replied Madge briefly. She turned and looked at her small sister thoughtfully. She wasn't very sure how much to tell Joey. She knew quite well that something, at any rate, must be told. The family baby had joined in all their councils ever since she could understand what they were talking about, and she knew Joey well enough to be sure that she would be intensely hurt if she were left out now. Jo was very clannish in feeling. What injured her brother or sister injured her. She would be wondering what had been in Captain Carrick's letter, and the chances were that if she were not told she would guess. Madge decided that it was better to tell her the whole truth rather than leave things to her vivid imagination.

"Jo," she said abruptly, "I'm going to trust you. I don't want any of the others to know, but you've always shared with us, and I'm not going to leave you out now. That letter from Captain Carrick told me that he was leaving Juliet on our hands. He can't afford to keep her, so he says, so he's dropped her on to us. It's very hard luck on her, poor kid, because she has no one for the present but us. He did suggest that we might send her to an institution if we didn't want to keep her. But that's impossible, of course."

"Oh, of course!" agreed Joey, her impressionable little heart filling with pity for the girl who was looked on as a nuisance by her own parents. "Oh, Madge! Poor Juliet! I'll be as decent to her as I can!"

"Don't let her know you know," warned the elder girl. "She would hate that. Just be nice to her as you are to Grizel, or Gisela, or Bernhilda. Remember, Jo, I've trusted you. Dick's cable was warning me about the Carricks, but it's too late now. The only thing we can do is to be as kind as we can to Juliet, and make the best of it."

"Rather!" But Joey's bright little face looked puzzled.

"Well! What now?" demanded Madge. "What are you thinking, Jo?"

"I was thinking, it seems such a horrid thing to do, to desert your own child! Mother and Father wouldn't have done it."

"I should think not!" Madge's thoughts went back to the long-dead father and mother who had loved their children so tenderly. "I've never heard of any other parents doing it either. Don't think about it more than you can help, Joey Baba. Now tell me about yesterday."

"We had a lovely time," responded Joey eagerly. "You'd have loved it at the Alte Post. And oh, the mountains! Madge, I love mountains!"

"Well, you've certainly got plenty of them here," said her sister. "Go on. Tell me what you did. Oh, and about that Berlin woman! What did Grizel say? I imagine she was frightfully rude, though Herr Marani didn't actually say so. But I know what she is by this time. Tell me all about it, Joey."

Thus encouraged, Jo gave a fairly accurate account of their various encounters with Frau Berlin, leaving Madge divided between laughter at the humour of it all, and horror at Grizel's behaviour.

"Grizel really is dreadful," she said at last. "I do hope you didn't join in, Joey."

"Madge! Is it likely? I've got a little common sense!" cried Joey, distinctly outraged.

"I should hope so," returned her sister; "but one never knows. Now don't get excited. I didn't really suppose you did. Well, it's time to go back now, so we'd better turn. Have you got any ideas for Thursday besides the Mondscheinspitze expedition? I've asked Frau Pfeifen to make some of the cakes for us, and I thought we'd get some tobacco. Herr Braun says the herdsmen always appreciate it, because, of course, they can't get it up there."

"Oh, that reminds me, Herr Marani is going to ask his mother to make some cakes for us," said Jo. "Gisela says she makes gorgeous cakes – all honey and nuts! The kind that melt in your mouth. Oh, and, Madge, I nearly forgot! He told me to tell you that Frau von Eschenau is coming to see you. He thinks she wants Wanda and Marie to be boarders. Won't it be topping if she does?"

"No, really?" said Madge, with quick interest. "Are you sure, Joey?"

"Well, that's what he said," replied Jo. "I say, aren't we growing?"

Madge laughed. "We are indeed! If we get any more boarders, I shall have to take another chalet for us to live in, or have school in, or something. Here we are! Now, Joey, remember! Not a word of what I have told you to anyone else."

Joey trotted off, and Madge turned into the dining room, where baskets piled high with brown rolls and glass dishes full of amber honey gave colour to the clothless table. The big, handmade cups and plates, with their cheerful decoration of unknown flowers painted in vivid colours, which stood at each place had come from the Tiern Kirche. The table looked un-English in the extreme, but very pleasant and inviting. Presently Marie came in bearing a huge earthenware jug in which steamed delicious coffee such as one rarely gets in England. She filled the cups by the simple method of dipping a mug into the boiling liquid and pouring its contents into each cup, while Madge arranged plates of the sugar oblongs, which were the joy of Joey, at convenient intervals down the long table. Her task completed, Marie carried the jug back to the kitchen, and then rang the bell which brought them all, fresh and summery in their white frocks, to the table.

Breakfast on Sunday was always a jolly meal, for rules were then relaxed, and everyone chattered in her native language. Mademoiselle, Simone, and Joey were carrying on an animated conversation in French, while Grizel and Margia Stevens argued amiably in English about the probable ending of some book they were both reading, and Miss Maynard and Juliet were describing to the others the walk they had taken on the previous day. Juliet, it is true, had little to say, but Madge noted thankfully that she looked more natural than she had done last night On the whole, the elder girl felt glad that she had taken her little sister into her confidence. It would make things easier, for she hated having any secrets from Jo. Besides, if anyone should be surprised when the next term found Juliet helping, Madge felt certain that her sister would put a stop to that by her own attitude in the matter.

After breakfast, the girls fled upstairs to make their beds and the staff foregathered in the little sitting room, where Madge told Miss Maynard that Juliet Carrick was to be a kind of student teacher next term, as her people had lost money, and had left her at the Chalet School for the present.

Miss Maynard was interested, but showed no curiosity. When Miss Bettany suggested that perhaps she might like to go and write her letters, she went off cheerfully, putting Juliet and her affairs completely out of her mind.

Madge turned to Mademoiselle with a sigh of relief.

"Thank goodness! I wasn't sure whether she would want to ask questions, and it would have been awkward if she had. I've told Jo about it, Elise. If I hadn't, she might have imagined things as being worse than they are And it's quite safe with her; she won't talk."

"No, that is true," agreed Mademoiselle. "Have you seen Juliette yet?"

"No; I'm going to see her presently and tell her what I've decided. Now I must hunt up my book." She turned to the bookshelves as she spoke, hunting for *The Little Flowers of St Francis*, which she was reading to the girls. Mademoiselle watched her with a sympathetic smile.

"You are very tender of Juliette's feelings, *chérie*. I can but trust that she will repay all your kindness to her! She has not proved an attractive member of the school so far."

Madge said, "I'm sure Juliet will do her best now, poor child."

There was a moment's silence, then Mademoiselle turned to the door with a little nod. "Perhaps you are right; we shall see! You are not wanting me this morning? Then I will ask Herr Braun to row me across to Buchau for High Mass."

"Yes, do," replied her friend absently. "Elise, why are those children so excited? Look at them!"

Mademoiselle looked out of the open window, to behold Margia, Amy, and Simone racing across the grass with eager faces. At the same moment music was wafted to them on the warm summer air.

"A band! A band!" cried Margia, who had shot ahead of the others. "Oh, Madame, a band – all violins and flutes and things!"

"Well, but why get excited about that?" asked Madge. "We've had bands here before – there was one last Sunday."

"Oh, but not like this! Big, very dark men, with flashing eyes!"

"They wear hankies round their heads," put in Amy, who had come up, panting, together with Simone. "Very bright hankies – all blue, and red, and yellow, and green! And huge silver rings in their ears!"

"The Tzigane!" exclaimed Madge, her eyes brightening. "Why, what fun! I wondered if there would be any of them round here this year. They're gypsies, children, and their music is often very wonderful. We must go and listen to them this afternoon. I wonder where they will be playing?"

"Gypsies? The people who make gypsy tunes like in Liszt's *Hungarian Rhapsodies*?" queried Margia, who was intensely musical, and meant to be a pianist some day.

"Yes, just exactly those tunes. You'll love them, Margia. They aren't a bit like other music, but something wild and untamed like the gypsies themselves. I do hope they've a good band! If so, we shall have a treat this afternoon."

At this point the others came to join them, ready for the

reading, and as they made their way slowly through the flower-sprinkled grass to the shade of the pines, Madge told them of the old superstition that the gypsies were cursed with wandering because one of their race had once denied rest and shelter to our Lord. The girls were delighted, and seeing this, she repeated the old legend of the attempt to steal the nails which pierced Christ's hands. "It was a gypsy who did it – or tried to do it," she said. "Partly, he wanted the iron; but partly, also, he had pity on Christ. For that pity, so the gypsies say, thieving is not counted by God as a sin in them, and they think nothing of it. They are a strange people. They are to be found in most parts of the world, and the Romany tongue is practically the same the whole world over. A gypsy from India would talk with a gypsy from our New Forest, and each would be able to understand what the other said. A true gypsy can never be happy within four walls. It is misery to them to be imprisoned in any way. They are very revengeful, too, and never forget a wrong. But then, it is said, they never forget a kindness either."

By this time they had reached their favourite spot, so they settled down, and, putting the Tzigane out of her mind for the time being, Madge read aloud to them about the gentle "Brother to all things".

When the reading was over she got up, closed the book, and strolled away, leaving the girls to chatter eagerly about the visitors. Every now and then bursts of music, sometimes cheerful and swinging, sometimes sad and wistful, but always with a peculiar haunting wildness in it, came across the meadow to them as they sat talking together, or wandered about among the dark pine trees at the edge of the forest. Joey, who had read *The Romany Rye* and *Lavengro*, told them all she knew, and the fascinating subject had still not been exhausted when the "tinkle-tinkle" of Marie's bell summoned them back to lunch. When the meal was over, they were wildly anxious to go to the Kron Prinz Karl at once, but Madge insisted on an hour's rest first.

"And no talking," she added. "Run along, all of you, at once."

When they had gone, she turned to the other two mistresses with a smile.

"Don't they think me unkind!" she said gaily. "Well, I don't know what you two people are going to do, but I'm going to write letters. Be ready in about three-quarters of an hour, if you want to come."

Left to herself, Madge sat down and scribbled a long letter to Dick, telling him the full story of the Carricks and the decision she had made about Juliet. The hour was just ended as she signed it, so she got up and went out to the meadow to summon her girls.

Presently they were all ready, and set off along the lake-shore road. Marie followed them behind, for Miss Bettany had decided that they should have tea at the Kron Prinz Karl, so had given her a holiday.

Good Herr Braun, the proprietor of the hotel, met them with a beaming face, and escorted them to three of the tables with their huge scarlet umbrellas nearest the Tzigane. How they all enjoyed that afternoon – even Juliet, and Simone, who was suffering from pangs of jealousy because Joey and Grizel had foregathered at another table! Many of their friends were there – Herr Marani, who brought over Frau von Eschenau for a chat with Madge; the Mensches, who had a table nearby; Monsieur and Madame Mercier with Suzanne and Yvette; and many others.

As Grizel said afterwards, it was so unlike England. There were the gaily dressed Tzigane playing as though they were music-possessed; the merry cosmopolitan crowd seated at the umbrella-shaded tables; the vivid blue lake waters before them; and, surrounding all, the great mountains, beautiful in the bright July sunshine.

They stayed a couple of hours, and then wandered back for their quiet talk, which was never omitted.

As they were going to bed that night, Grizel spoke what was in the minds of all of them.

"I think this has been a beautiful Sunday," she said. "If things were always like this it wouldn't be half so hard to keep rules."

"I s'pose it wouldn't really do if things were jolly always," said Jo. "It's because they're unjolly sometimes that we find other things topping, I think. It would be awfully dull if things were always the same."

"Yes, but some excitements are horrid, and we could do without them easily," replied Grizel.

In which she spoke more truly than she then realized.

Chapter Sixteen

THE MONDSCHEINSPITZE

IT MIGHT HAVE been expected that, after the delightful Sunday described in the foregoing chapter, things would take a contrary turn, and that there would be dire happenings. But for once Fate proved kind, and the week progressed quietly, such small events as Suzanne Mercier pouring ink over herself, and Grizel and Joey having what nearly amounted to a stand-up fight over Simone Lecoutier, not counting at all. The morning of the Head's birthday dawned in a kind of pandemonium, however. Margia Stevens had, the night before, hit on the original idea of serenading Miss Bettany under her window. The idea appealed greatly to them all, and, after a good deal of argument and squabbling, they had decided on "Who is Sylvia?"

"Of course, the name is wrong," said Margia, "but she'll know who it's meant for."

Six o'clock the next morning saw the long dormitory in the throes of getting up. From behind the yellow curtain which divided off the cubicles came subdued giggles and whispered remarks.

"Joey, is it fine? What's it like over the mountains?"

"Glorious," returned Joey, who had stripped her bed and was now sitting on it, waiting for her turn to go to the bathroom. "It's going to be a ripping day."

"Be quiet!" hissed Juliet. "You'll waken Miss Maynard if you shriek so."

"She's prob'ly awake already," returned Joey, not a whit disturbed. "Thank goodness! Here's Grizel at last! I thought you'd drowned yourself!"

"Rot! I've only been six minutes!" protested Grizel. "Buck up yourself! Margia and Simone have to come after you."

"What about my bath?" asked a little voice from the other corner of the room where Amy Stevens slept. "It's all cold still, isn't it?"

"Oh, bother! I quite forgot you hadn't to have cold baths!" Grizel paused in the act of putting on one of her stockings. "Juliet, what shall we do?"

"Marie will be up. Shall I go down and ask her for a kettleful of hot water? I'm just ready," suggested Juliet.

"Will you? That'd be topping of you. Yes, do go!" urged Grizel. "Hello, Joey, old thing! You can't have had much of a bath! You haven't been a minute!"

"Have, though! Tootle on, Margia! You're next, aren't you?"

Margia and Juliet vanished together, and presently Juliet

came back with a big jug of warm water supplied by good-natured Marie.

"Come along, Amy," she said cheerfully. "I'll tub you this morning. We can't wait till Mademoiselle comes."

"Oh, thank you, Juliet," replied Amy shyly; while Grizel stopped in the act of brushing out her curly mop to gape open-mouthed at her curtains. When had Juliet ever offered to help anyone like that before?

Amy herself was very startled. She had never liked Juliet, but was too shy to refuse the older girl's help, so submitted in silence to being bathed with much vigour and goodwill, if with some clumsiness. Juliet's whole-hearted rubbing with the towel brought an involuntary "Ow!" from her, but when the Senior, conscience-stricken, asked, "Did I hurt you?" she replied hastily, "No, oh, no, Juliet! And it's very kind of you to bath me. Thank you so much."

"Call me if you want anything tied or buttoned," said Juliet, as she returned to her own cubicle. "Margia will have to dress herself, and I'm practically ready, so I can help you easily."

Grizel restrained an exclamation of surprise in time. She stripped her bed in an awestruck silence which lasted until they were all ready to leave the room. Then Joey roused her.

"Aren't you feeling well?" she demanded bluntly.

"Yes, quite well! Why?" queried Grizel somewhat incautiously.

"You're so silent! You've scarcely spoken at all!" grinned Jo. "I thought something must be the matter!"

"So it is, Joey! Juliet did practically everything for Amy! Did you ever?"

"Well, that's nothing to be wondered at!" returned Joey smartly. "She's the oldest of us, and someone had to help Amy or else she'd never have been ready! You know what a perfect baby she is."

"Oh, yes, of course;" said Grizel uncertainly. "I expect you're right, Joey!"

"Course I am! Now come on."

They all slipped down the stairs and out into the glorious sunlight, collecting in a merry little group under Miss Bettany's wide-open windows.

"Let's start with 'Good King Wenceslas'," giggled Joey.

"Yes; I feel rather like Christmas carols too," agreed Grizel.

"Stop ragging, you two! We're waiting for you! This is the note." And Margia sang "Loo!" in a very true little treble. "Now! One, two!"

They all started off, and Madge, who had been sleeping the sleep of the justly weary, was roused by the notes of "Who is Sylvia?" sung fortissimo by the whole band.

She quickly guessed the meaning of the serenade, and sat up in bed with a chuckle. As they finished, she got into her kimono, and ran across to the window.

"Hello, everybody!" she called. "What a lovely awakening!"

"It's to wish you many happy returns, Miss Bettany," called up Grizel. "It was Margia's idea, really. Did you like it?"

"Yes; it was delightful. Thank you all very much! Now I'm

going to dress." She withdrew her head just as a tap at the door heralded Joey's advent.

"Hello! Many happy returns of your birthday," she said. "I've brought you this." She presented her parcel, and Madge opened it with delight.

"A picture of the Tiernsee! Joey! You gem! It's just what I've wanted," she cried. "You couldn't have given me anything better!"

"Glad you like it," returned Jo, as she turned her cheek for her sister's kiss. "Herr Marani helped me to choose it last Saturday. I say, can I help you to dress? I'll strip your bed; shall I?"

She suited the action to the word, and presently Madge sauntered downstairs, ready for the day, in her pale green frock. Marie was scurrying round getting breakfast ready. She stopped to offer her good wishes together with a bouquet of Alpen roses, which she had gathered the evening before.

"*Für Madame*," she said shyly.

"Oh, Marie! How good of you! And I love Alpen roses so much!"

Breakfast was a hilarious meal, followed by a cheerful rush to put in bedmaking and practice. Nine o'clock brought all the boarders, flower-laden and beaming. Gisela and Bette carried the basket containing the precious china between them, and Maria had another, full of *Grossmutter's* delicious cakes.

"Hurry up! Hurry up!" exclaimed Joey, dancing with impatience. "I've got the tray from Marie, and Mademoiselle is keeping Madame talking in the dining room till we're ready! Here you are! Now buck up!"

In the big schoolroom they arranged the dainty coffee service on the big black tray Joey had produced. Then they formed up in their usual lines, and Amy was sent to ring the bell. She came scampering back, proclaiming in a stage whisper, "She's coming!"

The sound of light, rapid footsteps followed, and then Miss Bettany came in and took her place on the dais. As she did so, a chorus of birthday greetings in German, French, and English came from the eighteen girls assembled below her. As they spoke, they all raised their bouquets – the day-girls had brought flowers for the boarders – and the beauty of the flowers, the goodwill and affection of the girlish faces before her, brought a little thrill to the young headmistress, and touched her charming face with rather more colour than usual. Then Gisela and Gertrud came forward, carrying between them the tray with its dainty burden of china.

The head girl looked rather flushed and nervous with her responsibilities, but she rose to the occasion bravely, and said in her clear, carrying voice, "Madame, be pleased to accept from us all this so small token of our feelings for you on this your feast day."

"Thank you, girls," said Madge, a little shyly. "It is very good of you indeed, and I cannot tell you how much I appreciate your kindness to me. If anything could have made it a happier birthday for me – the first birthday I have spent in the Tyrol – your thought could."

Then came the business of presenting the bouquets, and soon the table on the dais was heaped with lilies, roses, marguerites, gentians, single dahlias, Alpen roses, and peonies, until that end of the room was glowing with their colour and beauty. When, finally, little Giovanna Rincini had trotted up with her armful of lilies and dahlias, Gisela called for three cheers for "Our dear Madame!" which were given heartily, and then the serious business of the day was over.

"In half an hour we shall start," said Madge, smiling at them over the great heap of flowers. "First, I must place these in water and put them in a cool place. Then we must collect up all our possessions, and then we can set off! Joey, please go and fetch me some big bowls; and Grizel and Juliet, I want some water. Take them into the dining room; that is the coolest place, I think. Miss Maynard, if you will look after the younger girls, Mademoiselle will see to the food, and the prefects will help me to arrange the flowers."

They all flew off to do her bidding, and by ten o'clock a long string of girls was to be seen setting off up the path whch led to the Lauterbach Valley, through which they would have to walk in order to reach the mountain path that led up the Mondscheinspitze.

As long as they kept to the beaten track – that is, until they reached the white wooden railings that fenced off Briesau from the Lauterbach Valley – they walked in "croc", but as soon as the gate had swung behind them, they broke file, and wandered happily along in little groups, chattering happily among themselves. Gisela, Gertrud, Bette and Bernhilda attached themselves to Miss Bettany, and were soon eagerly comparing the differences of Cornish picnics and Tyrolean ones. Miss Maynard and Mademoiselle were discussing Paris, which the former knew very well, since she had been at school there. The little ones, needless to state, chased butterflies and gathered flowers; while Joey, Grizel, and Simone, for once in complete accord, strolled along amiably talking about their climb. Presently they came within sight of the Tiernjoch, even in this day of glorious sunshine dark and gloomy, with a hint of menace in its towering crags. Grizel stopped and tilted back her head, looking at it with a determined gleam in her eyes.

"I'll go up there some day," she said aloud.

Joey followed her eyes. "The Tiernjoch? Oh, Grizel, I wish you wouldn't!"

"Don't be silly! It's only a little climb! 'Tisn't even as if there were any glacier to cross!" retorted Grizel. "Why, there's no snow or anything!"

"It's such a cruel-looking mountain!" said Jo with a little shiver. "It looks as if it didn't care how many people were killed on it!"

"Joey! Tosh! That's only your silly imaginings!" began Grizel. Then the sudden whiteness of her friend's face made her sorry she had mentioned it, so she added, "Anyway, I'm not going today, or this week either, so keep your hair on!"

"I think you are unkind, Grizel!" broke in Simone unexpectedly. "Always you tease, tease, Joey! And she hates the Tiernjoch!"

"'Tisn't your business!" Grizel was beginning heatedly, when Joey stopped her.

"Oh, shut up quarrelling, you two! An' if you mention that beastly Tiernjoch again, Grizel Cochrane, I'll go away an' you can walk with someone else! So there!" And she marched ahead, leaving Grizel and Simone to follow meekly after her.

Luckily, at that moment, loud screams from Amy Stevens distracted everyone's attention to her, as she came flying down the slope, yelling at the full pitch of her lungs, "Ooh! Ooh! A snake! A snake!"

"What!" exclaimed Madge. She started forward, catching up the frightened child. "Amy! Are you hurt? Stop crying, dear, and tell me!"

"No, she isn't!" Margia supplied the information disgustedly. "She saw a little greeny snake curled up asleep by that stone, and so she howled! It never came near her!"

"Thank heaven!" Madge set the child on her feet again with a sigh of relief. There were very few snakes found round the Tiernsee, and, so far as she knew, the only venomous ones were vipers, which were even more rarely seen than the harmless green variety; but Amy's shrieks had scared her for the moment. "There's nothing to cry about, Amy," she added. "If you scream when you only see a snake, you aren't a very plucky person, are you? Now dry your eyes and stop crying. And, girls, don't go into the long grass, please."

"It will be all right, Madame," said Gisela seriously. "Snakes prefer the sun, and that grass is in the shadow, and is cold."

"Nevertheless, I shall feel safer if you keep more to the

path," returned her headmistress decidedly. "Frieda, I'm sure you've carried that basket long enough. Give it to Joey. And Grizel, take Juliet's for a while."

They went on again, Madge keeping a rather nervous eye on the Juniors. However, they soon had to leave the track, and strike across the valley to get to the mountain path.

"Do we cross here?" demanded Miss Bettany, eyeing what looked like a stony bed of a dried-up river somewhat doubtfully. "Isn't there a bridge?"

"Only a log further down," said Bernhilda. "You see, Madame, when the storms of autumn come, this is a torrent, and already three bridges have been swept away. The water comes suddenly, and there is nothing to break its strength. It is easy to reach, though. See; down here." And she pointed to some rough, natural steps which led down to the stony bed.

Already more than half the girls were struggling across, the unfortunate bearers of baskets uttering wild shrieks as the stones slipped under their feet, and they more than once nearly went headlong. At length they were all safely at the other side, and once more on the beaten path which led through grass and wild flowers to the foot of the mountain, where they all paused for a rest.

"Oof! Isn't it hot!" panted Margia, as she mopped her crimson face.

"I'm just comfortable," said Joey with an exasperatingly superior air, "but I'm awfully hungry! What's the time, anyone?"

"It is half after eleven," said Gisela, glancing at her pretty little watch.

"You must be slow, Gisela," laughed Juliet, showing hers. "I make it ten past twelve."

"So do I," said Madge, "and mine was right this morning. Miss Maynard, what does yours say?"

"Nearly quarter past," replied Miss Maynard, "but I may be a little fast."

"Well, anyhow, it's time for lunch," said Joey. "Do let's have it here!"

"Oh, yes!" agreed several voices at once. "I am hungry!"

Madge laughed and gave way. "Very well. I'm rather hungry myself; and it would certainly lighten the baskets!"

Accordingly they all sat down, and in a very few minutes the baskets were considerably lighter than they had been.

"It's funny how much hungrier one is out of doors than in," said Grizel presently, as she tackled her sixth sandwich.

"It is!" agreed Joey. "But I'm not so hungry as I was," she added pensively.

"After having only five sandwiches and six biscuits and two apples!" jeered Grizel. "There must be something up with you, Joey, old thing!"

"You can't talk!" said Joey contentedly. "You've had just as much. I say," she added in rather changed tones, "where's the lemonade?"

"Bette has it," said Gisela.

"I haven't," replied Bette. "I thought you had it!"

"No; I was carrying the apples. I was certain you had it!"

"Oh, no! I never had it!"

Madge began to gurgle with laughter. It was only too plain what had occurred to that lemonade.

"Sitting in the passage at home," she choked.

"Oh! And I'm dying of thirst!"

"And I!" "And I!" rose on all sides. "What are we to do?"

"Wait until we reach the alm. We can get plenty of milk from the herdsmen," said Miss Bettany somewhat unfeelingly. "I'm sorry, but it's your own faults."

"Then," said Jo, scrambling to her feet, "there's only one thing to be done – get up to the alm as soon as we can. Come on!"

There was common sense in her statement, so with loud groans the girls repacked the baskets and set off.

The climb up the Mondscheinspitze is remarkably easy. There is a well-defined path, which winds in and out among the dark pine trees, every now and then coming out into narrow – very narrow – grassy ledges. Presently, however, it left the woods, and they climbed up the bare limestone face of the mountain beneath the glare of the July sun. Tufts of grass, with wild scabious and white marguerites, punctuated the way, and gorgeous butterflies, brown and orange and scarlet and yellow, fluttered round them, so little afraid that often they settled on hat or frock, and little Amy Stevens cried out in delight when one balanced itself on her outstretched fingers, resting there for a moment before it fluttered off.

Madge was thankful for the distraction the dainty creatures afforded the girls; otherwise, the Juniors at any rate would have found the path more difficult than they did. As it was, she was very thankful when a triumphant cry from Joey, Simone, and Frieda Mensch, who had raced on, announced that they had reached the alm.

"Isn't it a gorgeous view?" demanded Jo, when they were all standing on the short, sweet grass. "Just look!"

They looked. At their feet lay the valley they had crossed that morning, cool and green, with the empty river bed stretching like a white ribbon down its length. In the distance they could see Briesau, lying like a toy village some giant child had set out; and beyond it, blue – blue – blue, the Tiernsee, a living sapphire, gleaming beneath the sun.

"Oh, wonderful!" breathed Madge softly.

They did not gaze long, however; they were all too thirsty. With one accord, presently, they turned, and made for the herdsmen's hut – and milk.

Chapter Seventeen

ON THE ALM

ALTHOUGH BOTH JOEY and Grizel had been up to the
Bärenbad alm many times since their arrival at Briesau, they
had never been inside a herdsman's hut, and great was their
interest in it.

Only one man was there when they reached the place – a
tall, lanky young fellow, in weather-stained green breeches
and ragged shirt, open at the throat. His black hair was rough
and long, and his face burnt brown with the weather. He
wore the little green Tyrolese hat with its cock feather, and
was sitting contentedly smoking a long china-bowled pipe,
such as most men smoke in the Tyrol. On seeing them
coming, he rose to his feet with a smile of welcome and a
hoarse-voiced "*Grüss Gott!*"

"*Grüss Gott!*" replied Madge briskly. "Can you sell us some
milk and cheese?"

"Yes, gracious lady. Will the gracious lady and the young ladies come in?"

Only the English girls availed themselves of this offer, so that they might look round at the little bare room, with its huge well in one corner, where a wood fire was burning although the day was so hot. A broad shelf ran round the room, well above their heads, and on this stood enormous earthenware pans for the milk and big cream-coloured cheeses. The one window was about two feet square, and set high up in the wall; a long wooden bench stood at one side, and next to it a huge cheese press; a door opened into another room beyond, where trusses of hay were to be seen. The atmosphere of the place was indescribable – a mixture of cheese, garlic, tobacco, and burning wood. The visitors soon left the hut for the sweeter atmosphere of the alm, where the others were gravely taking it in turn to drink out of an enormous bowl, full of rich, creamy milk, while their host stood nearby, still smoking, and gazing vacantly across to the mighty peaks on the other side of the lake.

When Miss Bettany presently brought back the empty bowl, together with the tobacco she had brought, and some kronen notes to pay for the milk, he smiled again, and answered her questions in his curiously hoarse tones.

Yes, he and four others were there for the summer. They had come up early in May, and would stay there till the end of September if the weather was good. Then the cattle must be brought down to the valley before the autumn storms began.

"But aren't you ever lonely?" queried Joey, who had accompanied her sister to the hut. "Don't you ever want to go down to Briesau?"

He turned indifferent dark eyes on her. "No, *gnädiges Fräulein*. There are the cows and the mountains. We are five, and I have my pipe."

"What do the cows do in the winter?" asked Madge, a fine instinct preventing her from asking what he did, though she felt curious about it.

"They live in the sheds in the winter," he replied, "and I go to my home in Scholastika. They do not need us in the winter, so we all go to our homes, and pray to *der liebe Gott* and the blessed saints for an early spring. Last winter it did not come, and some of us went hungry for a time."

"How dreadful!" said Joey with wholehearted sympathy. "I hope it's a good autumn."

"It will be as *der liebe Gott* wills," he replied, with the curious fatalism of his race.

Madge made arrangements for milk and cheese for the tea, and then went back to her flock. She found them all lying about in exhausted attitudes, and promptly proposed that they should have a rest before exploring the alm any further.

"It will be easier going down than coming up," she said. "We climbed in the noonday heat, but by then it will be cool, so we shall go twice as quickly. Half an hour, or even an hour's sleep won't do any of you any harm. I've got a book in my pocket, so I'll read and keep an eye on the time."

They promptly curled up in various attitudes,

Mademoiselle and Miss Maynard among them, and Madge was soon the only one awake. She glanced at her watch with a smile.

"A quarter past three," she thought. "I'll let them sleep for another half hour, and then we must have tea."

She turned back to her book. It was terribly hot – almost oppressively so, although the sun was not shining so brilliantly as it had done earlier in the day. The German print looked all funny and jumbled up; the page wasn't there any more. Madge was asleep.

Meanwhile, the sunlight faded away, hidden by the huge black clouds that began to marshal themselves in terrifying squadrons in the north-west. Even the faint breeze which had stirred the Alpine flowers in the short grass had died away. There was a waiting stillness, broken only by the occasional cry of a wild bird, frightened at what it felt was coming.

Joey was the first to feel it. She woke up with a sensation that something was wrong. The next minute she knew what it was. The electricity in the air was tingling through and through her. She sprang to her feet with a little cry, gazing wildly round her. The sunshine was gone; the whole place was wrapped in gloom. At the other side of the valley the mountains reared ghastly white heads against the blackness of the sky, and every now and then the lightning flashed across the awful inkiness, seeming to rip it open for a moment. There was no thunder yet, which made it all the more terrifying. Dashing to her sister's side, she shook her vigorously.

"Madge! Madge! Wake up! Wake up! Madge! I'm frightened!"

In a moment Madge sat up and regarded the awesome scene with horror in her eyes. The next instant she was on her feet.

"Thunder! What a fool I was not to think of it! We must get down at once! Girls! Wake up!"

They woke up at her urgent cries, and Simone and Amy promptly burst into tears. The Tyroleans were too accustomed to the terrible thunderstorms which come up with such terrifying suddenness to be scared, although the elder girls looked serious. They knew what thunder from the north-west meant.

Meanwhile, the three elders were taking rapid counsel, while Juliet and Gisela tried to console the two weepers. Joey was watching her sister's face anxiously, and Grizel was too excited to feel afraid.

Then, even as Miss Bettany turned to bid the girls hurry to the mountain path, there was a vivid glare, that seemed to rend the very clouds asunder, followed by a terrific crash, which scared what few wits Simone had left completely from her. She clung to Mademoiselle, screaming hysterically, and Madge realized that if they were to get her down the path at all they would have to carry her.

A sudden shout coming out of the gloom which had descended so rapidly made her turn, and there was the herdsman running towards them, beckoning to them as he did so. In a flash she realized that he meant them to come to the hut. The next moment the darkness descended completely, and overhead the lightning flickered and the thunder crashed almost incessantly. There was no question of going down yet. Even if Simone had kept her head it would have been impossible. The path was easy enough in daylight, but there were great tree roots sprawling across it at intervals, as well as occasional boulders which had worked loose and rolled into it. Any attempt to descend it now was more than likely to end in sprained ankles, if nothing worse. She made a swift decision. Even as the panting herdsman reached them, she spoke.

"Come! We must go to the hut! It is the only thing to do, and we can stay there till it is over."

Gisela, Bette, and Bernhilda had already collected the baskets together, and now they all turned and followed the man, who had picked up Simone with as much ceremony as if she were a bundle of hay, and was now leading them across the little plateau to the hut.

It was really quite a short distance, but to Madge it seemed never-ending, that strange walk – half walk, half run – in almost pitchy blackness, lightened only by the fearful glare of the lightning, while all round them the thunder roared frighteningly. Little Amy Stevens was between her and Miss Maynard, while the elder girls looked after the other Juniors, and Mademoiselle hurried gaspingly after them, with an arm round Margia Stevens.

Once they were all safely inside, the herdsman shut the door and set Simone down on the bench. She had stopped screaming now, but little heart-rending moans came from her lips every now and then. Leaving Amy to Miss Maynard's care, Madge went over to her.

"Simone," she said sternly, "you must stop crying at once – at once! Do you hear?"

"I… I have such fear!" sobbed Simone in her own language.

"So have the others," replied her headmistress, "but you are the only one who is behaving like a baby. Come! You must stop at once or I shall slap you!"

She nearly burst out laughing when she finished, for, as she glanced up, she had happened to catch sight of Joey's face, with eyes and mouth round O's of wonder. However, her dramatic speech had its effect on Simone, who gradually began to recover her self-control, and presently was able to sit up and drink the milk Gisela brought her.

Meanwhile, the herdsman had drawn the young headmistress aside.

"The gracious lady must stay here tonight," he said. "There is hay, and we can give bread and milk and cheese. To go down the path would be dangerous while the storm rages."

"But surely it cannot go on long?" said Madge in startled tones. "It is too heavy to last."

"It is from the north-west," he replied. "It will last many hours yet – four, or perhaps five; and then it will be night."

"Good heavens! How awful!"

She stood silent for a few moments, going over the state of affairs in her mind. Then she turned to the Seniors. "Gisela!

Bette! Is this true? Are we storm-stayed here for the night?"

"I am afraid so," replied Gisela. "When a storm comes from the north-west it does not die quickly."

"But how appalling! What will your parents think?"

"They will know we took refuge here," said Bette. "Everyone at the Tiernsee knows of the hut, and they will know that we should stay here. These storms come so quickly; often there is no time to do anything. Don't worry, Madame. They will be sure we shall be here, and quite safe."

"I wish I could think so!" murmured her headmistress. "Well, I suppose there is nothing else for it."

"Do you mean we're going to stay here all night?" gasped Grizel, who had been standing near. "How simply thrilling!"

"I'm glad you think so!" returned Madge dryly. "I'd be thankful to know we were all safe in our beds."

The herdsman, having given his opinion, was now busily engaged in carrying in great armfuls of fresh, sweet hay from a little shed which stood nearby. The rain had not yet come, and he had evidently made up his mind to prepare for the night before it did.

Grizel sprang forward. "Let me help!" she said in her pretty broken German. "Yes, do! I'd like it!"

"Oh, so would I," exclaimed Margia. "I'll come too!"

The man made no attempt to stop them, so they followed him out; and very soon one end of the room was thickly littered with the hay, which the elder girls shook up and covered with their raincoats. When that was done, he shut the door once more, cast a couple of logs on the fire, and then sat down on the bench and lit his pipe. He had done all he could, and now he was prepared to sit and smoke contentedly until he was sleepy, when he would go to bed in the next room.

A little silence fell on them all, which was suddenly broken by a "swish-swish!" and the rain had come. Such rain! Joey, opening the door to see, had to shut it again in a hurry or they would have been flooded out.

"Gracious Peter!" she remarked, as she came back to the others. "It's like the Flood! This is Mount Ararat, I shouldn't wonder!"

"Tosh!" retorted Grizel. "Mount Ararat has snow on it… I think!"

She finished rather doubtfully.

"Well, this has in winter," argued Jo amiably. "Anyhow, it's some rain!"

"Not unlike the rainy season in India," laughed Madge — the thunder had died away for the moment. "Do you remember how I told you about the time when we were flooded out the year before we came home?"

"Rather! Tell the others now!" said Joey. "It's like a story in a book!"

"It will take too long," replied her sister. "Ask me about it sometime when there isn't a thunderstorm going on. Just listen to it!" as a fresh rumble forced her to shriek the last words.

"It often does that," said Gisela. "It travels round and round the lake till it dies away. It will come back again and again before it is over tonight."

"Where are we going to sleep?" asked Amy with interest. "And oh, Miss Bettany, what is that funny thing on the wall?"

She pointed as she spoke to a zither which was hung up by a loop of soiled ribbons. The herdsman, seeing her point to it, got up from his seat and, taking it down, produced a little twist of wire attached to a silver ring which he fitted on his thumb, and then ran it across the string, producing a shower of silvery sounds.

"A zither!" cried Miss Maynard. "And I never noticed it!"

"*Gnädiges Fräulein* plays the zither?" queried the man, holding it to her.

"Yes; but you play first," she said, smiling at him.

He bowed somewhat clumsily, and then played them a simple little air, whose notes rippled through the hut like bird notes. When he had finished, he handed it to Miss Maynard, and she played a song which, she told them, she had learnt from the New Forest gypsies. Every now and then the thunder roared above the tinkling music, and made the nervous people start. The first awful gloom was wearing off, but the lightning flashes were as vivid as ever, and the rain still poured down ceaselessly.

Presently the herdsman produced a huge pot, which he slung on a hook hung over the fire by an iron chain. Into this he poured a panful of milk and, when it was heated, he invited them to dip big earthenware mugs, which he had brought from the inner room, into it, and drink. It proved very good if it did have a smoky flavour. Certainly, drunk in that room as an accompaniment to black bread and milk-cheese, it had a taste all its own.

When they had finished it, there was silence for a little. The close atmosphere and the warmth were doing their work. It was barely seven o'clock, but most of the Juniors were already nodding sleepily, and presently Amy turned to Miss Bettany with a request for bed.

"Please may I go to bed? I'm so sleepy!" she pleaded.

"I think most of you would be better in bed," said the young headmistress. "Come along, you people! You can slip off your frocks and lie down in the hay, and then we'll cover you up."

"In the hay?" Amy wasn't sure whether to laugh or cry.

Luckily, Maria Marani settled it for her. "It is topping!" she said cheerfully.

"Just like camping out!" added Grizel approvingly. "Oh, this is something like an adventure!"

The herdsman, seeing that bed seemed to be the order of the day, got up, lit two lanterns, hanging one on a nail near the door and, taking the other, slouched into the inner room with a muttered "*Gute Nacht!*"

"And that's that!" observed Joey, wriggling out of her frock. "I say, supposing the others come back, what a shock they will get if they walk in and see us lying round!"

"I hadn't thought of that!" Madge looked disturbed.

"I do not think they will come," said Gisela consolingly. "See, the door is barred. I think there is another hut at the other side, and they will spend the night there."

"Do you? Shunt along, Grizel! You've got three times your share of the hay – I mean bed! Righto, Simone! You can come next me, if you can keep your arms to yourself, that is!"

Thus Joey, as she slipped off her shoes and curled herself up. She suddenly sat up again to ask, "I say, does anyone snore?"

"Not unless it's yourself!" retorted Grizel promptly.

"Girls! Girls! Be quiet!" put in Madge, laughing. "You really must settle down and get to sleep! We shall have to be up at six to get down before Briesau is awake to see what scarecrows we are!"

Joey lay down, and presently they were all settled. Madge put out the lantern and lay down in her own place. It took her a little time to drop off, though everyone else quickly fell asleep – or so it seemed. But just as she was getting drowsy, a low voice said, "Madge!"

"Well?" she asked sleepily.

"We'll have a holiday tomorrow after this, shan't we?"

Madge sat up, fully awake.

"Joey Bettany, lie down at once and go to sleep, and don't let me hear you again till the morning!" she said severely.

There was a rustle in the hay and a little chuckle. Then silence.

Chapter Eighteen

THE CHALET MAGAZINE IS DISCUSSED

"OH, IT WAS priceless!" Grizel gave a little chuckle. "There we were, all grubby and untidy, and our hair full of hayseed, and all that walk to take! You'd have screamed if you'd seen us!"

She laughed again at the memory, and Wanda Von Eschenau joined her. Arrangements had been made for the next term, and Wanda and Marie were to join the Chalet School as boarders. In the meantime, they were to be with the girls as much as possible, partly with a view to learning English, so that they would be able to follow the lessons easily. Wanda already spoke fairly well, but Marie made funny mistakes at times. She and Joey and Simone were sitting in the grass some distance away, revelling in the warmth of the sun, while Wanda and Grizel were perched on the railings which cut off the path to Geisalm. Further along, Juliet was lying on the bank reading, while Margia, Amy and the two little Merciers were making wreaths of the big white marguerites which grew everywhere.

It was a Saturday morning; practice was finished, and the boarders were free to amuse themselves. Grizel was telling Wanda about the birthday expedition with its unexpected ending. The young Viennese, who lead the sheltered life of most girls of her class, was deeply thrilled, for Grizel told the tale well.

"It must have been full of terror up there on the alm," she said in her slow, careful English. "The storm was terrible, even here!"

"It was ghastly," agreed Grizel. "Simone shrieked like mad and Amy cried, and I'm sure I don't wonder! It must be awful if you're afraid of thunder! I'm not! But then, I'm not afraid of anything much!"

"You must be very courageous," replied Wanda simply.

Grizel coloured to the roots of her hair. She had not meant to boast, but she had to admit that her last speech sounded uncommonly like boasting.

"Sorry! I'm afraid that was swank," she said.

"Swank? *Was ist denn* 'swank?'" queried Wanda.

"Oh, bucking...er...boasting," returned Grizel hastily. "Er, I wouldn't use it if I were you, Wanda. It isn't good English – not proper, you know."

"What you call 'slang'. I see," replied the other girl. "But go on, Grizel. Did you meet with anybody?"

"Only cowherds," said Grizel. "Oh, but it was lovely, so early in the morning! Everything looked so new and well-washed after the rain! Except us, of course! I don't know about the others, but all us boarders had a hot bath and washed our hair. We had to, to get the hayseed out! Then we all went to bed and to sleep. I never knew bed could be so nice before," she added meditatively. "Sleeping on hay is fun all right, but you don't get much sleep! First of all, a beetle walked across Joey's face, and she yelled and hung onto my hair – suppose it was the handiest thing there was to hang on to! Then, when we had got over that excitement, Amy began to cry because the hayseed had gone down her neck and was tickling her. Then, just before dawn, an owl of sorts began to screech, and so did some of the little ones!"

"But how could you enjoy such happenings?" asked Wanda, wide-eyed.

"Oh, I don't know! You do, you know! It's something fresh – I s'pose that's it."

"Perhaps," said Wanda doubtfully. "But I should not like it."

"Oh, you will when you've been with us a while," said Grizel confidently. "Only, of course, there won't be any mountain expeditions next term."

"No, not with the snow here," agreed the young Austrian. "How shall we amuse ourselves, then, my Grizel?"

"Oh, I don't know! Dancing and games, I suppose. P'raps we shall get up a play. Just the usual things one does do in the winter. I'm tired of these old railings now – they're so jolly hard! Let's walk along to the other end. Gisela may be coming. She often does on Saturdays, and so do Bernhilda and Frieda Mensch. It makes it jollier for Juliet and me. Most of the others are rather babies, you see. Coming, Juliet?"

Juliet raised her head. "Where to? Oh, the other gate? No, thanks, Grizel. I want to get on with my book; and anyway, it's too hot to move."

"Lazy old object!" laughed Grizel. "All right! Come on, Wanda! Let's leave her to it!"

They went off, laughing and talking cheerfully, while Juliet, uncurling herself from the little heap in which she had been lying, gazed after them thoughtfully.

She was not jealous, although Grizel had very little to say to her nowadays. In Grizel's eyes, Juliet had become suddenly and tiresomely "good"; Wanda was fresh, and the English girl was rather given to running after fresh things. One thing thought Juliet, as she sat hugging her knees in a brown study, Grizel could come to no harm with Wanda, who had been trained on the most conventional lines, and was often horrified at her new friend's tomboyish ways. It was rather a relief to the elder girl to know this, for she could not forget Grizel's declaration of a fortnight or so ago that she would be off up the Tiernjoch the first chance she got, and she didn't care who said what! City-bred Wanda was most unlikely to attempt such an expedition. The Barenbad alm was as much as she could manage, though Marie and Wolfram were ready for anything, and Kurt, the elder boy, went on climbing and hunting expeditions with his father every day.

Meanwhile, the younger children had grown tired of their wreaths, and were making their way slowly towards the boat-landing to watch the steamer come in. As they strolled along, they saw a couple of big boys come racing down the path towards them, followed by a little girl of about nine. Instinctively the children moved to one side, and the two lads tore past them without giving them a glance. The little girl turned and looked at them, however, with a look of friendly curiosity, before she galloped after the others.

"Wonder who they are?" commented Jo in German, which language she now spoke as fluently as she did English. "They looked rather jolly, didn't they?"

"I think they are English," said Simone gravely.

"*Das Mädchen* was not," corrected Marie. "She hadn't the English view."

"Appearance, you mean," observed Margia. "Amy, come back! You'll fall in."

"It wouldn't matter if I did, 'cept for having to change," replied Amy.

"Well, that would be bother enough," said Margia, as she hauled her little sister back to safety.

"It wouldn't be yours anyhow!" snapped Amy.

Margia released her little sister in sheer amazement. It was the first time that Amy had ever attempted to have an opinion different to hers, and she gasped with wonder.

Joey laughed at her startled face. "Margia, if you open your mouth like that the mosquitoes will dash in to their doom. Be always kind to animals, wherever you may be. If a mosquito is an animal!"

"Oh, don't talk rubbish!" burst out Margia. "Amy, you must be ill!"

"No, I'm not!" returned Amy pettishly. "But I'm not going to be pulled about."

"Oh, say no more, Margia!" interposed Simone. "It is but that Amy grows up."

"Well, but—" If her gentle little sister had slapped her in the face, Margia could not have been more surprised.

"Never mind now," said Joey tactfully. "I want to talk about my idea – at least, it's Gisela's really," she added truthfully; "but don't you think it would be topping to have a school mag?"

"Gorgeous!" said Simone, who had picked up this expression from Jo.

"It would be like the school tales," said Marie thoughtfully.

"There's the Mondscheinspitze picnic for one thing," said Joey. "That would be a topping thing for a mag!"

"And your day at Innsbruck and Frau Berlin," added Margia; for all the school knew of that episode by this time.

"Yes; and the day we went boating and the storm came on. And we do play cricket and tennis with ourselves," said Jo thoughtfully.

"Then let us ask Gisela, shall we not?" suggested Marie.

"An'… an' I'll write a poem for you," proposed Amy cheerfully.

They all stopped still with one accord and stared at her. She blushed crimson, but stood her ground.

Joey was the first to speak. "I say!" she said, and whistled loudly.

"Amy!" cried Margia. "What do you mean? You know you can't write poetry."

"I can, then!" retorted Amy. "I writed some last night!"

"Let's see it, then!"

"Can't! It's in my cubey under my pillow!"

"What is it about?" demanded Marie.

"A river. The one beside the Kron Prinz Karl."

"That's not a river; it's not big enough," declared Margia.

"Well, I've called it a little river," returned Amy defiantly.

"Oh, Amy, do let us see it!" pleaded Simone. "I think you are awfullee clevaire! I could not do it. I! No, truly!"

"I tell you it's in my cubey," said Amy, nevertheless softening before Simone's compliments. "I'll get it when I go to wash my hands for *Mittagessen*."

"There's Gisela, with Wanda and Grizel," put in Joey. "Let's scoot and ask her."

But Amy had caught at her arm. "Joey, don't let Grizel know!"

"Why ever not?" demanded Joey in surprise.

"She'll laugh if you do! Don't tell her, Joey! Not yet, anyhow!"

"Grizel Cochrane shan't laugh at you!" said Margia determinedly. "Why should she?"

But all Amy could be got to say was, "She will! I know she will!"

"Oh, all right then! But we can ask Gisela about the mag," said Joey. "Come on, everybody! Gisela! Gi-se-la!" Gisela, who had been chattering gaily with Wanda and Grizel, lifted her head.

"Yes! I come!" she called back, and set off at a run, heedless of Grizel's impatient, "Oh, don't bother with the kids just now, Gisela!"

"What is it?" asked the big girl, as she reached the Juniors. "Is there anything wrong?"

"No, nothing. Only, do you remember what we were talking about the day we decided to get my sister's birthday present? Gisela, let's have a school mag!"

"Yes; and you be editor," added Margia.

Gisela looked thoughtful, and at this moment Wanda and Grizel came up with them.

"Well! What's the worry?" demanded Grizel. "Anyone dead yet?"

Joey turned on her like a flash. "Grizel! I hate that horrid sneery way of talking you've got lately! You're always making fun of us! It's horrid of you!"

"Keep your hair on!" said Grizel easily. "No need to get hot about nothing!"

"I'm not!" retorted Joey. "And anyhow," as an unholy memory came to her, "anyhow, I didn't ask to have my hair rinsed in holy water!"

"Joey! What do you mean?" cried Wanda, astounded.

"Ask Grizel! She knows!" said Joey with somewhat malicious delight.

Grizel, crimson and furious, glared at her tormentor. "You little pig, Joey!"

"Well, you did, didn't you?" Then Joey's malice vanished in a chuckle. "I say! Do you remember the man's face when he heard you? Oh, wasn't it funny?"

"It was only a mistake," said Grizel with an unwilling laugh.

"But what was it?" asked Gisela, bewildered. "Please tell us, Grizel."

"Oh, it was only that I mixed up *heisses* and *heiliges*," explained Grizel. "Jo's a horror to drag it up like that! Oh, well, let it alone now, and let's get on to the magazine."

"It is an English institution," observed Wanda. "I have read of it in my story books. Papa has given me several, you know, as he wished Marie and I should know something about life in the English schools."

"But you can't always go by stories," said Joey. "Some of them are awful tosh – like that *Denise of the Fourth* one you showed me, Gisela."

"There is one about a girl who was a Guide," began Gisela doubtfully, "but I did not quite understand it. It is not the kind of guide we know here."

"Girl Guides, was it?" asked Joey with interest.

"It was a Girl Guide," said Wanda. "Her name was the same as yours, Gisela, but they called her 'Gilly'. I liked the book very good."

"You should say 'very much'," Grizel corrected her. "Well, we can't do anything about the Guides just now, though it's jolly well worth thinking about. Let's get on to the magazine.

And this afternoon, I vote we play cricket. Wanda is keen to learn; aren't you, old thing?"

"I should love it," said Wanda.

"It is a top-hole game," said Grizel. "You'll soon learn it. Now, about the magazine."

"I have never seen an English school magazine," began Gisela, "but I have read of them. We must have for editor one who can write the… the… editorial, and also arrange. Then we must have articles upon our games and the happenings of this term. There should be stories and poetry, and a letter from our Head. There are only eighteen of us, but I think we might do it. It is an English custom, as Wanda says, and we are an English school, and I should like to do it. Bette and Gertrud and Bernhilda wish it too. What do you think, Joey? Would Madame allow it?"

"Rather!" said Joey enthusiastically. "She'd be awfully keen, I know."

"Then what do you say? Shall we see what we can do about it?"

"Yes, let's!"

"It's a ripping scheme, Gisela!"

"But we… we, too, Gisela! We shall be members of the school soon. May we not write for it?"

"Well, I–I–I'll let you have some poetry!"

This last was Amy, of course. The Seniors looked at her with much the same surprise as the others had done.

"Poetry, Amy? Why, you don't even know what poetry is, do you?" teased Grizel.

"Yes, I do! It's lines that rhyme! So there, Grizel Cochrane!" flashed Amy, her fair little face burning with a mixture of shyness and indignation.

"Oh, my hat! There is a cat! On the mat!" mocked Grizel. "Your poetry anything like that, Amy?"

"It's a jolly sight better than anything you could do, anyway!" declared Margia, coming valiantly to Amy's assistance. She might sit on her little sister for her own good, but she wasn't going to have Grizel Cochrane doing it if she could help it.

Grizel tilted back her pretty head and laughed aggravatingly. But Joey now took up the cudgels.

"You're horrid just now, Grizel! I don't know what's the matter with you!" she said with more vehemence than politeness.

"Don't get excited, babies—"

"Grizel!" At the sound of their headmistress's voice they all turned round.

"What is the matter with you, girls?" asked Miss Bettany, as they faced her.

Gisela rushed into the breach. "Madame, it was just a little argument. And please may we have a magazine for the school?"

"A school magazine?" She looked at them with twinkling eyes. "Yes, if you will promise not to quarrel over it, and not to leave all the work to one person, I think you may."

And so was the idea of *The Chaletian* born.

Chapter Nineteen

SOME PRANKS

"ONLY THREE WEEKS till the end of term! Nothing much can happen in three weeks!" Thus Madge Bettany, as she sat in her bedroom, talking things over with Mademoiselle Lepâttre. "Our first term," she went on dreamily. "Well, it hasn't been a bit what I thought it would. For one thing, I never expected we should get such a large school together so quickly. Eight or ten was the most I had hoped for. But here we are with eighteen, and at least seven more for next term! It isn't bad, is it?"

Mademoiselle nodded her head slowly. "It has gone well, *ma chérie*," she said gravely.

"The girls are so keen on being really English," went on the young headmistress. "Even the Juniors are infected with the desire. The other day I heard Suzanne Mercier and Berta Hamel discussing some prank or other, and Suzanne asked very seriously, 'Are you sure it's English?' Berta wasn't certain, so they went off to discuss it with Joey."

"Has it occurred yet?" asked Mademoiselle with a smile.

"I haven't heard anything, so I don't suppose it has."

"I wonder what it is?" ruminated the elder woman. "They think of things so extraordinary, these little ones. I am sure Simone would never have thought of cutting off her hair a year ago."

"It's far better for her," said Madge decidedly. "She really had too much. She's much better in every way, I think; and she's losing the tragic look she used to have, and she does things… well… off her own bat!"

"My dear!" Mademoiselle was genuinely horrified at the slang, but Madge only laughed.

"Awful, isn't it?" she said cheerfully. "Mercifully none of the girls heard me. Do remember, Elise, that I've not been a Head for three months yet! You must allow me a little slang just very occasionally."

Mademoiselle joined in her laughter, which was cut short by a piercing shriek.

"Mercy!" gasped Madge. "What on earth has happened?"

She fled to the door, tore it open, and ran down the stairs, to meet a scared and horrified Bette and Bernhilda, who both exclaimed, "Oh, Madame! Come quickly! Come at once!"

"What is it? An accident?" she gasped with whitening face.

"No… no! It is much worse! It is witchcraft!" wailed Bette.

"Witchcraft! Nonsense! There is no such thing as witchcraft!" she said sharply, nevertheless following them along the narrow passage to the little boarded-off compartment where the "Splasheries" were. Arrived there, she gasped at what she saw. Then, realizing what had happened, she burst into laughter. Each of the two basins was full to the brim of sparkling, sizzling bubbles! Even as they looked, the foaming began to subside, and in another minute or   two the bowls held only ordinary water – or what looked like ordinary water.

"Oh, Madame, what is it?" sobbed Bette in German. "I did nothing! I only poured in the water, and Bernhilda also, and it foamed up at once! Oh, is it witchcraft?"

A sudden gurgle outside the window, followed by a "Hush!" drew the Head's attention for a second, but she took no further notice.

"Oh, Bette! You silly child!" she said rather impatiently. "Of course it isn't! Haven't I told you there is no such thing as witchcraft? All that has happened is that those young monkeys have powdered the bowls with sherbet or salts or some fizzy stuff! Of course it bubbled up when you poured the water in! But that's all it is!"

Had she been able to see through the bushes which grew against the side of the house, she would have seen four faces grow rather blank at her omniscience.

"I say!" murmured Joey. "I forgot they would probably fetch my sister, and it's a trick my brother told us of. He did

197

it at his school."

"Will she be angry?" asked Berta, a trifle apprehensively.

Joey considered, her head on one side. "Shouldn't think so," she said finally. "There's nothing wrong in it — it's only a lark, and it doesn't hurt anyone. That idiot, Bette! Fancy believing in witchcraft at her age!"

"But lots of them do," argued Simone, with somewhat incautious loudness.

"Shut up, idiot!" hissed Joey. "D'you want them to come and catch us? Come along! We'd better clear out now!" And they promptly vacated their position and decamped to the ferry-landing.

Meanwhile, Madge was busy soothing the injured feelings of the Seniors. Bette was furiously angry at having been so taken in, and even Bernhilda the gentle was inclined to be indignant.

"It is an impertinence," she said in her soft, careful English. "Is it not, Madame?"

Madge nodded. "Oh, yes! But it is the kind of thing that often happens with Juniors, and I advise you to take no notice this time. If they do it again, of course, the prefects should take it up. It's not bad mischief. You people must learn to distinguish between bad mischief and nonsense like this."

With this she left them, to go and relate the occurrence to their compeers, while she herself chuckled over it with Mademoiselle and Miss Maynard, who had just come in.

"It's healthy mischief anyhow," she said, "so I shan't interfere. There's *Mittagessen*."

At *Mittagessen* the four Juniors kept giggling together, and many were the meaning glances shot at Bette, who held her head very high, and was remarkably chilly in her behaviour to them. Bernhilda had cooled down, and was able to laugh at the affair, but Bette was half Italian, and her indignation still ran hot. Gisela and the others had enjoyed the joke, even while they admitted that it was "an impertinence" and, as the head girl said, it was better than the defiance of Grizel and Juliet of the previous week.

There were three bedtimes during the week at the Chalet. Amy and Margia Stevens, and the two little Merciers, who were boarders till the end of term, as their parents had been obliged to go to Paris owing to the sudden illness of Madame Mercier's mother, went at seven, Joey and Simone at eight, and Juliet and Grizel at nine. On Saturdays and Sundays they all went at the same time – half-past eight on Saturdays and eight on Sundays. When seven o'clock came that evening, the four Juniors trotted off quite happily. Miss Maynard went up to brush hair at half-past seven, and see that they were all safely in bed. She found them, as she afterwards said, "rather gigglesome", but as the story of the powdered basins – they had used sherbet, as Madge had surmised – had gone round the school by that time, she set it down to that. At eight o'clock punctually Joey and Simone said goodnight and retired in their turn. It was Mademoiselle's duty to go up half an hour later to see that they were all right. Juliet and Grizel were considered old enough to be responsible for themselves.

When half-past eight came, Mademoiselle was in the

middle of writing a letter, so Miss Maynard good-naturedly offered to run up for her. The Frenchwoman accepted the offer, and the mathematics mistress ascended the stairs lightly. She expected to find the two in bed, ready to bid her goodnight, so she was considerably startled to find Joey in her dressing-gown, grimly unpicking the top of her pyjama legs, while Simone was wrestling with a sleeve of her nightdress.

"Girls!" exclaimed the mistress. "What is the meaning of this?"

"All our night garments are sewn up," said Simone mournfully.

"Some joke!" remarked Joey. "Look, Miss Maynard! Stitched top and bottom of legs and sleeves, and the top of my trousers too!"

Miss Maynard's eyes twinkled, and she bit her lips. "H'm! So the biters were bitten," she said softly. "Well, I will give you five minutes longer. Be quick!"

She knew better than to look through the other curtains to see if the Juniors were asleep. Certain little rustles and snorts made it quite evident that they were not. She took no notice of the suspicious sounds, but simply waited by the window until the other two were safely in bed, and then withdrew, remarking that she hoped they would all – with an emphasis on the "all" – get off to sleep quickly.

"Pigs!" remarked Joey, as soon as she was well out of the way. "Little horrors!"

Four separate giggles answered her, but no one spoke. She gave a snort and turned over, burying herself beneath the sheets. Simone had done the same.

"An' the worst of it is that it completely put the lid on our stunt!" she groaned next morning when she and Simone had finished telling the other four what they thought of them. "We'd intended ragging the Senior cubicles, but I thought we'd better get ready for bed first, and then we found what you'd done! An' Maynie came up before we were half ready."

"Well, why didn't you tell us?" demanded Margia. "Then we'd have helped, and left you till tonight!"

"Well! Of all the cool cheek!" gasped Joey. "Margia, you're the limit!"

"It's your own fault!" retorted Margia. "You said we hadn't any rags yet, and it would be a pity to finish the term without."

"Yes; but I never meant you to rag us! An' that reminds me, is the piano done?"

"Uh-huh! Amy did it when she had finished her practice."

"Good enoughsky! No one saw you, did they, Amy?"

Little Amy shook her head till all her curls danced. "No one! It will be fun!"

"Well, it's Grizel's practice first! Won't she be mad?"

"Hopping mad," agreed Marcia. "There's the bell! Come on!"

The conspirators scurried into lessons. and only saved themselves from complete disgrace by the most valiant efforts. Amy, her mind wandering to the latest joke, when asked to explain what a delta was, said dreamily, "It's another name for the keyboard of the piano – the white keys!"

Miss Bettany dropped the blackboard chalk in her surprise. "Amy!"

"I beg your pardon, Madame," she faltered. "I-I—" She stopped, unable to go on.

"I see," said Madge drily. "Will you kindly pay attention to the lesson? What is a delta?"

Amy managed to stumble through a fairly accurate if somewhat lengthy explanation.

Joey and Simone, doing algebra, came off little better. Joey's simple equations were a hopeless muddle, while Simone's had neither beginning nor ending.

Frieda, Anita, and Sophie stared at them in amazement, while Miss Maynard scolded them sharply for carelessness and inattention.

Much they cared, however! They were only longing for two o'clock and the beginning of practice time. They had not dared to meddle with the music-room piano, for this was one of the days on which Herr Anserl came up from Spärtz to give music lessons. He was a magnificent teacher, and a musician to his fingertips, but he was terribly short tempered, and any pranks would have sent him storming off to Miss Bettany. His pupils all regarded his lessons with a mixture of terror and amusement. He told Grizel that she had the fingers of a machine, and the soul of one too, which offended her dreadfully, but she dared not show it. Joey he raved at for her lack of a sense of time, while Juliet's stumbling performances brought German phrases and epithets rumbling from his very boots. On the other hand, he had once told Margia Stevens that if she worked hard and thoroughly for the next six years, she might make a performer who would not disgrace him. Margia was the only one of the younger girls to go to him, the others being taken by Mademoiselle.

Simone learnt the violin, and so did Gisela Marani and Gertrud Steinbrücke, so they three went down to Spärtz on one afternoon in the week for their lesson.

After *Mittagessen*, they were allowed to do as they liked until two o'clock, when preparation and practice were the order of the afternoon. The schoolroom piano stood in the Senior classroom, and while the Juniors did prep under Miss Maynard, the Seniors had an English literature lesson with Miss Bettany, and Grizel practised under Mademoiselle's eye, so that she should work as accurately as possible. The partition between the preparation room and the Senior room was of light matchboarding only; the windows were wide open, and it was possible to hear everything that went on in the next room. The Juniors listened eagerly. They heard Grizel settle herself down and touch the notes tentatively before she began. Then Joey stood up.

"Please, Miss Maynard, may I take my French to Mademoiselle?" she said. "I don't quite understand her corrections."

"Yes, Joey, if you must," said Miss Maynard, glancing up from her work.

Joey escaped, and hastened into the other room. It was no part of their plan to let Mademoiselle find out what they had done. She would probably be angry, and report them to the Head, and they did not want that.

"*Eh bien*, Joey, what is it?" asked Mademoiselle, as she made her appearance.

"It's this exercise, Mademoiselle," replied Joey meekly. "I don't quite see where I've gone wrong. Should I have used the subjunctive mood?"

Unsuspectingly, Mademoiselle took the book from her and looked it over.

"Yes, my child, it is here," she said. "If you use '*est-ce que*', you must follow it with the *subjonctif*, which you have not done. Grizel! What, then, are you doing?"

She might well ask! Grizel was supposed to be practising modulatory exercises, but even they were no excuse for the hideous noise she was producing.

"I – it's the keys, Mademoiselle," said Grizel. "They are so slippery."

"Slippery? Bah! It is your own abominable carelessness! Begin again, and with more care, I pray you!"

Hunching her shoulders and compressing her lips, Grizel started again, with much the same results. For once, it was a cool day, and chilly fingers combined with slippery keys proved too much for her. Suddenly it dawned on her to look at her fingertips. They were powdered with white! In a flash she realized what had happened: the Juniors had covered the keys with French chalk! Nearly choking with anger, Grizel took out her handkerchief and dusted the keyboard as unobtrusively as she could. Furious though she was, she could not give them away to Mademoiselle, who was busy instructing an extraordinarily stupid Jo.

As for Jo herself, it was all she could do to keep a straight face. She was unable to see Grizel's expression, but a back can be very expressive at times, and Grizel's looked as if she had swallowed a poker whole. When, presently, she had apparently listened to all Mademoiselle's explanations, and was dismissed, the Middle girl literally fled out of the room and, collapsing at the foot of the stairs, rocked backwards and forwards with laughter. The sound of footsteps overhead made her pull herself together with a mighty effort, and getting up, she went back to the prep room, where for all the amount of work she did, she might just as well not have been.

Never had the afternoon seemed so long to the Juniors. When at length Miss Maynard said, "Five minutes to four! Pack up your books and get ready for tea!" they all sighed audibly with relief, much to her astonishment. She had barely taken her departure before a righteously indignant Grizel dashed in.

"Where's Joey Bettany?" she cried. "Jo, you little horror, how dared you mess up the keys like that?"

"I didn't!"

"She didn't!" "It wasn't Jo!" exclaimed several voices at once.

"But she knew all about it! I know that!"

"Jolly well I did! But I didn't do it," returned Jo stoutly.

"Then who did? I never heard of such nerve in my life! Who did it?"

"Me," said a small voice, and Grizel turned to stare incredulously at the baby of the school.

"Amy! You!"

Amy raised angelic blue eyes to the startled face above her. "Yes, it was a joke!"

"Well! I – I'm jiggered!" declared Grizel flatly.

She went slowly out of the room to her own quarters, where all the coaxing and teasing of the other Seniors could not get out of her what was wrong with her, and it was only after Gisela and Bette had heard from the delighted Juniors what had occurred that they understood. Then they were almost as startled as Grizel herself. Amy was the last person they would have suspected of such a trick. Margia, Joey, Maria, even Suzanne might have done it. But Amy! The Seniors were completely flabbergasted.

As for Amy herself, she was in high glee over it, and cut capers to such an extent that she called down upon herself a sharp reprimand from Miss Maynard, who coached them for tennis, and who, of course, had no idea why Amy Stevens was behaving with such sudden wildness.

On their way home after tennis in the evening, Gisela summed up the state of affairs rather neatly to Bette.

"Amy is becoming a schoolgirl and ceasing to be a baby," she said. "But one doesn't expect it so suddenly."

"No," agreed Bette – they were talking in their own language – "but I think you are right."

"I know I am," said the head girl with finality.

Chapter Twenty

AND STILL MORE!

THE JUNIORS, HAVING begun to play pranks – all, it must be admitted, of fairly harmless character – found it too pleasant a pastime to give up. The night after the affair of the French-chalked piano keys, Juliet, on going to bed, barely suppressed a wild yell when she entered her cubicle, for there, sitting up in her bed, was a figure that looked curiously lifelike in the half light. A closer inspection informed her that the creature was made of her own pillow, decked in her own pyjama jacket, with a boudoir cap, hastily manufactured out of two handkerchiefs, stuck on top, while beneath this an amiably smiling face drawn in coloured chalks on a sheet of white paper made the thing natural enough to have scared her badly for the moment.

Grasping the ridiculous object, she marched into the cubicle where Joey Bettany, who had caught the extraordinary sound she had made, was choking her laughter with the sheet.

"Joey!" said Juliet indignantly, "did you do this?"

"I-I—" Joey was incapable of uttering more at the moment. The sight of the weird object completely upset her.

Dropping it, Juliet took her by the shoulders and shook her. "Joey! Stop giggling, and tell me if you were so stupid!"

"Well, stop shaking me then!" retorted Joey, as well as she could for lack of breath.

"You deserve more than shaking, you little horror!" declared Juliet, releasing her as she spoke.

"If anyone hears you, there'll be a row," said Joey calmly. "It's lights out for me, and you're not supposed to talk to me now."

Juliet was rendered speechless by her virtuous air, but she soon recovered herself.

"Well, upon my word!" she said. "For cool cheek, that beats everything! It would serve you right if I took this thing to Madame!"

"You won't, though," returned Joey with confidence. She was leaning back against her pillow, smiling up at the older girl as she spoke.

Juliet suddenly laughed at her. "No; you're quite right, I won't! But be careful, my child! I'll have my r-r-revenge, so don't forget!"

"I won't," replied Jo cheerfully. "What! Must you go? So sorry! Goodnight!"

She turned over on her side and snuggled down, and

Juliet, with rather a grim smile, left her. All the time she was preparing for bed she was turning ideas over in her mind. Just as she was kneeling down to say her prayers, a smothered shriek from Grizel brought her to her feet with a bound.

"Grizel! What on earth's the matter? Are you hurt? Oh—"

"Those little beasts!" spluttered Grizel, as she drew her curtain back. "Look at that! Two brushes in my bed!" She held them out as she spoke.

"Little horrors!" laughed Juliet. "I had an effigy in mine!"

"They must have gone mad!" declared Grizel. "It's all Joey, of course! She thinks of the things, even if she doesn't do them."

"She does not!" said a third voice indignantly. "'Twas me did that!"

"Girls! What are you thinking of? Juliet! Grizel! Why are you not in bed?"

They all jumped as the outer curtains parted to show Miss Bettany.

"Why are you not in bed?" she repeated. "And why have you drawn back the curtains between your cubicle and Juliet's, Grizel? You know it is against the rules!"

Silence answered her. On hearing her voice, Grizel had dropped the brushes, so she did not see them. As no one seemed to have an answer ready, she bade the two Seniors hurry into bed.

"I will see you in the morning," she said coldly. "I am very disappointed in both of you. I thought you could be trusted to keep the rules!"

With this she left the room, while two unhappy people stared at each other. Then Grizel drew the curtain again and retired to her bed, after she had pushed the brushes underneath it. Juliet followed suit, and a deadly silence filled the room. It continued next morning and, when Grizel met Simone on the stairs, she drew to one side. Simone lifted her dark eyes to the Senior's face with the glimmer of a smile, but Grizel tilted her head and stalked downstairs with an offended dignity that was rather marred by her missing the last step and staggering somewhat ignominiously across the hall.

"Grizel is furious!" reported Simone to the others. "She would not regard me."

"If you mean 'look at', I'd say so," murmured Joey. "When are you going to my sister to say it's your fault?"

Simone's eyes fell, and she began to play nervously with the end of her girdle. "I-I don't know," she stammered.

"Why not? I should go after breakfast an' get it over."

"Ye-yes!"

Joey turned and looked at her incredulously. "You surely don't mean you're goin' to funk it?" she demanded.

"N-no! No! Of course I will go! Will… will Madame be very angry?"

"Couldn't say! Shouldn't think so," was the laconic response.

"Oh, Joey, do not be angry with me!" pleaded Simone,

half crying. "I will go certainly, and say it was my fault."

"Righto!" said Joey. "Come on to breakfast – there's the bell!"

Simone would have made only a poor breakfast had Joey not kept a watchful eye on her. As it was, she was persuaded to eat her usual meal. And then Joey went with her as far as the study door.

"Buck up, old thing!" she said cheerfully. "She can't eat you, an' I'll wait for you here."

Thus adjured, Simone went in after tapping at the door. Miss Bettany looked up in surprise when she saw her; she had been expecting Grizel and Juliet.

"Well, Simone," she said, "what is it?"

"Please, Madame, I am come to say that it was my fault," said Simone.

"Your fault? What is your fault? I don't understand."

Simone took hold of her rapidly departing courage with both hands and said, "The... the disturbance last night... I did it!"

"You did it? But it had nothing to do with you!"

"Yes, Madame. I had put two brushes in Grizel's bed."

For a moment Madge's lips twitched. Simone's expression was so serious. Then she pulled herself together. "That was very silly," she said gravely.

"Yes, Madame. I know it was," agreed Simone. "But you will forgive them, since the fault is to me?"

"'The fault is mine'." corrected her headmistress. "I will see Grizel and Juliet, Simone. And please don't do such a silly thing again. Run away, now."

Greatly relieved, Simone trotted off, and a minute or so later Grizel and Juliet presented themselves, inwardly quaking a little. They met with an agreeable surprise.

"Simone has been to me," said Miss Bettany soberly, "and she tells me that it was her fault that there was a disturbance in the dormitory last night, so we will say not more about it. But remember that for the future even brushes in your bed will not be accepted as an excuse for breaking rules. You may go now."

"Jolly good for Simone," said Grizel. "I didn't think she had it in her."

The next joke was a harmless one, which nobody minded except the perpetrators, but which had far-reaching consequences. Two days after Simone's confession, Joey and Grizel came up to Gisela and solemnly informed her that on the fifteenth of July, which was St Swithun's Day, it was the custom in all good English schools to sip a cup of water, which was passed round, and wish as one did so.

"But first you must take it to any foreign mistress in the school," said Grizel impressively, meaning, of course, that the water should be offered to Mademoiselle.

As the two practical jokers had already played tricks of a similar nature on her, Gisela looked at them sharply. Neither had the ghost of a smile on her face, and Joey's expression was super-angelic – a bad sign, which her sister would have recognized at once. Gisela, however, was not so experienced, and she was completely taken in.

"The fifteenth – that is tomorrow," she said seriously. "I will remember!"

"What a lark! Didn't think she'd be had so easily!" chuckled Joey.

"Neither did I," replied Grizel. "Shan't we crow over them tomorrow!"

Unfortunately, Gisela had misinterpreted one part of Grizel's speech. In her eyes, of course, all three mistresses were foreigners, and both Joey and Grizel were thunderstruck when, just before prayers, the head girl advanced to the little dais where the staff was, and offering the cup of water, murmured in her pretty English, "The cup of water for a wish, as is the custom in all English schools on St Swithun's Day."

There was a moment's silence. Miss Bettany looked puzzled, Miss Maynard choked audibly, and Mademoiselle wore an outraged expression. Then the headmistress, with one rapid glance round the room, took in the affair at once. Quietly she accepted the cup, and drank from it.

"Thank you, Gisela," she said, as she returned it. "And now we will have prayers."

The ensuing events were lost on Joey and Grizel, who were almost petrified with horror. They were more horrified when, after she had given out the notices for the day, Miss Bettany added, "I should like to see Josephine and Grizel in my study now, before lessons." Then she dismissed the school and went to her own room.

The culprits presently appeared. She waited till they had shut the door.

"Now," she said, "I want to know what Gisela meant."

"It… it was only a lark," mumbled Joey at last.

"Please speak correct English, Josephine. Repeat your sentence."

"It… it was only a joke," repeated her small sister rather faintly.

Miss Bettany's eyebrows went up at the statement.

"A joke? I'm afraid your sense of fun is too elemental to appeal to me. I see nothing humorous in a silly trick like that. Who suggested it?"

Joey went scarlet; Grizel hung her head and said nothing. Truth to tell, she was rather scared. She had never encountered her headmistress in this mood.

"Who suggested it?" repeated Miss Bettany, in a voice that intimated that she meant to know sooner or later.

"It was me," said Grizel at last, as sulkily as she dared.

"Indeed? Your grammar seems to stand in as much need of correction as your idea of humour. Well, I am going to send for Gisela, and you will both apologize to her before me for your silly impertinence towards her." She rang her little bell as she spoke, and presently Marie appeared and was dispatched for Gisela.

Presently Gisela appeared, wearing a rather startled expression. "You have sent for me, Madame?" she said.

"Yes, Gisela. Josephine and Grizel wish to express their regret for being impertinent enough to play a silly trick on you about St Swithun's Day observances."

Gisela's face cleared at that. "But it is all right," she said. "I knew when I had offered you the water that it was a… a take-in!"

"Nevertheless, it was very impertinent of them," replied Miss Bettany. "Girls!"

"I'm sorry," said Joey. "I suppose it was cheek, Gisela, but I didn't think of it; honest injun!"

"It is all right," repeated Gisela.

"Now, Grizel," said the headmistress.

"I'm sorry," mumbled Grizel.

After dismissing the head girl, Miss Bettany said a few more words on practical joking, and then sent them to their form rooms, where Jo, at any rate, was soon immersed in her history. Not so Grizel. She was intensely proud, and hated apologizing to anyone. Besides this, her headmistress's strictures on her sense of humour had offended her dreadfully. She sulked till halfway through the morning, then the sudden memory of a joke she had once heard of as being played on a master at her cousin's school came to her.

"I'll do that!" she thought. "Perhaps that may not seem kiddish! At any rate it'll be something to rag me for! That idiot of a Gisela!"

The joke in question required careful preparation, and Grizel was rather doubtful as to whether she could get the materials she required. Fortune, however, favoured her. On the landing near the big dormitory stood an old armoire in which Mademoiselle kept such simple medicines as they were likely to need. As a rule it was kept locked, but Amy had fallen down and bumped her head, so Mademoiselle went to fetch some cold cream for the lump. She left the cupboard open, and Grizel, passing at the time, saw her chance – and took it.

The fun started next morning when Mademoiselle came to give B division their German lessons. Both Grizel and Jo came for this. Jo's German was fluent enough, but her written composition was weak, so Madge had ordained that she must attend the lessons of B division as well as those of A. Happy-go-lucky Jo accepted her lot quite calmly, and rejoiced in the fact that, at any rate, she was missing hated geometry, and might have been much worse off.

The first half of the lesson was devoted to the correction of a previous composition; then Mademoiselle turned to the blackboard.

"We will now do some oral composition," she said in German. "I will write the title on the board, and then we will all make sentences. We will, today, talk of the mountains. Margia, give me the German for 'the mountains'."

"*Gebirge*," said Margia promptly.

"The article?" said Mademoiselle, waiting, chalk in hand.

"Oh! '*Die*', I think," said Margia, somewhat doubtfully this time.

Mademoiselle beamed approval on her, and turned to write it up. In vain she struggled with the chalk. Not one mark could she make.

"I do not understand," she said, lapsing into her own language in the stress of the moment.

"P'raps the chalk is wet," suggested Joey. "If it is, it doesn't write, I know."

"Perhaps that is the reason," agreed Mademoiselle, looking at the chalk dubiously. "Margia, my child, go to the stationery cupboard and fetch me a fresh piece, if you please. There is no more in the desk."

Margia darted away, and presently returned with a new stick. But for all the impression it made, she might just as well never have fetched it.

"But this is an extraordinary occurrence," Mademoiselle was beginning, when the door opened and the headmistress entered, white with anger. Mademoiselle was too full of the unusual behaviour of the chalk to notice anything wrong.

"Madame," she began eagerly, "the chalk will not write!"

"I know," said her Head in low tones. She advanced to the board and drew her hand down it in one sweep. Then she looked at her palm. "As I thought," she said. "Which of you has vaselined all the blackboards?"

There was a deathly silence. Everyone was staring with fascinated eyes at the headmistress, whom they seemed to be seeing for the first time. Miss Bettany suddenly struck the desk with her hand. Everyone jumped.

"Who did it?" she demanded. "Is there a coward in the school?"

On the word, Grizel sprang to her feet, head up, eyes blazing defiance.

"I did it!" she said, as insolently as she dared. "I—"

"Hush!" There was that in the one word which checked the rush of speech to her lips. "You say you did it, Grizel Cochrane?"

"Yes."

"Go to your room," said Miss Bettany quietly, "and wait there till I come to you. I am ashamed to think a girl I had counted as a Senior should cause so much trouble by her childishness and impertinence. Go at once!"

Grizel went.

Chapter Twenty-One

PLANS

JUDGEMENT HAD GONE forth. Grizel was to be left severely alone by the rest of the school. No one was to speak to her, and she was to speak to nobody. She was to sit by herself in classes, and her meals would be brought to her in the schoolroom. When the others were at games, she was to go for a walk with whichever member of the staff could take her. This was to last for two days, and it was the severest punishment that had ever been given at the Chalet School.

In vain did Joey plead that the fault was largely hers, since it was she who had suggested that it would be a pity to let the term go by without some practical jokes. In vain did Mademoiselle, who was fond of the troublesome child, appeal against the sentence. Not even could Gisela, speaking for the school, avail anything. Miss Bettany had made up her mind that punished Grizel was going to be, and nothing could save her.

In the interview she had had with the girl, Grizel had proved herself defiant in the extreme. She possessed a temper which, once aroused, took some time to cool off. She had hated having to apologize to Gisela the day before, and the two affairs together had roused all the worst in her. Finally, Miss Bettany had given up trying to make her see reason, had named her punishment, and left her to herself, hoping that a little solitude would bring her to her senses.

"Oh dear!" sighed Joey in the lunch hour, when they were all wandering about doing nothing in particular. "I wish I'd never heard of the word 'joke'!"

"Is Madame very angry?" asked Gisela, slipping an arm through hers.

"She's rather mad," acknowledged Joey. "I think Grizel cheeked her."

She threw a wistful glance at the window of the little room where Grizel was, presumably, confined. Then, turning to the elder girl, she went on: "Grizel's got such a beast of a temper. When she gets her monkey up, she doesn't much care what she does."

"'Gets her monkey up?'" repeated Gisela with a puzzled frown. "I do not understand."

"Sorry! That's slang, I'm 'fraid," apologized Joey. "Loses her temper, you know."

"Your English slang is so incomprehensible," complained the head girl.

"Yes, I s'pose it is. But it's jolly expressive. Hello! Here's the postman! He is late today. *Grüss Gott*, Herr Sneider!"

The postman returned her greeting amiably, handed her the letters and departed.

"One from Dick – that's my brother – for Madame," commented Joey, "two for Maynie, and one for Margia and Amy. None for me. What a swizz!"

"There is the bell for *Mittagessen*," said Gisela. "Come! Let us go in!"

They went in, Joey leaving the Tyrolean in order to take the letters to her sister. Madge was standing by the window, her lips set and her eyes thoughtful.

"Hello," she said, when she saw her small sister, "what is it? Oh, letters!"

"Letter from Dick," said Joey, "and it's *Mittagessen* now!"

Madge's face relaxed as she took the letters. "All right. You can come here after, and we'll read it together. Take the others to their owners, will you?"

Mittagessen seemed never-ending to Joey. She bolted her own food, and when Simone accepted a second helping of *Pflaumekuchen*, cast a look of deep reproach at her.

However, everything comes to an end sooner or later, and at last they all rose, and grace was said. To Madge, two minutes later, appeared a flushed and excited Joey, who could scarcely be induced to sit down.

"Buck up and get on! Do!" she urged. "I'm dying to hear what Dick says."

Madge laughed. "Here goes, then!" she said, as she

smoothed out the thin foreign paper.

Dear Kids, (Dick had written)

Thanks awfully for your last letters, though it took me all my time to read Joey's. What on earth she wrote with I suppose she knows! Some of the words looked as though a good-sized black beetle had fallen into the inkpot and then staggered about on the paper. They don't seem to teach the young to write nowadays.

"Cheek!" interjected Joey swiftly. "He needn't talk; his own fist's bad enough for anything!"

I'm glad the school's going so well; but my dear kid, have nothing to do with Carrick. He's an awfully bad hat. They do say that he was practically kicked out of here — had made the place too hot to hold him. But it's only gossip so far, and there may be no foundation for it. All the same, a chap from the Hills told me that they'd sent that unfortunate kid of theirs to some school up there, and then tried to clear out and leave her on the Head's hands. Luckily, the old lady contrived to track them, and they were obliged to stump up what they owed and take the girl with them. One's awfully sorry for her. She seems to have a rotten time from all I can gather. Mrs C. has a vile temper, they say, and he isn't much better. It's an awful life for a girl to go dragging about like that! If Carrick wants you to have Juliet — isn't that her name? — as a boarder, don't you do it! I wish to goodness you had someone more reliable to look after you than Mademoiselle Lepâttre. I know she's a jolly good sort, but women are so helpless! They ought to have a man to look after them.

I'm awfully glad to hear that the piccaninny is going strong and getting fat. Austria seems to suit her. That cinema stunt was rather cheek, I thought. I'm thankful it got no further. I certainly don't want my sisters stuck up in every cinema for any idiot to see!

There's precious little news to tell you. We are busy with some experiments at present. The Gobbler (Dick's superior) has some wild notion of growing European fruit trees here, so we're mucking about in a fair-sized clearing growing good old plum and apple. This, of course is in addition to our ordinary work. I blessed him the other day, I can tell you. He had us pruning and planting the whole day, and the mercury doing the high jump for all it was worth.

The rains are going well, and there's a chorus of frogs outside my bungalow at the moment. This is beastly weather. The one consolation is, that anyhow the snakes are lying pretty low. My bearer caught a whacker the other night – a king cobra – so he's introduced a mongoose to the household in case the mate is anywhere round. We've called the little lad "Binjamin", after Stalky's Binjamin. Remember? Well, there's nothing more to tell you, and I'm dead tired, and just going to turn in when I've finished this screed. Remember what I say, and leave Carrick alone.

Salaams.

Dick.

There was a little silence when Madge had finished. Then Joey broke it.

"Dick's too late," she said. "We've been and gone and done it! Poor Juliet!"

"Poor Juliet indeed!" sighed Madge. "Oh, Joey Bettany, you've got a lot to be thankful for, let me tell you!"

"I know," said Joey soberly. "You're a sport to me, Madge! And Dick's another!"

"We're all you've got," said Madge briefly.

"Some people haven't as much," replied Joey, leaning her head against her sister. "Look at Juliet! And then Grizel hasn't anyone much. You can't say her father's up to much, can you? Poor old Grizel!"

Madge slipped an arm round her little sister. "You're right there, old lady. But Grizel must come into line with the rest of you. You're up to monkey tricks as well, I know, but you haven't been impertinent too. I know you think I'm being a perfect beast to her, but she can't be left to go on like that, can she?"

Joey acknowledged the truth of this. "No; I see your point. But, Madge, old thing, I do think she's sorry by this time! Can't you go and see?"

Madge shook her head. "No, Joey! She won't be sorry yet. Now it's time for prep, and you must toddle off. Come along early tomorrow morning and we'll have a palaver. It's only a fortnight to the holidays now, and then we'll have a good time together." She gave her sister a little squeeze and then sent her off to her preparation.

Left to herself, she faced the Grizel problem once more. She knew that it would take a lot to make that young lady say she was sorry, and yet she had determined that apologize Grizel must and should. The point was, how was she to be brought to it? She recognized the truth of Joey's statement that Grizel hadn't "anyone much". In some ways she was more to be pitied than Juliet. From all accounts, the latter had been accustomed to little different treatment from what she had received; but Grizel for five years of her life had been the spoilt darling of her grandmother, the next few years had been a hard discipline for a wilful, petted child; and apparently too much freedom from such discipline had gone to Grizel's head. Nothing else could explain her present defiance.

Later in the day she went to see Grizel again, but found her stonily silent and absolutely unrepentant. The interview did no good, and she left the girl with a hopeless feeling that something was all wrong here. Grizel herself was still too miserably angry to care what happened.

"I hate her. I hate them all!" she thought to herself. "I'd run away if I'd anywhere to run to! Oh, I wish I was dead, I do!"

She leant her forehead against the edge of the window frame, staring miserably out at the dark pine woods and the slopes of the Bärenbad alm. Presently she shifted her position, so that she could look up the long valley towards the Mondscheinspitze, with the Bärenkopf in the distance, and, towering over all, the Tiernjoch, with its sinister shadows. Even on a summer's day, when the other peaks gleamed white in the glory of the afternoon sun, it looked dark and lowering. Her mind went back to the stories Herr Mensch had told them about it. How, one winter, sixty years ago, there had been a fearful avalanche down its slopes, which had partly buried a little hamlet that stood at the foot of it, and how, when spring had brought the thaw and the snow had melted, the houses were so buried in rocks and earth that it had been well nigh impossible to dig them out. There were other gruesome stories, too, of travellers who had been caught in the treacherous mist on its slopes and had never been seen again – or else had been found, a little heap of broken bones, at the bottom of the ravine which made one of its chief dangers. As she stood looking dreamily into the distance, she heard footsteps under the window, and then Wanda's precise English.

"Where is Grizel, Margia? I should like with her to speak."

"Grizel's in a row," replied Margia's voice. "She vaselined the blackboards, and was awfully rude to Madame about it. So she's not to be with any of us till she says she's sorry."

"Oh, I am so sorry!" said Wanda. "Poor Grizel! How unhappy she must feel at having been rude! But how did she dare?"

"Goodness knows! She dares anything! She's going to climb that old Tiernjoch some day, she says," floated up Margia's clear notes.

"Oh, but I do not think she can mean that!" replied the young Viennese. "That is only talking, as Joey says."

They moved on then, but the mischief had been done. So

that was what they thought, was it? That it was all talk on her part? Well, she would jolly well show them! She would show them that very day! No, the next day! She would get up early, and when they came to find her she would be gone! She'd show them all what she dared to do and what she daren't! She'd make them very sorry they'd treated her like this!

Miss Maynard entered at that moment to tell her to get ready for a walk, and she had to change her shoes and find her hat. Throughout the hour and a half, during which they went round the lower end of the lake to Buchau, where they caught the steamer back to Briesau, she remained obstinately dumb. Miss Maynard made one or two remarks, then, finding her efforts vain, lapsed into thoughtfulness on her own part, leaving Grizel to herself.

When they returned, the young lady was taken back to her room, and Miss Maynard brought her a couple of books and her embroidery before she withdrew, closing the door quietly behind her. There was no question of locking her in; the door was merely shut. Naughty as she had been, it never dawned on Miss Bettany to think that the girl would abuse the trust reposed in her; and in her normal frame of mind, Grizel would as soon have thought of trying to fly as of betraying that trust. But she was not normal at present. The one idea of "showing them" filled her mind to the exclusion of everything else.

It would be an easy matter to get away. She must wake early – by four o'clock at latest. That would give her a start of four hours, since nobody was likely to come near her much before eight. By that time she hoped to be well on her way to little alm halfway up the mountain, where herdsmen attended to the cattle which were grazed there in the summer. The question of food was rather a difficulty for the one little shop the place boasted would not be open at that hour, and Grizel knew that bread and cheese was all she was likely to get from the herdsmen; and the bread would most likely be reeking of garlic, which she detested. Finally, she decided that she must save all she could from her supper. She hoped they would bring her plenty.

She strayed over to the window, and stood with her head thrown back gazing at the great gloomy mountain. Joey Bettany, passing beneath with Simone on her way to tennis, glanced up and saw her, though she did not see Joey.

Half-past seven brought Marie and her supper. Grizel's spirits went up with a bound as she took in the bowl of soup, the rolls and the butter, the large slice of *Kuchen*, and the glass of new milk. The soup and the milk would do for the supper, and the rest she must put away for the morning. Perhaps there would be some apples in the kitchen. Things were going well for her.

Later, she heard the others coming back from cricket and tennis. Joey was talking. "Look! Alpengluck!" she said, her words carrying easily in the still air.

"Bother!" Juliet chimed in. "No games tomorrow, then, and it's Saturday!"

She heard no more, for just then the Head came in to say goodnight, and see that everything she needed was there.

Miss Bettany had meant to say something to her, but the hard, defiant look Grizel turned on her forbade anything of the kind. She realized that, in the girl's present mood, discussion would be worse than useless.

"Goodnight, Grizel," she said quietly.

"Goodnight," mumbled Grizel.

Then the door closed and she was alone.

Chapter Twenty-Two

GRIZEL RUNS AWAY

"SATURDAY MORNING! THANK goodness, no lessons!" And Margia heaved a sigh of relief.

"Lazybones!" jeered Juliet from her cubicle, where she had been reading for the last half an hour.

"The hols will be here soon anyhow," said Joey Bettany. "Let's hope it's decenter weather than this! A horrid grey day! I do hate them so!"

"There's mist on the mountains!" Margia had climbed out of bed, and was contemplating the Bärenbad, the Bärenkopf, and their fellows with pensive eyes. "Can't see the top of old Mondy, and the Tiernjoch is lost!"

"It'll rain later," observed Juliet, shutting her book with a sigh for her disturbed peace. "We shan't even get a decent walk."

"Frau Mensch asked Simone and Grizel and me to tea

today," observed Joey in rather muffled tones, since she was buried beneath her *plumeau*. "I suppose we'll go, but it's rotten for Grizel. I wish she hadn't cheeked my sister!"

"It is quiet without Grizel," observed Simone, who was sitting up in bed hugging her knees. "And it will be not nice – I mean horreed!" as a groan from Joey reached her, "to have to say Grizel is being punished."

"Don't you worry! They'll know all about it!" Joey assured her. "I saw Frieda's eyes nearly jumping out of her head yesterday when she answered Mad— my sister! Where's my dressing-gown?"

She scrambled out of bed, wriggled into her dressing-gown and bedroom slippers, and vanished in the direction of her sister's room.

"It's rotten for Joey," said Margia, who had gone back to bed again. "Madame is her sister and Grizel is her chum. Whichever she sides with, it looks mean for the other! I do think Grizel is an ass!"

"Whose turn is it to go first to the bathroom today?" inquired Juliet.

"It is me!" said Suzanne Mercier in her shy soft voice.

Both Suzanne and Yvette had very little to say at any time, and their voices were so seldom heard, that, as Grizel had once remarked, they might just as well never be there more than half the time. Now, Juliet nearly jumped.

"I always forget you two are there," she said. "If you're going, Suzanne, you'd better toddle along. I can hear Marie coming with Amy's water."

She got up as she spoke, and fished out her bedroom slippers and rolled up her sleeves, preparatory to giving Amy her bath. That she should do it had become quite a recognized thing now, and to Juliet it was a great thing that she could help even in so little, as some return for her Head's goodness to her. She could never help contrasting Miss Bettany's quiet acceptance of the state of things with the behaviour of her Anglo-Indian headmistress under similar circumstances. That lady had been mainly concerned about the loss of her fees. Of Juliet's feelings she had thought not one jot. Juliet had not suddenly become an angel as a result of her present Head's treatment of her. She was a very human girl; but she was deeply grateful, and since she was thorough in whatever she did, she was making valiant efforts to become the same sporting type of girl as that to which her headmistress belonged. This bathing of Amy, which had been a self-imposed task, sometimes bored her very much, but Miss Bettany's thanks had filled her with a determination to go on, and, as a result, she was learning that a duty undertaken for love of a person isn't half so tiresome as one which is thrust on one.

As for Amy, she had quite overcome her fear of Juliet, and chatted gaily as the elder girl sponged her down and then rubbed her dry.

"There you are!" said Juliet finally, as she finished drying between the little pink toes. "Now buck up and get into your clothes! Who's in the bathroom now?" she went on, raising her voice slightly.

"Simone," replied Joey, who had come back from her

sister. "I'm next, an' then you. Oh, an' Madame says go past Grizel's door quietly, as she wants her to get a good sleep 'cos she seemed so tired last night."

"All right," said Juliet briefly. "Stripped your bed, Joey? I say, I don't think we'd better put the *plumeaux* over the balcony today. It looks as though there was going to be a splash!"

"'Twon't come yet," said Joey, the weather-wise. "Prob'ly not till this afternoon. It's going to be a beastly day," she added, shaking her pillow vindictively. "I jolly well wish it was over!"

Nobody seemed in a particularly happy mood that morning. The girls were subdued under the consciousness of Grizel's disgrace. The staff was worried for the same reason. In the kitchen, Marie was accusing her small brother Eigen, who came to help with odd jobs, of having helped himself to the apples she had left in a big dish overnight.

"Sixteen apples I leave," she scolded, "and now there are but ten! Where are the others, rascal? Thou hast eaten them! Thou hast stolen!"

Eigen, a stolid person of eleven, looked at his sister solemnly. "*Nein, Marie,*" was all he said in answer to her accusations.

"But I say thou hast! Who would take them if thou didst not, *junge Taugenichts*?"

"*Nein, Marie,*" said Eigen serenely. All he knew was that he hadn't touched the apples, whatever his sister might say, and he cared for nothing else.

Madge, hearing the disturbance in the kitchen, went

to discover what it was all about.

"Why dost thou scold, Marie?" she inquired in fluent German.

"This rascal, Madame, he has stolen six apples… six."

"Good gracious!" observed Jo, who had followed her sister. "He'll be ill!"

"*Nein, Marie,*" observed Eigen, still as placidly as ever.

Marie turned to her mistress with outflung hands of helplessness. "You hear him, Madame! That is all that he says! He who has stolen!"

"*Nein, Marie!*" was the parrot-like response of the accused youth.

"Wait, Marie," said Miss Bettany, checking the flood of exclamations which she could see to be on Marie's tongue. "He is a good boy. If he says he did not touch the apples, then I do not think he did. Eigen, hast thou seen the apples of which Marie speaks?"

Eigen looked at her hopefully. He had quite given up expecting any sense from his sister. He said, "*Nein, gnädiges Fräulein.*"

"Very well!" Miss Bettany turned to Marie. "I am sure he speaks the truth, Marie, and one of the young ladies may have felt hungry during the night and taken them. I will inquire, and, meantime, say no more about it."

Her young mistress left the kitchen, followed by Jo, who was wondering rather miserably how things would go that day.

"It's going to be simply horrid!" she decided, as she

attacked her roll and honey with considerably less appetite than usual. "Oh, I wish it was over!"

Inquiries about the apples did not solve the mystery. No one had touched them, and Juliet, who was a light sleeper, and who had, in any case awakened early, was positive that no one had left the dormitory till the rising bell had rung. "Except Joey," she added.

"Joey came to see me," said Miss Bettany, "so that's all right. Well, I'm sure that if Eigen says he hasn't touched the fruit, he hasn't. I imagine Marie didn't count very carefully when she put them out. That's more likely than that Eigen should have taken them when he says he didn't. Now, go and make your beds and then get ready for a good walk. It's going to rain later on, so you won't get games this afternoon, I'm afraid. Jo, you and Simone are going to Seespitz to the Mensches, so you'd better not go with the others. Get your practising and mending done this morning instead of going for the walk, and change before *Mittagessen*. Herr Mensch rang me up last night to say he was going to take you all for a motor ride up the Tiern Valley, and would be at the fence gate for you at two o'clock, so you must be ready. What he will do if it rains I can't tell you!" thus forestalling the question on Joey's lips. "Now run along, all of you, and get on. Please go quietly."

She had said grace previously, so they all got up and went upstairs in a subdued manner. As she passed the door of Grizel's prison with Simone close beside her, Joey heaved a little sigh.

"What is it then, Joey?" demanded Simone.

"I don't know. I feel as though something horrid was going to happen," returned her friend. "Sort of foretelling, you know! Spooky and awful!" she added incoherently.

"I do not understand," said Simone, who might well be forgiven for not understanding.

"Oh, well, I can't explain!" replied Jo impatiently. "Come and make your bed!"

They were halfway through, when the chink of china on a tray and the sound of careful footsteps told them that breakfast was going to Grizel.

"It's awfully jolly to have your breakfast in bed," grumbled Margia. "I wish I had! Worth being naughty for! I say! What's that?" as a startled cry reached her ears.

Before anyone could answer her, there came the sound of hurrying feet, and Miss Bettany flung open the door of the dormitory.

"Girls! Which of you has seen Grizel Cochrane this morning?"

A startled silence followed her question. Finally Juliet answered.

"I don't think any of us have, Madame. Isn't she in her room?"

"No. The windows are wide open and her clothes are gone! Are you sure you haven't seen her?"

You could have heard a pin drop as they digested this information.

"D'you mean you think she's... run away?" ventured Margia at last.

"Of course she hasn't!" exploded Joey. "She's broken bounds, that's all! An' I think she's a beast!"

"Hush, Joey!" said Miss Bettany. "Of course she hasn't run away, Margia! For one thing, she has no money, and for another, she hasn't anywhere to run to. But it's very trying! I did think I could trust you girls!"

She turned and left the room as she spoke, leaving a startled group behind her. They did not quite know what to think. Up till this moment they had felt a good deal of sympathy for Grizel; and her brilliant idea of vaselining the blackboards had rather captivated them. But this was quite another thing. It was untrustworthy, and, as Margia said later, "not cricket". With all her wilfulness, Grizel had never yet failed to play the game, and the shock of discovering that she could fail rather stunned them. Presently Juliet went back to her task of bed-making, and they all followed her example in a deathly silence that said far more about their feelings than any amount of speech could have done. Whey they had finished, Joey and Simone went to their practise, while the others got ready for their walk with Miss Maynard. Presently they set off, passing Madge and Mademoiselle on the way, the one going over to Buchau to make inquiries as to whether Grizel had been seen about there, while the other was going down to Spärtz by the mountain path on the same quest.

For some forty minutes Joey worked away steadily at her scales, her mind anywhere but on what she was doing. Suddenly she jumped up.

"The Tiernjoch!" she gasped. "That's where she's gone!

Up the Tiernjoch! Oh, she was looking at it last night! That's what she was thinking of! I must go and fetch her back!"

With Jo the impulsive, to think was to act. She dashed along to the cloakroom, tore madly into her mac, dashed into Simone, and gasped, "Simone, Grizel's gone up the Tiernjoch! I'm off to fetch her back! You must stay and tell Madge when she comes! Goodbye!"

Before the astounded Simone had taken in half the sense of what she said, she had gone. Thus it happened that a distracted and worn-out Madge was met some hour and a half later by a tearful Simone, who sobbed out that Joey had gone up the wicked Tiernjoch to find Grizel.

Chapter Twenty-Three

ON THE TIERNJOCH

TO GO BACK a few hours to the time when Grizel awoke in the early greyness of the morning is now necessary. When she had got into bed, she had banged her head on her pillow four times, saying solemnly "Four o'clock!" as she did so. She woke up just as the old grandfather clock below chimed four times. For a minute she listened for the breathing of the others, then she remembered. She was by herself as a punishment, and she was going to climb the Tiernjoch that day. "At last!" she thought, as she climbed cautiously out of bed. Shivering a little with cold and excitement, Grizel began to dress in the half light. She was soon ready, and then, picking up her electric torch, she stole downstairs in her stockinged feet to the kitchen to see if Marie had, by chance, left any food about. She found the apples on the kitchen table and abstracted six, dropping five of them into her knapsack and beginning on the other. There was nothing else, however, and she dared not risk opening the cupboards in case any of the door should creak. Still, six apples, two rolls of bread, and a slice of Marie's *Kuchen* were not so bad.

The next thing was to get out. It would be madness to attempt to open the doors. What she decided on was almost as mad. The window of the room opened on to the balcony that ran all round the house. Grizel clambered over the railings, hung for a moment from the ledge of it, and then dropped. Mercifully, it was only ten feet above the ground, and she had learnt how to fall easily, so beyond a bumped elbow she came to no harm.

When she reached the fence, the cows that were pastured in the valley were coming along, led by the big cream-coloured bull who was lord of the herd. The boy who was herding them looked curiously at her, but made no comment. Probably he thought that she was waiting for the rest of a party. When they had passed, Grizel set off again, this time at a reasonable jog-trot pace, which she knew she could keep up for some time. When she had reached the tiny hamlet of Lauterbach, the last remnants of the darkness had gone and it was broad daylight.

A man was chopping wood for the fires outside one chalet, and he was whistling a jolly tune as he worked. Two or three goats, tethered nearby, bleated at the sound of her footsteps, and a baby kid came skipping alongside of her, its head cocked inquiringly on one side, its yellow eyes full of innocent inquiry which won her heart instantly.

"Oh, you darling!" she cried, trying to catch him in her arms. But Master Billy was as shy as he was curious. With a terrified "Ma-a-a!" he made a side dash away from her, and raced for home and mother.

Grizel threw back her head, laughing happily at the sight. The peasant looked at her, and grunted "*Grüss Gott!*" She answered him, and then went on. All remembrance of the fact that she was in disgrace and had no business to be there had faded from her mind in her enjoyment of the morning. Even the actual ascent of the great mountain that hung so threateningly over the upper end of the valley was forgotten.

Like a good many unimaginative people, Grizel possessed the gift of living in the immediate present. Where Joey and Madge would have been dreaming of the mountain summits and the joy of the hard climb, she was simply wild with delight in her present surroundings. As she swung along, she began to sing one of the folk songs she had learnt in her English school. She finished the song with a wild flourish of her stick, and discovered herself at the foot of a narrow path that wound up and up between bushes and rocks. A tiny stream trickled down far above her, looking like a silver thread in the cold light.

Grizel stopped and debated with herself. Should she eat her breakfast where she was, or should she go on till she reached the alm where she would buy her milk?

"I'll eat an apple," she decided, "then I'll go on. Coo! What a scramble!"

She sat down on a convenient rock and bit firmly into an

apple. "Jolly it is, early in the morning!" she thought, as she flung the core into nearby bushes. "Well, I must pull up my socks and get on with it!"

Accordingly, she shouldered her knapsack once more, picked up her stick, and set off cheerfully up the narrow path, whistling cheerily as she went. Presently, however, the track left the bushes, and twisted about round boulders and over heaps of broken stones which she found tricky to negotiate. She had been right. It was a scramble! Up and up she clambered, unheeding of her legs and shoulders, which were beginning to ache with the unaccustomed exercise.

"The Sonnenscheinspitze was a circumstance to this," she thought, as she toiled onwards, "and as for the Mondscheinspitze, it was a baby's crawl! I hope it gets better further on!"

Far from getting better, however, it got worse, and Grizel was forced to stop more than once to rest. "Oof! This is some climb!" she sighed, as she sat down for the third time to mop her streaming face. "However they get the cows up here is beyond me!"

As a matter of fact, the cows reached the alm by a path which came over the shoulder of the mountain, and was much easier; but Grizel could not know that. Presently she set off again, and this time she succeeded in reaching the alm. She nearly came to grief over the last few steps. The alm itself overhung the path, and, in order to get on to it, she had to catch at a tree root and haul herself up. She was almost there when her hand slipped and she nearly fell. If she had gone, it would have meant a fall of twenty feet or more, for just here the rock had broken away. Luckily, she managed to scramble to safety somehow, and reached the short, sweet turf, where she lay with beating heart for the next few minutes.

Presently she got to her feet. With all her faults, Grizel was no coward. A weaker character might have given in at this point, but she simply set her teeth and went on. The alm is a long one here, and the herdsmen's hut is built in a crevice in the rock, so it was a good ten minutes before she reached it. The men had long since gone to their day's work, and there was only a lad of sixteen or seventeen in the hut. He stared at her, but made no comment. When she asked for milk in her best German, he brought it to her in a big earthenware mug, and stood watching her while she drank it. Never had anything tasted so delicious to her as that draught of sweet milk, rich with yellow cream. When she had finished, the boy took the mug, saying in curiously hoarse, thick tones something of which she caught only the last words: *ein Nebelstreif.* Grizel did not understand, but she was not going to let him know that if she could help it; so she looked as intelligent as she knew how, nodded her head, and said, "Oh, *ja, ja!*"

Again the boy spoke, this time saying something about *keine Aussicht.* This, Grizel knew, meant "no view", so she shook her head this time, saying, "*Nein, nein! Keine Aussicht!*" which seemed to satisfy him, for with the usual "*Grüss Gott!*" he turned and went back into the hut.

Grizel looked after him doubtfully before she turned and went on her way. Walking over the short, springy grass was a treat after the hard, toilsome scramble over the rocks and shale. She had got her second wind, and went on joyously, munching an apple as she went. It struck her that it was getting rather misty, but she had no means of knowing the time, as she was not wearing her watch, and she supposed it to be the morning mists, which would soon disappear. It was then about eleven o'clock, as a matter of fact; and at the foot of the mountain Joey Bettany was eyeing the path up which her friend had come with dubious eyes. Ten minutes took Grizel to the far edge of the alm, and once more the path began to wind upwards. It was easy going at first, but soon became more difficult. The mist-clouds closed in round her, and presently she found herself struggling upwards, surrounded by white walls of mountain fog, which hid the path from her and deadened all sounds save those of her own footsteps. She was plucky enough, but the deadly silence and the eeriness began to frighten her. Some of the terrible stories Herr Mensch and Herr Marani told them came back to torment her now. She was worn out, and the climb was becoming more and more difficult. Over and over again she was obliged to sit down and rest, and after each halt she felt herself becoming stiffer and stiffer. Then suddenly her foot struck a loosened stone and set it rolling. She heard it go a little way, then there was an awful silence, and at the same moment the clouds lifted just sufficiently to show her that she was standing on the edge of a precipice!

As the realization of the fact came to her, Grizel felt the last remnant of her courage oozing away, and clutched at it desperately. If she had followed the inclination of the moment, she would have flung herself down on the ground and screamed. Luckily, she did nothing of the kind. More, she even tried to take a step or two forward. Then, as the mists came swirling back once more, she gave it up. She knew where she was, for Herr Mensch had described the ascent to her more than once. She had reached the worst bit of all. Here, for one hundred and fifty yards, the path, barely three feet wide in most places, and even less in some, crawled along the edge of a precipice which went sheer down to the valley below. On the other side a wall of stark rock rose, also sheerly, giving no hold of any kind. This was the part where anyone in the least degree nervous was roped, and it was where the worst accidents always occurred. What made things worse was the fact that she had no idea how far along she had come. With a pitiful attempt at self-control, she sat down, slowly and carefully, curling herself up against the rock wall. Little shivers, partly of cold, partly of terror, ran up and down her. Lying there, with only a narrow shelf of rock between her and instant death, Grizel prayed as she had never prayed before. At first the words would not come. Then gradually the old familiar "Our Father" rose to her lips. That comforted her. "Our Father, which art in heaven," she prayed aloud, the sound of her own voice helping to steady her. "Our Father, oh, send someone! Please send someone quickly. Our Father—"

"Grizel, Grizel!" The cry came faintly through the mist.

She sat up. Joey! It was Joey's voice! "Our Father," she sobbed. Then, "Joey! Joey!"

"Hold on a tick! I'm coming! Where are you?"

Grizel pulled herself together. "Joey! I'm on the precipice! I'm lying down! Look out!"

Almost at once a figure loomed up out of the mist, and then Joey, feeling her way carefully, was beside her. She was sitting down, pulling her into her arms, holding her tightly, saying, "Grizel! Grizel!"

"Our Father," began Grizel dully. "Oh, Joey. He sent you at last!"

Then darkness swept over her and, to Joey's utter dismay, she fainted. It was only for a few moments, however. She struggled back to consciousness, and with consciousness came terror, complete and overwhelming. She clung to the younger girl, shaking from head to foot, while Joey, with wide, straining eyes trying to see through the mists, held her tightly, murmuring words of comfort to her.

"Grizel! Darling! Don't cry! It's all right! Honest injun, it is! There! Don't cry, Grizel! Joey's here! Joey's got you safely! It's all right!" Over and over again she repeated it, till finally the meaning of her words reached Grizel's brain, and she began to pull herself together.

"Joey!" she said presently. "Oh, Joey! How did you know?"

"Where to come to, d'you mean? I guessed! Grizel, are you better? Don't you think if we went on hands and knees you could get back to the rocks? We aren't awfully far along, I know. Two minutes would do it. Can't you try, Grizel?"

But Grizel dared not. "Joey, I daren't! Oh, Joey, I know I

should slip and fall! I daren't move! Don't you move either, Joey! If you do, we shall go over! Don't move, Joey! Please don't!"

"But, Grizel, old thing, it's awfully cold, and you're wet through! Do let's have a shot at it!"

But Grizel's nerve was gone. She could only clutch her friend, crying piteously, and, mercifully for both of them, she made no attempt to move. Had she done so in her present state of mind, there is little doubt but that both of them must have gone over the edge. Finally, Joey gave up her coaxing, and settled herself as comfortably as she could to await the rescue she felt sure would come soon. Grizel, lying closely against her, had ceased to cry. Now she seemed drowsy and dull. With a sudden throb of fear, Joey Bettany faced a new danger. She had read of the death sleep which continued cold brings on, and she realized that already Grizel was only semi-conscious. At all costs she must rouse her.

"Grizel!" she said imperatively. "Grizel! Wake up! You can't go to sleep!"

Grizel muttered something drowsily, but made no movement. Joey slapped her face smartly, and nearly brought disaster on them both as the elder girl stirred.

"Grizel! Grizel!"

"Yes, Joey! I'm here!"

"But you must stay here!" sobbed poor Joey. "Oh, Grizel, don't go to sleep!"

"I'm not; but I am so tired," murmured Grizel.

"I know, but oh, you mustn't! Oh, I can't bear it!"

Her tears fell on Grizel's face, and did more to wake her than anything else would have done. Joey crying was a wonder not to be understood.

"Don't cry, Joey! It's all my fault, and I'm sorry now! Oh, and if we both die it will be my fault, and Miss Bettany will never forgive me or look at me again!"

Joey began to gurgle hysterically at that. "Don't be s-silly! If we both die we shall be d— What's that?"

She sat with head upreared, listening for the sound her quick ears had caught. It came again – the long, melodious call of the mountaineer.

"Grizel!" she cried. "We're found!" Then, with all her strength, she cooeed.

The yodel came again, nearer this time, and, as she answered it, Joey noticed that, at long last, the mists were thinning. Then came the sound of careful footsteps, and, finally, the dear familiar figure of Herr Mensch, looking more like a benevolent giant than ever. Behind him came the slighter form of Herr Marani, and behind him again two of the herdsmen, who had been pressed into service. To a skilled mountaineer like Herr Mensch the narrow path presented no difficulties. With one big stride he had stepped across the two girls, then, turning round, he bent down and picked up Grizel, while Herr Marani helped Joey to her feet. The next few minutes were dangerous enough, for Joey's cramped muscles would not work, and she nearly fell. Luckily Herr Marani had her firmly, and twenty minutes later they were on the alm, where Madge awaited them with white face and eyes dark with the agony she had undergone. If Herr Marani would have allowed her, she would have carried Joey herself to the herdsmen's hut, where a potent drink of hot milk, mixed with brandy from Herr Mensch's flask, was given to them before they made the final descent to the valley.

Two hours later the sun appeared in full glory, gilding all the peaks and driving away the last rags of mist from the sinister mountain which had so nearly added two more to the toll of its victims.

Chapter Twenty-Four

CONSEQUENCES

IT WAS THE day after Grizel's grand escapade, which had so nearly ended in terrible disaster, and it was a day which none of the girls ever forgot. The sun shone gloriously the whole time, as if to make up for his behaviour of yesterday. The Tzigane band had come up the lake again, and was making music outside the Kron Prinz Karl. But all this meant nothing to the school, for Grizel was ill with bronchitis, and Joey Bettany had never come out of the sleep into which she had fallen after they had laid her in Herr Mensch's car, which had been awaiting them at the foot of the mountain.

Herr Marani had gone hotfoot to Innsbruck to fetch the doctor, and he had said that the awful nerve strain through which the imaginative, highly strung child had gone might result in brain fever. That could only be decided when she came out of the heavy stupor in which she lay, and which might last for two or three days yet. Grizel's case was far simpler. It was a straightforward attack of bronchitis, the natural result of having been for hours in the clinging mists. It was, of course, made worse by the fact that she had gone all to pieces when she found herself in her own bed; but with careful nursing – and they could be sure of that – she would soon be all right again. Joey's case was far more doubtful. Then he left them, promising to return the next day. Frau Mensch had appeared in the morning and carried off Amy and Margia, and Frau Rincini had sent Bette over to fetch the little Merciers. She had offered to have Simone as well, but Simone had begged to stay, and Juliet had offered to look after her, so they had given the child her way.

Midday had brought Frau Marani with an offer to nurse Grizel, and Madge herself had never left Joey for a minute until the doctor had arrived, and with one glance at her white face had sternly ordered her out.

"It will make things worse if you are ill," he told her. "Go and have some food, and then a little walk. Tonight you must sleep, while the young lady – ah, Fräulein Maynard! – watches. Nothing will occur for some hours yet." Then the anguish in her eyes touched his compassion, and he added, "She looks better – seems more natural. Now go and rest."

Madge did as he told her as far as going out was concerned. She had gone to the pine wood, and was wandering up and down, when Simone had caught sight of her, and breaking away from Juliet, had rushed across the meadow and caught her arm with hot little hands. Now, as she saw the child's face, all puffed and swollen with crying, Miss Bettany felt suddenly that she had been neglecting her duty. She slipped an arm round Simone, who promptly began to sniff again.

"The doctor says nothing will happen for some hours yet, but he thinks she looks more natural. Don't cry, Simone."

Simone made a valiant attempt to check her tears and succeeded. "I do love Joey so much!" she said quaveringly. "Oh, Madame, if there is one little thing I can do you will tell me?"

"Yes," said Madge. "I can tell you of one little thing now. You can stop crying and try to be brave. Tomorrow there will be school as usual. Joey is far above the schoolrooms and I know you will all be quiet. We shall break up on Tuesday or Wednesday, instead of a week later as I had intended. I want you to be very brave, and work as steadily as you can for the two days. If the others see you and Juliet," – she smiled at the other girl, who had now come up with them – "trying to go on as usual, they will try too, and that will make things easier for us all."

"I will try," said Simone very soberly. "I will try ver' hard."

"I'll do my level best," Juliet promised, "and I will look after Simone, Madame."

"Thank you, both of you," said Madge. "Now I must go back, as I may be needed."

She turned and went back to the Chalet, feeling fresher for her little rest, and more able to cope with things. She found Joey lying as she had left her, with the doctor sitting by her side. He looked up as the girl entered, but made no other movement. Madge bent over the bed, looking at the dear, funny little face with a world of love in her eyes. Was it her imagination, or did Joey really look more like herself? She glanced up at the doctor inquiringly, and he nodded his head.

"Yes, it is really so. I begin to have hopes of her. We cannot yet say definitely, but the pulse is stronger, and the temperature has risen no further. Now go and change your clothes, and have a bath and wash your hair!"

Madge quite literally gaped at him, wondering if she had heard aright.

"Yes, I mean that," he said, nodding his head again. "Go to the hotel with this note and have your hair shampooed. There is more than time for it, and it is a better tonic than any I can mix for you in my dispensary."

Sheer astonishment rendered her dumb and obedient. She had thought as she mounted the stairs that she could only leave the bedroom again when she knew that Joey was safe. Now, clutching his note, she made her way to the Kron Prinz Karl, where the Tzigane were playing a plaintive, haunting waltz, to which people were dancing on the grass at the side.

The von Eschenaus were sitting at one of the little tables, and when Frau von Eschenau saw her, she came quickly over, taking her arm.

"*Mein Fräulein*, we are so grieved – Marie has cried herself sick for grief! Tell us, how is *das Mädchen*, and if there is anything we can do?"

"Thank you," said Madge. "There is really nothing. Joey is

much the same, and I've come to get my hair shampooed. The doctor sent me."

Frau von Eschenau stared. "To get your hair shampooed?" she repeated doubtfully.

"Yes, I have a note for Herr Braun."

"Then come this way, and we will find him. Doubtless he will be in the *Speisesaal*."

The good-natured Viennese led her into the big dining room, where Herr Braun was engaged in directing the laying of the tables for dinner. When he saw them, he hurried forward, exclaiming. Madge gave him the doctor's note, and he read it through with wonderment in his eyes. Then he nodded his head wisely.

"It is well, *gnädiges Fräulein*. If *das Fräulein* will come through here, it shall be done."

He led her into the hairdressing room, and forty minutes later Madge was going back to the Chalet feeling refreshed and ready for anything. She peeped into Grizel's room, where good Frau Mensch sat knitting, one watchful eye on the bronchitis kettle. Grizel was sleeping, propped up with pillows to relieve the breathing. She looked flushed, but there was nothing alarming. The illness would take its natural course and the doctor was not alarmed about her. So much Frau Mensch told the young headmistress, her busy fingers never ceasing their work.

"He will stay here for tonight," she continued in her low, murmurous voice that made the guttural German sound soft and musical. "I think he expects that little Jo will come to herself before the morning. Mademoiselle has come in, but she knows nothing about sick-nursing and would be useless. Frau Marani will come tonight and watch by *das Mädchen*, for Fräulein Maynard must sleep, and you will be with the little sister. *Na, mein Liebling*," as Madge tried to thank her, "it is nothing – we are glad to do what we can. You and she are very dear to us all, and we of the Tyrol do not show ingratitude. See! *Das Mädchen* is waking – she opens her eyes."

"What is it, dear?" said Madge. "Do you want to know about Joey? She is still asleep. The doctor is staying here for a while."

"Will... she... be... very... ill?" The words came slowly.

"She is very tired," said Madge evasively, "but she hasn't got bronchitis like you. Now you must rest, you naughty child. We want you to get well again as quickly as possible. The holidays are very near, you know." She bent to kiss the girl, and Grizel relaxed.

"I'm glad," she said. "It wouldn't have been... fair if Joey ... had to be ill... for me."

Madge left her after that, and went back to the other sick-room. The doctor looked at her keenly but, beyond a grunt, he said nothing. Throughout the long night he sat there, watching the little white face on the pillow, Madge watching with him. Once only he left her, to go and see Grizel, and came back with the news that she was decidedly stronger. At ten o'clock Frau Marani appeared, and Frau Mensch want back to the hotel at Seespitz. Five o'clock in the morning brought Miss Maynard to insist that Madge should lie down on the couch and rest for a couple of hours, while she watched in her turn. At seven the doctor went to ring up his partner in Innsbruck and warn him that he should stay where he was for that day. Later, Marie came with hot coffee, rolls, and butter, of which the doctor insisted Madge should partake, and at five to nine she went downstairs to see to work for the day.

The girls came with grave faces, and kind messages and offers of help from their parents. The whole lakeside knew of poor Grizel's escapade, and a good many people had since learnt of the dreadful possible result for Joey, so there were many inquiries.

Amy Stevens' first care was to grab Juliet and demand in an awestruck whisper, "How is Joey? Has she come awake yet?"

"Not yet," said Juliet, who looked white and heavy-eyed. "Don't ask Madame any questions, Amy, will you? She's so fearfully worried."

"Course I shan't!" returned Amy indignantly. "I say, isn't the bell late?"

"There won't be any bell at all today," explained Juliet. "Just go straight in to prayers,"

"Juliet, will you come here one minute?" said Gisela. "We want to know about Joey and Grizel too. How are they both?"

"Grizel is getting on fairly well," replied Juliet. "Joey hasn't roused up yet. They can't say till she does what will happen. The doctor expects it will be today, and he is staying. He was here all last night too."

Prayers were very solemn that morning, and when they were over, there was a little stir among the girls. Madge looked at them.

"Joey is much the same," she said. "There is no change – yet."

She left the actual schoolwork to Mademoiselle and Miss Maynard, flitting in and out at intervals.

The weary day wore on, and still there was no news from the room at the top of the house. The girls behaved like angels, as Miss Maynard said afterwards. There could be no music lessons, of course, and Mademoiselle had rung up Herr Anserl to tell him.

The one bright spot during the day was the fact that Grizel, reassured by their repeated statements that Joey was asleep, and also by Madge's obvious forgiveness, was improving rapidly, temperature going down, breathing easier.

At about three o'clock, as Madge was wearily trying to help Amy Stevens disentangle a glorious muddle of rivers and lakes in her map of Asia, word came down that the doctor would like to see her for a moment. She fled up the stairs to her bedroom. The doctor was standing by the bedside, one hand on Joey's wrist. He looked up as her sister entered.

"*Ah, mein Fräulein,* I have sent for you, for I think she is beginning to arouse. Please stand just there, where she can see you."

Madge took up the position he pointed out, and stood, her eyes fixed on Joey's face. There was no doubt that she was coming out of the stupor. Her lashes flickered more than once, her lips were parted. The only question was, would she wake up the old Joey, or would it be to the babbling delirium of fever?

There was a silence in the room that could be felt. The only sound to be heard was the breathing of the four people – Frau Mensch was by the window – and the ticking of the doctor's watch. Then, slowly, slowly, the long black lashes lifted and Joey looked full at her sister.

"Hello!" she murmured. "I'm awfully tired! Hai–yah!" She finished with a little yawn, turned slightly, snuggling down into the pillow, and fell asleep.

"*Gott sei Dank!*" said the doctor quietly. "She will do now; there is no further danger. Hush, *mein Kind*," for Madge had begun to cry. "It is well now!"

"I know," sobbed Madge. "But oh, Herr Doktor, the relief!"

He signed to Frau Mensch, who led her down to the study, and let her cry away the last of the awful weight that had been hanging over her. When, finally, the tears were all dried, she found a dainty meal of soup, roll, and grapes awaiting her, and when she had finished, Frau Mensch suggested bed.

"I must tell the girls first," said Madge. "I will make myself tidy, and go and tell them."

Ten minutes later Miss Bettany, who looked like herself once more, entered the room where they were all anxiously awaiting her news. She looked at them, but no words would come to her lips. It was Bernhilda the quiet who helped her out.

"Ah, Madame," she said, "there is no need to say anything. Joey will get well."

Madge found her voice. "Yes," she said. "She is sleeping now, and all is safe once more."

And there were rejoicings in the Chalet School that afternoon.

Chapter Twenty-Five

Frau Berlin Again

"Oh, I say! Isn't this perfectly golloptious!"

"Joey! What an appalling expression! Where on earth did you get it?"

"What? 'Golloptious'? I heard those schoolboys we ran into at the Tiernsee use it."

"Well, I wish you wouldn't. It's all very well for schoolboys, but it isn't pretty for schoolgirls, so cut it out!"

Joey cocked her black head on one side consideringly. "Getting a bit old-maidish, aren't you, old thing?" she said. "Don't do it, Madgie Machree!"

"Joey, you little brute! I won't be called such awful names! And you might show a little more respect for your headmistress. You get worse and worse every day!"

"Poor old darling! Never mind! Wait till we get back to school again, and then you can be as crushing as you like. This is holiday time, and there's no one to hear us for once. I think it was topping of the Maranis to take Grizel and Juliet away for the week and let us be on our own for a bit. And this really is a gorgeous place! I never imagined anything like it!"

Madge nodded as she glanced up at the great peaks of the Rosengarten Gebirge which towered above them. Their own limestone crags in the North Tyrol were magnificent, but they were not to be compared with these. As far as they could see, lofty pinnacles of rose-hued rock lifted magnificent heads to the summer skies. Every here and there, cataracts flung themselves downwards in silver ribbons which leapt from rock to rock, all hurrying to join the river which dashed past, making thunderous music as it went, for the two previous days had been very wet, and all the springs and mountain streams were flooded.

Neither Madge nor Jo had been in the South Tyrol before, though both knew the North Tyrol very well, and when Frau Marani had come with the suggestion that Grizel and Juliet should go to Vienna with them for a week while the two sisters had a little holiday to themselves, it had been Joey's idea that they should come here.

"We can't go too far," she argued. "For one thing, we can't afford it. We've never seen Meran, or Botzen, or Primeiro, or any of those other places, and the Mensches say the Dolomites are just gorgeous. It's warm there, so it'll suit us both, and it's been rather chilly here lately. So let's go there; shall us?"

Madge had laughed and agreed. There was nothing to

keep them at the Tiernsee. Miss Maynard was spending the holiday with her family in the high Alps, and Mademoiselle had gone home to her beloved Paris, taking Simone and the two little Stevens with her. The Maranis' kind invitation had settled Juliet and Grizel, and so, seven days previously, the two Bettanys had left Innsbruck, en route for Botzen, by way of the magnificent Kuntersweg Gorge. Botzen they had loved, and Meran was a dream of delight. They had left the little Roman town only that morning to establish themselves in the tiny village of Paneirimo, in the Rosengarten Valley; and here, on the morrow, the other two girls would join them. Joey now turned and slipped an arm through her sister's. "It's been jolly on our own!"

Madge nodded, but said, "I told them at the Chalet to forward letters here. You might run and see if there are any, Jo. I forgot to ask."

"Righto!" And Joey dashed off, to return in a very few minutes waving a whole budget. "Here you are! Dozens of them! At least there are ten – eight for you and two for me. This is from Simone, and this looks like Marie von Eschenau. Madge! You aren't paying any attention! What on earth's the matter? Who's your letter from? Is there anything wrong? What is it?"

Madge pulled herself together with an effort and turned to her little sister. "It's rather dreadful news in one way. Joey. There has been a terrible motor accident in Rome, and Captain and Mrs Carrick were in it."

Joey looked serious. "Are they awfully hurt?"

"Mrs Carrick was killed at once," said Madge, "and Captain Carrick died two days ago. He has left me Juliet to bring up, as they have no relations."

Madge gathered up her letters and went to her bedroom.

Joey sat looking after her. She was silent for a minute, then she turned to her own letters. "Let's see what Simone's got to say!"

Meanwhile, Madge Bettany sat in their bedroom re-reading the letter written by a doctor of the hospital where Captain Carrick had died. After describing generally his injuries, the writer had continued: "Captain Carrick told me that his daughter was with you, and that you would be her guardian. He made a will before he died, leaving all he possessed, including some very valuable jewellery belonging to his wife and a sum of one hundred thousand lire, in trust to you for the girl. He asked me to say he hoped you had forgiven the trick he played on you, and would undertake the trust. The money, I gathered, he had won at the tables at Monte Carlo. He died three hours after he had made the will."

The letter concluded with a request to know how the jewels and money were to be sent, and a suggestion that Madge should come to Rome to fetch them, when "my wife will be delighted to welcome you to our home as our guest".

When she had finished re-reading this startling communication, Madge sat thinking hard. In one way, this event settled the Juliet difficulty, but it by no means completely solved it. Pondering over the problem seemed to bring her no nearer its solution, so she shelved the matter for the moment and turned her attention to her other letters. One was from Mrs Dene, who had written to make final arrangements for Rosalie, who was coming to the Chalet School next term. Another came from Mrs Stevens, thanking her for the care of Margia and Amy, and enclosing a very welcome cheque for the next term's fees. The third she took up was on very expensive paper, in a most illiterate hand, and bore the postmark of Bradford, which puzzled her extremely.

"Bradford!" she said aloud. "Who on earth do I know in Bradford?"

"Open the letter, old thing, then you'll find out!" observed Joey's voice from the doorway.

Madge literally jumped. Joey happened to be wearing plimsolls, and her steps had been quite noiseless.

"Sorry!" she observed, as she dropped down beside her sister. "I didn't mean to startle you. I'd finished my letters, so I thought I'd come and see what you were doing. I say! If Captain Carrick has left Juliet to you, how does he imagine you're going to manage for money?"

"There's money for her," returned Madge. "You needn't worry, Joey. But I'm rather afraid we shall have to go back to the Tiernsee tomorrow. They want me to go to Rome to see about Juliet's affairs."

"And who is your Bradford pal?" said Joey.

Madge opened the letter and glanced at the beginning. "'Honoured and respected Madam.' Good heavens! Who on earth can it be from?" She turned to the end, but found no enlightenment there. The signature, finished off with a flourish, was 'James H. Kettlewell'.

"James H. Kettlewell! Never heard of him!" began Joey.

"No; and yet it's vaguely familiar." Madge thought hard for a minute. "Joey! I've got it! Do you remember the man in the Paris train who gave us gooseberries? His name was Kettlewell, and he told us he lived at Bradford!"

"So he did! Whatever can he be writing about? Buck up and see!"

"Ahem! 'Honoured and respected Madam,'" began Madge, "'I take my pen in hand to inscribe this present epistle to you.'"

"Coo! What elegant English!" commented Joey.

"Be quiet! If you interrupt, I won't read it to you at all!"

"Sorry! I'll be good! Do get on! I'm dying to know what it's about!"

"Where was I? Oh, yes! 'It is with the greatest diffidence that I venture to approach you on such a subject, knowing, as I do, the delicacy with which it should be treated, especially to a high-up lady like you—'What on earth— ? Is the man mad?"

"Oh, get on!" implored Joey impatiently. "Don't be so aggravating!"

"All right! It's my letter, remember! Let's see… 'lady like you. Believe me, honoured Madam, I should not have the … the… oh… the temerity to approach you thus were it not that I feel—'" Her voice died away as her eyes wandered down the page. Then she suddenly sat bolt upright with horror. "Joey! It's a very private letter! I—"

"I s'pose you mean it's a proposal!" Joey interrupted her. "Oh, I knew what was coming after the very first sentence! Oh, I say!" And she went off into fits of laughter.

Madge shook her slightly. "Joey, behave yourself! It's not a thing to laugh at! If I'd known, I'd never have read it to you. I thought it was just an ordinary letter. You must give me your word of honour never to mention it to a soul!"

"What do you take me for?" Joey was righteously indignant. "Of course I shan't."

"Oh dear! This is dreadful!" Madge had turned over the page and was reading on.

"But of all the weird things to happen!" Joey got up and strolled over to the window. "I scarcely ever thought of him again. He was awfully sweet and kind, of course; but I must say it seems a mad thing to do when he'd only seen you once. Why, he couldn't know if you were good tempered, or a decent housekeeper, or... or truthful, or anything!"

"Oh, Joey, be quiet!" exclaimed the exasperated Madge. "You'd talk the hind leg off a donkey! Oh dear! Why does everything come at once?"

"It's rotten luck, old thing!" Joey's teasing mood had suddenly vanished. "You have had a time of it since we came to Austria! Let's hope next term is quieter than this has been! One thing, Grizel can't go off climbing mountains!"

Madge got up, folding her letter and putting it back into its envelope.

"Joey, I don't want you to think I'm always saying 'don't',

but I'd rather not talk about that affair just yet, it's too soon after!"

She cast a thought to those dreadful hours when it had been doubtful what was going to happen to the speaker, and suddenly hugged her. "It was all very horrible. We won't talk about it at all, Joey. Let's see what the other letters are."

There was nothing exciting in them. Two of them were from the aunts in England, one from an old school friend of Madge's, and the last asked for a prospectus of the school.

Later they strolled along by the banks of a rushing stream.

"It's been a weird affair all round!" said Jo, as she stood throwing in pebbles, trying to make them skim the surface of the water.

"What has?" demanded her sister.

"Why, all this – coming to Austria, and having the school, and Juliet, and... and James H. Kettlewell's letter, and everything!"

"Yes; but I don't see why you call it a weird affair!" Madge was deeply interested. Jo's imagination often helped to throw new light on matters, and she wondered what new light was going to be thrown on the Chalet School.

"Why, it's this way. We come out to the Tiernsee because we're frantically poor. You decide to start a school, and it goes like... like fun. We do heaps of things in one term, and we grow from three to eighteen. Then, when the school is just going like everything, you get a chance to chuck it if you want to, and get married. We're jolly lucky, I think!"

Madge nodded. "Yes, that's quite true. But oh, if we're going to have the same sort of excitements each term that we've had this, I shall want to give it up!"

"Still, they haven't been bad excitements, 'cept the last – not really bad! Madge! Did you ever! There's Frau Berlin!"

"Frau Berlin? Where? Joey, don't point! It's frightfully rude!"

"There! By that house! Well, I'll be gumswizzled!"

"Joey!"

"Well, but did you ever! Glory! She's coming along! Wonder if she'll know me?"

But she passed them without a look, while Joey gazed at her with wide-open eyes.

"She'll recognize Grizel," she said, when the tartan-clad lady had finally waddled out of hearing. "Oh, Madge, if she does!"

"I'm not going to risk any more fusses," said Madge with determination. "If there's the slightest chance of that, back we go tomorrow."

"P'raps it would be best. I say, I'm awfully hungry! Let's go back an' see if we can get anything to eat. It must be nearly lunch-time."

As Madge was hungry too, she agreed, and presently they were enjoying a substantial meal. Just as they had reached the dessert stage the door opened, and in rolled Frau Berlin!

"That settles it!" murmured Miss Bettany. "You may pack up tonight, for as soon as Grizel and Juliet arrive we go back to the Tiernsee. I think I must go to Rome after all, so that will be all right. It will just fit in nicely."

As soon as they could, they left the *Speisesaal* and retired to their room.

"That's the finish!" said Jo, as she finally rolled into bed at about half-past nine. "There can't be anything more after this."

However, the morrow was to bring them just one surprise more.

Chapter Twenty-Six

A GRAND WIND-UP

"WHAT DO YOU think? An old pal of yours is here, Grizel — a very dear friend!"

Grizel, thus greeted by a wildly excited Joey on her arrival at Paneirimo, looked at her suspiciously.

"Who on earth is it?"

"Guess!"

"Can't! Can't think of a soul likely to be in Austria! Who is it, Joey?"

"Think, Griselda! Think of someone you met a short while ago!"

"But I haven't met anyone except people you have too. Why is it a pal of mine?"

"Someone you had a fearful row with," Joey prompted her, jumping tantalisingly up and down.

"I can't think— Joey! You don't mean Frau Berlin?

Oh, it is, it is!"

"Well done you! Yes, it is. Well, what do you think of it?"

"My dear! It's awful! Has she seen you yet? Does she know, d'you think?"

Joey shook her head. "Don't think so! Anyway, we're not staying. Madge won't risk it."

"What d'you mean by not staying? Where are we going?"

"Home! Oh, you don't know yet, of course!" Joey cast a wary eye at Madge and Juliet, who were walking ahead. "Come on down to the river. We aren't going till the afternoon train, and we're to spend the night at Innsbruck. It's rather awful in some ways, but on the whole, I think it might be worse. My sister had a letter from Rome yesterday, and Juliet's father and mother are dead."

Grizel gasped. "Joey! Oh, how dreadful! Poor Juliet! What will she do?"

"Her father's asked Madge to look after her, and he's left her some money to do it with," said Joey. "That's one reason why we're going home. Madge has to go to Rome to get it. We're going back to Briesau, and Miss Maynard is coming to look after us. She was coming anyhow, so that's all right. What sort of a time did you have in Vienna?"

"Top-hole!" And Grizel plunged straightaway into an account of her adventures. When, finally, they turned their steps towards the hotel, they saw Madge coming to meet them. She was by herself and was walking rather slowly.

"Have you told Juliet?" said Joey in hushed tones as she reached them.

"Yes; I want you two to be very kind to Juliet. She's been through a good deal lately, and, naturally, she is very much upset. I needn't tell you not to hang round her or do anything silly like that, but just be as nice as you can to her. We are going back to Innsbruck this afternoon, and then tomorrow we shall go up to the Tiernsee, and I shall have to leave you there, as I must go to Rome to settle up affairs for her. Miss Maynard will be with you, and I want you to give her as little trouble as possible. I'm sorry I can't send for her to come here, but under the circumstances, I'm afraid it's rather impossible."

Grizel coloured furiously, although her headmistress had not attempted to make the last remark specially pointed. She knew well enough, however, that her behaviour at the Alte Post was mainly the cause of their leaving Paneirimo that afternoon. She said nothing, but followed Joey into the hotel with unaccustomed meekness. Madge, herself, had said nothing about what had occurred on that Saturday when Grizel had followed her own wilful way and tried to climb the Tiernjoch; but Frau Marani had had no scruples, and she had told the girl very plainly of what they had feared for Joey during the two long days which had followed. Grizel had had a dreadful shock, and she was never again so thoughtless.

"Where is Juliet?" asked Joey, as they reached the foot of the stairs.

"Upstairs in our room," replied Madge. "Yes, go to her, you two. Take them both out and show them the place, Joey. There are one or two odds and ends of packing I want to finish up, and I'd rather not risk a fuss with that Frau Berlin, as you call her. So keep out of the way till luncheon. Our train goes at three, so you won't have much time here. Make the most of it."

Upstairs in the big, airy room with its twin beds they found Juliet standing at the window staring listlessly out at the mountains. She was not crying, as Joey had half feared, but she had a white, worn look, as though she had been ill, and her eyes were heavy and weary.

"Come an' see the mountains, old Ju!" said Joey, slipping her hand into the elder girl's. "They're topping, though not a bit like ours at home, of course!"

"Yes, do come!" urged Grizel, "And oh, Juliet, that awful woman's here!"

"Which one?" asked Juliet, though with a complete lack of interest in her voice.

"Frau Berlin – the one who was such a pig the day we went to Innsbruck to get Madame's birthday gift. Don't you remember?"

"Oh, yes, I remember. All right, Joey, I'll come."

But though she let them pull her downstairs and out into the sunshine, it seemed as though she didn't really care much what she did. The shock of hearing what Madge had told her, even though the news had been broken to her with great tenderness, had dazed her for the time being. Through all the chatter of the other two she was conscious of just one thought: "If only I could have felt they loved me!"

However, the fresh air and sunshine did her good, and

when, finally, Miss Bettany came to summon them to lunch, she looked better than she had done.

No contretemps occurred with Frau Berlin, for she did not appear. Nevertheless, Madge felt very thankful when she found herself safely in the Innsbruck train without having had a scene. Juliet settled herself in a corner with a book, but she did not appear to read much. Most of the time she was gazing unseeingly out of the window. The other two had retired to the far end of the compartment which they had to themselves, and at Joey's bright suggestion embarked on a game of Roadside Cribbage. Madge, sitting with one eye on the silent girl opposite her and the other on the *Wiener Zeitung*, occasionally heard exclamations of "Three goats – thirty!" "Waterfall – five!" "Mule – oh, bust it! Back to the beginning!" but paid no attention. She was not desperately interested in her paper either. For the most part, her thoughts were with the coming term. She could have twenty-six girls this time, and of these, twelve would be boarders. If the school went on growing, she knew that she must either build on to the present Chalet, or else take another somewhere near. She was not quite certain what to do. Herr Marani and Herr Mensch were very good friends to her, but she wished heartily that Dick were at hand to advise her.

As she was thinking of this, she suddenly became aware that the train was slackening speed, and even as she looked up to see where they were, it began to rock violently backwards and forwards with a sickening motion. She had barely time to leap to her feet before, with a mighty crash, the carriage gave a final lurch and collapsed on its side. Above the noise she heard the screams of the three girls, mingling with shrieks from the other passengers. Mercifully, Joey had flung herself on the floor, dragging Grizel with her; and by a positive miracle, neither Madge nor Juliet had been badly hurt, though the former was, like everyone else, slightly stunned, and Juliet, as they found out after, was badly bruised. Also, being thoroughly English, they had had the window wide open, and so had a means of exit. The door, when Miss Bettany tried it, was jammed.

"It's a good thing none of us is fat," she said with a shaky laugh. "Come along, you three; I'm going to push you through the window. Grizel first."

Grizel had the sense to make no protests; besides, she was still rather dazed, so she allowed her headmistress to push and tug till she was through, and then, as the fresh air began to clear her stupefied brain, she reached down and helped to pull Juliet up. Joey was an easy matter, and she was soon standing on a heap of stones, looking very white and scared, while the two big girls dragged her sister out. They had just pulled her clear when, from the front of the train, came the dreaded cry of "Fire!"

"*Feuer! Feuer!*" shrieked a fat woman, who was badly jammed in the window-frame of the next compartment.

Madge flung a hasty "Stay where you are! Don't dare to move!" at the terrified girls and dashed to the rescue. The scene was becoming ghastly. The big engine and three of the long carriages lay on their sides in a narrow gorge-like way.

The foremost carriage was already wrapped in flames, and their roaring rose above the screams and cries of the people still imprisoned in the other carriages. The three remaining on their wheels had disgorged all their passengers and already men were tearing along, working madly to save those in such deadly peril. Madge Bettany contrived to take in all these things as she made that frantic scramble on to the side of the carriage, where a terrified fat woman, with grey hair streaming wildly round her, was struggling madly to get free of the window-frame which held her gripped as in a vice.

Through all the horror of it the English girl contrived to keep her head.

"Steady!" she said, as she took the gripping hands, and though the language was a foreign one and a hated one, her voice brought self-control to the maddened woman.

"I cannot get free," she panted in German. "*Fräulein—*"

"Keep still a moment! Now! Ready! Then, as hard as you can!"

There was a struggle, a sound of rending and tearing, a sudden gasp, and then the other woman suddenly shot out over the wheels and onto the heap of stones, her clothes in shreds, but otherwise safe. Madge sprang down beside her, and then she felt the world turning black, and she fainted. When she came to herself she was lying on a coat in a field. Joey was kneeling beside her, crying vehemently, and a big fair man whom she did not know was holding something to her lips. With an effort she pulled herself together and pushed it away.

"No, no," she said.

"Oh, Madge!" sobbed Joey. "O-ooh! I thought you... you w-were dead!"

"Hush!" said the man. "She'll be all right in a minute, kid. It's only whisky and water I'm giving you, madam. Better take a little to buck you up!"

"No, I'm all right!" With an effort she sat up, pushing the hair off her face. Joey promptly flung her arms round her, hugging her tightly. Juliet and Grizel seemed to have vanished.

"Oh, Madge darling! Oh, I had such a fright! Oh, Madge!"

"There! That'll do," said their benefactor. "You're not helping her, kid. Let her alone for a minute or two to come round. It's quite all right – the other kids are safe enough, and – oh, you plucky girl! It was one of the bravest things I've ever seen!"

"It was nothing," returned Madge, who was rapidly coming to herself. "Joey! Don't strangle me, child! Let me get up!"

She contrived to get onto her feet, but was glad enough of the arm the stranger flung round her as she swayed for a moment.

"There!" he said rather roughly. "Come over here and sit down a minute! You can't do everything at once! I'll send the other kids along, and you'll be all right in a minute. No, there's nothing you can do. Everyone got clear but the driver. He fell on his head, poor chap! Even your fat rescue is recovered enough to fuss about having no skirt on—"

"Yes; and oh, Madge, who do you think it is?" interrupted Joey, with considerable lack of both manners and grammar. "It's Frau Berlin!"

"Oh, goodness!" and Madge began to laugh weakly.

"Isn't it rum? And we left Paneirimo because of her and Grizel, and then you save her life! Yes, you did. The carriage got on fire just as you slithered down. If it hadn't been for you, she'd have burnt to death! She was only bumped a bit, and she wanted to kiss you, only that man came and hiked you off into this field, and she suddenly found her clothes were all torn, so she wouldn't follow us! Grizel and Juliet are over there. They aren't hurt, and nor am I. Do buck up, Madge!"

Thus Joey, in a breathless, hurrying tumult of words.

"That man" stood to one side, smiling, as the elder girl managed to take it all in. Then Grizel and Juliet appeared, and all the excitement began over again. At length he interfered.

"Now then, you kids, let's go and see what we can do about getting on. I know this place, and we're about ten miles from anywhere. Besides, Miss—?"

"Bettany," supplied Madge. "These are my sister Joey, and two of my pupils – Grizel Cochrane and Juliet Carrick."

"Ah, thank you," he replied. "My name's Russell – James Russell, at your service. Well, as I was going to say, Miss Bettany, you had better get somewhere where you can lie down for a bit. There's a main road goes past here somewhere, and, with luck, we ought to get a lift in something. If you will take my arm, I think we can get there all right, and we can't do anything here."

There was common sense in what he said, so they set off, Madge beginning to realize how very shaky she still felt. The girls were upset too, and it took them some time to make the road. Luckily, just as they reached it, a peasant came past with an empty hay cart. Mr Russell quickly came to an arrangement with him, and a couple of hours later they were safely in the *Gasthaus* of a tiny village. They stayed there all night, their new friend going on to Innsbruck after leaving his card with Joey and getting the Chalet address, so that he could wire to Miss Maynard not to expect them for another day. The morning found them all very tired and worn out, but Madge wanted to get back to the Tiernsee and home, so they set off, and finally arrived at the Chalet, where they were rapturously welcomed by an anxious Miss Maynard, who had been feeling very worried. Mr James Russell had been better than his word, for he had gone up to the Tiernsee and given her a full description of what had occurred.

"I'm thankful you've all arrived safely," said the young mathematics mistress. "I couldn't feel sure you wouldn't have another awful adventure."

"I think I'd rather keep out of adventures for some time to come," laughed Madge rather shakily. "Teaching and school generally will be enough for me for the next three or four years, I can assure you."

"Oh, I expect we'll have some more adventures presently," said Joey.

And so they did. But that, as Mr Kipling says, is another story.

Postscript

In the final lines of *The School at the Chalet,* Elinor Brent-Dyer drops a hint that further adventures are awaiting Joey Bettany and her friends. But when the book was first published, in October 1925, not even the author could have foreseen that the adventures of her Chalet School characters would eventually fill more than sixty books, published over a period of 45 years, and be famous today as the longest series of girls' school-stories ever known.

During the years before World War II there were many stories about fictional schools outside Britain, but Elinor Brent-Dyer was the first author to use the Austrian Tyrol as a setting. Her inspiration for *The School at the Chalet* grew from an idyllic holiday she had spent, probably in 1924, at a Tyrolean lakeside village known in real life as Pertisau-am-Achensee. In the stories, Pertisau is renamed Briesau, and the lake becomes the Tiernsee. But many local places appear under their real names, including Seespitz, Gaisalm, Buchau, Seehof and Scholastika; and no one fortunate enough to have visited Pertisau, with its glorious setting high in the mountains above the Inn valley, could fail to recognise it in the early Chalet School stories.

That Elinor Brent-Dyer fell in love with the Tyrol, and

with the Achensee region in particular, is reflected in the many affectionate descriptions of scenery, people and local customs that she gives in the early books; and a capacity for capturing something of the character and atmosphere of places was undoubtedly among her gifts.

Later in the series, the Chalet School was to change its location several times, leaving the Tyrol during *The Chalet School in Exile*; this book was written after Hitler's annexation of Austria in 1938, and the story, part of which relates the thrilling adventures of Joey and her friends during their escape from the Gestapo, shows an awareness of the real-life international situation at the time that was unusual then in children's fiction.

Over the years, the Chalet School gradually acquires many new characters, both staff and pupils, but most of those first introduced in *The School at the Chalet* remain important throughout the series. Madge, Grizel, Gisela, Juliet, Simone, Margia, Bernhilda and Frieda are among those who reappear regularly; while Joey Bettany continues, right to the end, to play a leading role, despite being by then grown-up, married, a well-known author *and* mother of a large family! Links with the school are also maintained by Joey's many daughters and those of countless other former pupils, who all eventually turn up at the Chalet School, while some members of staff remain from the school's earliest days until the final book.

Many readers have come to look on the Chalet School characters as personal friends; and it seems that Elinor herself, in the course of writing the long series, began to identify closely with Joey. For although she differed greatly in appearance from Joey – being neither black-haired nor slender – and lived a very different, far less adventurous life, there are strong indications that much of Elinor's personality was unconsciously absorbed into her favourite heroine. As put by a friend who knew Elinor for more than forty years: "Joey was Elinor as she would like to have been".

However, certain things about Elinor can only be inferred, for in real life she seldom talked about personal matters. As a result, only a few people ever knew she had had a beloved younger brother, who died tragically, aged only seventeen, from meningitis; or that, in the previous year, a sixteen-year-old schoolfriend had been stricken with a fatal bout of tuberculosis – a disease that is rare today in developed countries, but one that is much dreaded and sadly prevalent throughout Britain during Elinor's early life. No wonder that illness plays such a prominent part in Elinor's books, for in those days, long before the discovery of antibiotics, illnesses that can now be speedily cured would often prove fatal. And, viewed in this light, Madge's constant anxiety about Joey's health is understandable.

Other aspects of Elinor, such as her love of music, history, legends and foreign travel – not to mention continental food! – are clearly shown in her stories. And, in making her own Margaret Roper School in Hereford non-denominational, Elinor was probably modelling it on the Chalet School, where Protestants and Roman Catholics play equal roles in a way that was quite unusual for those days. Other links between the fictional and real-life schools are easy to find – Elinor even chose for her pupils in Hereford a uniform exactly like the Chalet School's! Not that Elinor was really suited to being a headmistress: she was far too erratic and disorganised, and would sometimes become so absorbed by her writing that she completely forgot to turn up for a lesson! Nevertheless, she had real gifts as a teacher – something else that shines through in her books; and despite her reputation for eccentricity she has left affectionate memories with many people, including former pupils.

Elinor Brent-Dyer was a prolific writer, but it is unquestionably the Chalet School series that keeps her name alive. The stories, which have now been continuously in print for over seven decades, are still selling well; and each year the paperback editions introduce new fans to the books. Today, Chalet enthusiasts can be found not only throughout Britain but in numerous further-flung parts of the world. Many of them belong to one – or sometimes both! – of the two fan clubs, the New Chalet Club and Friends of the Chalet

School. Fans hold regular meetings; and in 1994 they helped to organise celebrations of Elinor's centenary in a wide variety of places, including Australia, during which memorial plaques were erected in South Shields (Elinor's birthplace); Hereford (where she ran her school); and Pertisau (the setting of the early stories).

The Pertisau plaque stands on the wall beside the parish church, and it highlights the crucial importance of Elinor's Tyrolean holiday, as well as paying her a fitting tribute. Translated, it reads:

In memory of the well-known English writer
Elinor M. Brent-Dyer
1894–1969
Pertisau inspired her in her stories of
The Chalet School.

HELEN MCCLELLAND
President, New Chalet Club